THE BOOK OF ETTA

ALSO BY MEG ELISON

THE ROAD TO NOWHERE SERIES

The Book of the Unnamed Midwife

THE BOOK OF ETTA

MEG ELISON

This is a work of fiction. Names, characters, organizations, places, events, and incidents are either products of the author's imagination or are used fictitiously.

Published by 47North, Seattle

www.apub.com

ISBN-13: 9781503941823
ISBN-10: 1503941825

Cover design by Christian Fuenfhausen

Printed in the United States of America

THE BOOK OF ETTA

CHAPTER 1

On the map, all the roads led to Estiel.

Eddy didn't like that. He hated how inevitable it felt. Touching the star on the faded map, he had asked his mother why Estiel was the bigger city, with the giant arch and the huge tall buildings, when it hadn't been the state capital in the old world.

"That's just not how it worked," Mother Ina would say tiredly. "I don't know why, my living child. That was before my time."

He thought of the skeletal silver arch against the black sky, the smell of smoke in the back of his throat.

How does a memory make me sick? How does it make me feel like running from somewhere I am not?

He was a few days away from the city on foot. He knew the southern routes better, knew where to find water and the safest places to rest. On the map, old names were scratched out and new names were written in. A faded red star at the crux of all roads read *S-T-L*. Eddy traced the roads with his finger, but he never went over that spot. He sought out the little signs his fellow raiders had supplied. Here, you'll cross the herds moving in season: a set of wide horns. There, a big building in the process of falling down: a number 7 lying on its side. Here, a town that did not admit black people: a smudged, filled-in circle inside an X. There, a town that trades in slaves: three links of chain.

As a child in his small town called Nowhere, Eddy found the maps foreign and exciting. They confirmed something he had always believed: that the world outside was different and there were all different people in it. He couldn't wait to become a raider, mark up his own maps, go everywhere. Not just Estiel. Even then, the way the lines on the map puckered toward it made it seem like a mean old mouth.

He was forty miles south of the city when he found Chloe. This spot had been his camp many times, often for moons on end. The round gray birds, partridge and grouse, were thick here. In some seasons, wild chickens and pheasants in brown and red and checks mixed among them. The partridges were slow and showed little sign of contact with people. Eddy would pick off one or two, snapping their necks and plucking them at his leisure.

The old woman who held Chloe's tiny hand was gray-haired and short, her spine bent like a question mark. Her belt was circled around with blades. Rusty razors alternated with broken knives, their tangs showing empty screw holes. Sharpened hunks of tin glittered in the sunlight. Her mouth had the sunken look of a recently filled grave; Eddy knew she would be toothless, but he didn't expect the black stumps that showed when the hag smiled. Her eyes were covered by black plastic glasses that wrapped around her head, chipped and fogged but still transparent enough to see through.

The hair on Eddy's arms stood up suddenly, in hard little bumps identical to those on the half-plucked bird he was working on. He got to his feet slowly, feeling the presence of the gun at his back suddenly take on weight.

Black teeth and split lips opened, but what came forth didn't sound like words at all. Eddy stared in amazement, trying to puzzle it out.

Her accent was deep bayou south, traveling through the marshland of her mouth and landing in the Midwestern air sounding like no human language. He cocked his head to the side, affecting mild confusion to mask bolting horror.

Her man walked up slowly, carefully. This time Eddy put his hand on his gun and left it there.

The man was tall and thin with long, slender arms. He wore a cap made of an inexpertly skinned animal, and bad tattoos marched up his arms. "Ho, there. Ho, there, son. No trouble, now. No trouble at all. We thought we might bring you something nice."

Wee that wee mat brang you sumpn nahs. Eddy turned it over and over in his head, trying to make it into words.

"This here is the last girl in the world."

It came together all at once, the way a heavy summer rainstorm breaks in an instant and soaks the ground. He understood. They were selling the girl. Their talk was sloppy, slow, like something clotted pouring through a ragged hole. But once he got the feel of it, he could understand them.

He shifted his stance. "Is that right? The last girl in the world?"

The old woman's head rocked in a wild nod on her tortured spine. "That's right. The very last one. Of course, I don't count anymore. I can't tell you how many old women there might be. But girls . . . now that's different. This here is the last one."

Eddy tried to remember the last time he had seen a girl this small on the road. He tried to remember how many girl children had died being born back home, how many women had died trying to have them. It didn't make the girl any more or less precious. He didn't feel like doing the math.

The old woman touched the girl's blonde hair as though it were the finest merchandise before yanking the child forward, leading her roughly by one hand.

Eddy let his eyes rake over the child. Thin enough to make him wince. Dirty and scabbed and dull in the eyes past all recognition.

If this is the last girl child on earth, he thought, *surely she deserves better than this.*

He kept his hand on his gun.

The man spoke up again. He wore a long cloak that had been patched and mended with some care. The main body of it had once been made of velvet. He had stubble but had shaved fairly recently. His eyes were clear, and Eddy could see the ropes of his muscles when he moved his long arms.

"Will you just look at that? Pretty as a pitcher and no trouble at all. Just does exactly what she's told. Watch this."

He gave a short whistle and the girl turned toward him mechanically, following as devoid of will as when a flower turns to the sun. As the man lowered his pants she shoved one small, filthy hand in to root for her salvation, her face turned away.

Eddy saw her seize upon the man's member and resignedly tuck herself toward him, saw the habit and economy in her gestures. He knew the girl had been born in captivity, never known a free day in her short life. He saw the way the man sagged, hips forward, whole body relaxing as the child moved to service him. The old woman did not trouble herself to look away.

"I don't want to watch that," Eddy said, struggling to keep his voice unconcerned. "Let's hear the price."

The man shrugged and pulled the child's hand out of his pants, hitching and tying them back into place. "Man doesn't need to be shown, I reckon. You know what you're getting. We want a gun."

"I don't have one." He said it too quickly. There were only a few guns in Nowhere, and only a few girls this young. If he was careful, he could change one of those numbers today. He let a beat pass, took a breath and let it out slowly. "I have throwing knives, and I'm pretty good with those. I could show you."

A look passed between the cloak and the old woman. "Any drugs, then?"

Eddy thought a moment. "Yes. Yes, I might have something that you want."

He picked up his pack, laid there beside the bloody feathers. He reached into the exact pocket, knowing precisely what he wanted and finding it with his fingertips. He pulled out two small vials of clear liquid, made by Alice.

He held the two vials up between two fingers. "This is a powerful painkiller. If you drink the whole vial, you'll sleep deep enough to have a bone set or a bad tooth removed. If you drink half, you can come through a bad infection without pain. If you just take a drop or two, you feel fine and kind of sleepy. I'll give you both for the girl."

They shared another look.

"The drug and the knives," the hag said. "Both."

Eddy looked at her belt of blades. "What are those for?"

She looked down like she hadn't known she was wearing it. "Oh, these? Just for my own protection."

The silence hung.

The tall man reached out, taking a step forward. "I want to try it first. I ain't trading you the last girl on earth for some water."

Eddy stepped back, flinching at the man's sudden movement.

Damn it. Try for some control.

"Here. I'll break the seal and show you. You just put a few drops under your tongue. No more than four, though."

He took a knife off his belt and ran it around the wax seal. His palms were slick and it took a minute. He held the other vial in his teeth. When Eddy handed it to the man in the cloak and cap, he took extra care that their hands did not touch.

Eddy opened the second vial and pressed his dry lower lip against the mouth of the bottle. He tilted his head back, pretending to tap out drops. Nothing entered his mouth.

The man watched this, then opened his own mouth and dripped the liquid beneath his tongue. Eddy got the impression that he wanted the drugs mostly for amusement and not because he had sickness or pain. The old woman watched them both, moving her jaw from side to side, grinding her teeth.

The little girl stood motionless, her bare feet in the dirt. Toes pointed in. The feathers of small birds blew on the wind.

Eddy wasn't completely sure how this would go. When the tall man's eyes rolled back in his head and he started to pitch forward, Eddy pulled out his machete and advanced toward the old woman. He watched dapples of sunlight glint on her belt of knives as she trembled.

It was always old women who did the cutting on girls who were too small to fight. Men did the trading, the buying and selling. Every camp seemed to have an old woman who knew the anatomy well enough to condition a girl but not to ruin her. Eddy understood what men were, and how they lived and died selling girls just like this one. He did not, never could, understand the old women who helped them do it. He raised the machete, ready to split her skull in two.

At the last second the woman bolted, suddenly spry, zigzagging past the trees.

The last girl in the world did not turn to watch her go.

She did not react when Eddy walked up, swearing, and kicked the limp body of the man in the cloak. She said nothing while Eddy roughly searched the man's pockets. This yielded an inferior knife and a compass.

He heard the man's breathing, slow and without urgency. The man would just slip away, no fuss and no struggle. Eddy wished the girl had seen him kill them both. It would have done her some good. Still, the old woman was out alone now, with only her knives and her skill to peddle. She wouldn't live long.

Eddy was fine with that.

He didn't touch the girl. He didn't try to make her meet his eyes or take his hand. He sat down, opened up a canteen, and set it near her. It brimmed over with water, the drops running down both sides in the sunlight.

As soon as he was out of arm's reach, the girl seized the canteen and drank in hasty gulps. She let it fall to the ground, empty. She didn't replace the cap or say anything.

He didn't talk to her. He smiled as nicely as he knew how and returned to plucking the birds. When they were spitted and roasting, he let the smell of it bring her closer. When she came near enough that he could see her trembling, he tore off a hot leg and blew on it.

The bird's bones were tiny and he had to hold it between two fingers as it smoked.

"My name is Eddy," he said softly. "I'd like to know your name. You don't have to tell me, and I will still share food with you, even if you don't. But it would be better for us to share dinner if I at least knew what to call you."

He sat waiting, trying to encourage her with eye contact but not dominate her.

"Ch . . . Chloe." She said it very quietly before reaching out with both hands to snatch the partridge leg. She curled her tiny hands around it and brought it to her mouth.

"Careful, it's still—"

The girl had eaten every shred of meat and was gnawing the knuckle.

"Well alright then, Chloe." He pulled the whole bird off the spit and onto his metal plate. With two knives he held it down and cut it in half. He held the plate out to her, one thumb holding down his own dinner.

She snatched her half up and sat down in the dirt, teeth buried in the thigh meat.

"Alright then," Eddy repeated, smiling.

The girl had been the perfect reason to avoid the city. Eddy told the people of his village that he raided in the city with the Arch every summer. He brought back all kinds of useful objects to prove it.

The truth was that Eddy had not been to Estiel since he was seventeen years old, a still-green raider with only two years behind him. His very first solo raid at fifteen had taken him straight into the heart of the city, cocksure and invincible. He had come back with precious, irreplaceable things.

He was a hero.

Like a hero, he'd walked out of Nowhere in his sixteenth year, a little taller and stronger but not much wiser. He left on the same warm spring day, intending to return at the end of the summer. He followed the same route and raided the same part of the city.

He had walked back to Nowhere in the dead of winter with nothing but his gun. He had lost every ounce of extra weight on his body and shaved his head. He spoke to no one until three whole moons had passed.

When his voice had returned and he was no longer starving, he told them he had gotten lost. When he left the following summer, he followed those same roads, all of them leading toward Estiel under its dead rainbow. He never got close to the city. He raided other places and found people to trade with and returned a hero once more.

The reputation had stuck, and Eddy rescued girls and women to keep it safe. To cut off questions about when he was going to settle down.

Chloe was the first girl he had found this year. It seemed like a good omen to have rescued one so soon.

Eddy walked to the gates of Nowhere holding Chloe's hand. The child was sleepy and sick of walking, he could tell. She did not complain.

He whistled the signal, and a half-covered face appeared in the guard tower above a shotgun.

"Your name?"

Eddy lifted the child up onto his hip. He was too weary to be glad to be home, but he hoped Chloe would be happy here.

He pulled back his hood to show his shaved head. The spotter would know his face in the afternoon light.

"Etta, daughter of Ina. And this is Chloe, daughter of the Road."

The gates opened and they walked through. Etta turned to the little girl and spoke softly in her ear.

"I don't know what they told you," she said. "But you are not the last girl on earth."

CHAPTER 2

David, son of Jenn, came down the ladder from the guard tower and pulled his mask down. He dropped the butt of the gun gently to his toe and held the stock.

"Etta! You're early! And nice to meet you, Miss Chloe." He waved to the little girl, who turned away from him to burrow herself deeper into Etta's arms.

Etta put a hand on the back of the girl's head as people began to appear and look them both over.

Etta spoke to the child without looking at her. "We're okay. This is the safe place I was telling you about. This is Nowhere. Remember the stories?"

Chloe's matted blonde hair bunched and crawled as she nodded. "Are we going to your house?"

"No, kiddo. We're going to the Midwife."

The infirmary was far from the gate. Etta walked straight, acknowledging greetings with nods and waves, not excited to see anyone.

"Where have you been, Etta?" a tall redheaded woman called out, with two men carrying baskets of clothes behind her.

"Not far, Chrissy. I'm back early because of the little one."

Chrissy waved to the child beside Etta. Chloe ducked her head again, but shyly lifted her hand before dropping it at her side.

"Your mother will be glad to see you!" Chrissy gestured for the men to precede her and walked after them.

"I'm sure." Etta made herself smile.

The doors of the infirmary were painted with a scene that was new to Etta: a fat duck roosting on a clutch of three eggs that all looked like tiny moons. She knocked and waited.

A harried-looking face appeared much lower than Etta's. "Yes?"

"Sylvia!" Her smile was genuine this time.

The short woman opened the door wide. "You're home so early!"

Etta wrapped her arms around the short woman, who buried her head in Etta's leather coat. "I missed you too much." Their embrace was awkward with the little girl between them, beginning to squirm.

"Now who is this?" Sylvia's voice was muffled.

Sylvia pulled away and looked at Chloe. Etta put the child down slowly, but firmly.

"Sylvia, I would like you to meet Chloe. Chloe, this is Sylvia, daughter of Sylvia. She is the Midwife—the doctor I told you about. She will protect you and help you, just like I did. Maybe better."

"Nobody could be better." Chloe spoke with the hitching thickness of a child headed for tears.

"That's not true, child." Etta put her hand on the small blonde head. "Sylvia here knows how to make you stop itching, for one."

She scooped the child up again in one motion, nudging Chloe's skinny legs to either side of her right hip. Etta thought Chloe was four or five, based on the way she spoke and thought her way through actions. The child was tall, if that guess was correct, but so underweight that Etta was sure her own pack was heavier. They walked a few feet like that and Etta put her down on an exam table. She looked into the child's scared brown eyes.

"Sylvia would like to check you out to make sure you are healthy. That's her job, she takes care of people's bodies. I'm going to stay with you, but the Midwife needs permission to touch you. Will you tell her that's okay, or no?"

Chloe looked down and didn't speak.

"She will be gentle and careful, and you can say stop anytime. Can you say 'Stop' for me?"

"Stop." Barely audible.

"Say *'Stop!'*" Etta said it loudly but didn't yell, popping the *p* just a little.

Chloe did not say it.

Sylvia stood with her hands folded, waiting.

"Chloe, remember when we were in the woods and I heard something? And I told you not to move?"

Nodding.

"Can you say that? Say what I said."

Chloe smiled a little. "Don't fucking move!"

Etta laughed. "Just like that. How about if you want to stop, you say 'Don't move'?"

Nodding again.

"Okay. Chloe, does Sylvia have permission to touch you gently and carefully?"

Nodding. Eyes wide.

Sylvia stepped forward, making eye contact with the girl. "Thank you. I promise I will listen to you."

Sylvia squeezed the girl's hand. Chloe looked at her other hand, turning her head away.

The Midwife checked the child's joints and looked for wounds. She noted that the girl was scarred all over, with an arm that had been broken and healed without proper setting, but alright. Etta watched, arms folded.

"Chloe, are you itchy?"

"Mhmm."

"On your head?"

"Mhmm." The child scratched vigorously as if the mention of it had reminded her.

Etta fought the urge to do the same.

"Other places?"

"Mhmm." Chloe scratched at her vulva through her cotton shift. The garment was filthy, but Etta hadn't been able to get the child to wear anything else. Below the shift, Chloe wore scavenged leather cowboy boots two sizes too big. On her feet were two precious pairs of Etta's wool socks. She hadn't wanted to wear those either, until Etta had showed the girl her own feet, unblistered and whole.

"Okay." Sylvia dipped her hands in a basin of warm water. "First thing is you need to have a bath and get some new clothes. Next thing is I think we have a home for you. There is another little girl there. Would you like to meet her?"

Nodding.

Etta came near the child again. "I have to go for a little while to have my own bath and see some people. Sylvia is a good Midwife, though, and she will take care of you. I trust her. Is that okay with you?"

Chloe looked bewildered, but nodded again. Etta kissed her own fingertips and laid them on the child's forehead. For just that second, Chloe closed her eyes.

Sylvia set Chloe in a shallow tub with strong soap and added a few inches of hot water from the big pot mixed with cold from the basin. She watched as the child began to wash herself and left her to it. She met Etta in the hall.

"Where did you get her?" Her brow was furrowed.

"Outside of Estiel."

"Alone?"

"No, she was being sold. A man and an old woman. No idea where they got her. She doesn't remember anything before them."

"Did you kill them?" Sylvia seemed curious but unconcerned.

"Him." Etta studied her fingernails as she spoke. They were short and filthy.

"Is she cut?"

"I don't know. I didn't look and I can't ask her. The old woman had knives on her belt." She shrugged. "I headed straight here after that. It's been a few days."

Sylvia made a face. "Well, she's covered in both lice and fleas. You probably are, too. You'll have to see to that. I'm gonna place her with Ani and her daughter. I know she's ready for a foundling and will be happy to get a sister for Belle. Unless you want to take her."

Etta shook her head.

"Alright. Scrub up before you see your mother." Sylvia kissed Etta lightly on the cheek. "Glad you're back. Stay a little while."

Etta nodded but did not commit. She turned and left.

She went to the bathers. They had been through all this before. They took her clothes and pack, scrubbed them all down with lye, and then did the same to Etta herself. Etta carefully shaved her black skin with her sharpest razor and then allowed the washers to grease her down with their special preparation of lanolin with lavender and peppermint. It went on as thick as tree sap and burned in that cold, minty way. Etta felt like she was on fire, but it was a pleasure to burn. She felt clean, and she knew this would keep the bugs away.

Lanolin was expensive in Nowhere, but they always had some for her. Peppermint and lavender grew wild, and both helped to cut the smell of sheep. Etta, fragrant and tingling, paid the bathers handsomely with seven new books from her bag and a small tin of stale but prized cocoa.

The washer men smiled to each other and agreed to tell no one of the cocoa so they could split it amongst their house. The books they agreed they would share, once they had read them first.

Bald and burning beneath her clothes, Etta headed to the shrine of the Unnamed.

The Unnamed Midwife had been a founder in Nowhere. She had been from the old world, a trained nurse and Midwife who had lived through the dying and seen how it all came down. She had left behind her journals, which told the whole story—her own as well as the world's. It was known by every man, woman, and child in Nowhere. They kept their own journals as a way to carry on her work.

The Midwife's journals and the books that they salvaged told them everything they would ever know of the world before the plague. There had once been a world that held as many women as it did men. Women had been free, and childbirth had been simple, hardly ever deadly. The Unnamed had lived in that world, and had learned to live in one where each city held perhaps one living woman for every ten men. She had written what it had meant to go from being free to being hunted, when one world became another. She was the change, and the strength to survive it.

The Unnamed was Etta's hero. Not as a Midwife, but as a survivor, a person who could be anything they had to be to survive.

Handwritten copies of her story, copied every year by young scribe boys, were stacked on a wood table. The leather of their bindings shone where they had been handled a thousand times. Gold beeswax candles burned day and night so that the room smelled faintly of honey. The twining figure of a caduceus was carved into the floor. The people of Nowhere said that the Unnamed had had a tattoo of that strange image on her chest, but Etta didn't believe it. It wasn't in the book, and it seemed too dreamy for the woman who had practically built the settlement of Nowhere by herself, and written its history besides.

On the wall behind the books, there was no image of the Unnamed. Instead, a salvaged old-world mirror hung with dark drapes around it. If you were looking for the Unnamed here, you had to find her in yourself. Etta saw her own reflection and sighed, choosing to look instead at the floor. She knelt for a while with her head down. She drifted off to sleep in the quiet glow of candles.

"Did you bring her an offering?"

Etta started and came to her feet quickly but unsteadily.

She knew the voice belonged to her mother, but at first it scared her as much as if it had been a stranger. She stood a minute, hands on hips and head down.

"Mother."

"Etta, my living daughter." Ina came forward and wrapped her thin arms around Etta. Etta let herself be held, but she shifted uneasily until her mother let go.

"You're home early! Almost a moon!" Ina's eyes were bright and clear, and she had good, strong teeth. She had been nearly forty when Etta was born. She was not the oldest woman in Nowhere, but she was close.

Etta nodded. "That's right. I found a girl, too little to travel with me, and not far from here. So I turned back."

"Where is the child?" Ina's lined face lit up with joy. She was not wearing her wooden baby belly, the symbol of her status as the Mother of a living child; she must have come in a hurry when she heard Etta was back.

"Sylvia had to clean her up. She's getting homed with Ani and Belle."

"I see."

Etta did not look up to see her mother's disappointment. She didn't have to, she knew that look and that tone.

"Well, come on home anyway. Your room is all made up. Some of the ranger boys brought back apples, and I dried a bunch for you. And I got you a gift." Ina held out an arm so as to lay it around Etta's waist and bring her along. Etta debated it for a second, then let it happen. They walked out of the shrine together.

Ina's home was formerly officers' quarters on the base that had existed before Nowhere. It featured a broad front window and granite countertops in the kitchen. The unbroken front window was an enviable sight, since there were no glaziers in Nowhere. Ina took great care of her house and lived stubbornly alone, after a few years in the House of Mothers. Her lovers came and went, but she could live with no one but herself.

She put on a teapot and filled her strainer with her own blend of mint leaves and dried peach slivers.

Etta sat at the kitchen table and unrolled a long leather strip.

"Brought you something."

"Did you, now?"

Etta pulled more than a dozen pen nibs out of the pockets in the roll, stacking them in front of her.

"Clean metal, all of them. More than I've ever found." Etta was pleased with herself. She waited.

Ina looked over her shoulder and nodded. Her hands were drawing forth a pan of cornbread from the cabinet.

"Cornbread's cold, but there's plenty of butter. I think there's bacon in the smokehouse, I can go get it."

"I'll go, Mother."

"Alright, then." Ina watched her living child go.

Then they sat together for a long time without speaking. Etta ate slowly, methodically, as though she could pack more away if she set a pace. Ina nibbled at everything.

"So where did you find the girl? What's her name?"

"Chloe. Just outside of Estiel, a couple of days ago."

Ina sipped her tea. "You were back awfully quick."

"So?"

"That's where you found the twins, too. Right?"

"Yes." Etta ate another piece of bacon, relishing the salt. She did not look at her mother. "So?"

"So nothing. Just thinking about it."

Etta slurped the hot tea with honey. It was the only sound for a few minutes.

"You could have kept Chloe, you know. You could bring her here."

Etta said nothing.

"Eventually I'll be gone. You should think about getting you a Hive. Settling down."

Many of the women in Nowhere kept Hives—groups of men who shared the duties and joys of marriage with a single woman, like the queen among bees. No one knew where the custom had come from, but the Unnamed had written of it, and included the stories of others from all over who lived the same way. With one woman for every ten men, it seemed a very sensible arrangement.

"I don't want a Hive, Mother."

"Or some children. You could have a daughter, or two daughters. You wouldn't even have to settle for sons. You always seem to find girls." Ina had abandoned the pretense of eating.

Etta set her fork down. She stared at the table. "Mother. Listen to me. I do not want to get pregnant. I don't want any man, or any men. You know what I am. I don't want to be a Mother, or a Midwife. I'm a raider. That's what I do."

"Even the Unnamed knew she had a purpose, Etta. If you want to be like her, you could—"

"I *am* like her. I am. That's the point."

"That's not the point. The point is you have nothing to put before her as an offering. You never bring her any blood, even bad blood."

Etta turned her head away. "I still follow her." She waited a moment, staring at the floor. "And I know all about blood."

Ina got up and crossed to her daughter's side of the table. She reached into Etta's bag and whipped out the journal stuck in the back there, purple leather and decorated with flowers. A gift Ina had given Etta when she had gotten her first blood. It was this that she was supposed to offer to the Unnamed: not the blood of the slavers she killed, but the blood a woman gives in the endless and doomed pursuit of having children.

Ina flipped the book open with one hand and smacked it down, laid open. The pages on both sides were utterly blank. No histories of the girls she had saved on the road. No stories of how she lived or the long-gone world she raided goods from. No Book of Etta.

"You're not following shit."

Etta sprang up and snatched the book, stuffing it back in the bag and packing up everything. She pulled her leather jacket back on, her breath coming hot and fast through flared nostrils.

Ina tried to put a hand on her shoulder, but Etta jerked away.

"Child, I just want your life to have meant something. What does it mean if you live and leave nothing behind? No child, no book. You're a dead end." Ina's gnarled hands curled in empty space, coming to rest against her lower belly.

Etta looked at her mother's hands lying there. She fought rage, then guilt. She held on to her pack.

I leave behind six women and two girls. Free. So far.

"Thanks, Mother."

"Where are you going?"

"Back on the road."

"Oh, where to this time? How far away do you have to go to understand what this life is really about?" Ina's eyebrow cocked high in her thin face.

Etta clenched her jaw and opened the front door.

"You've lived your whole life in this village, Mother. You have no idea what you're talking about. Go back to your kitchen."

She slammed the door and faced the darkening orange sky. She didn't want to hit the road without a good night's sleep. She looked both ways on the path and made a decision.

She was going to Alice's.

Alice, daughter of Carla, lived alone. She had a small Hive of two men, Antoine and Ian, but the two of them lived together and she visited when she felt like it. Her home was the back half of a small building, with a low bed surrounded by her collections of rocks and shells and crystals. The front half was her lab.

Etta let herself in, sidling past the surfaces that she knew, without looking, were littered with glass vessels and delicate tools. The lab windows were open up high, but the spring air could not dispel the odors of blood, urine, acids, and indefinable stinks that Etta couldn't place.

Alice slept soundly in the back. Etta could hear her snoring softly. She slid her pack off when she reached the doorway, slipping out of her shoes and leaving them beside it. With her hands, she parted the curtain of wooden beads that separated the space.

The bed was greeny-gold, eerily lit by Alice's handmade solar lamps. She coated ceramic pots with paint that stank and left them out all day to absorb sunlight. On a clear day like today, the pots glowed brightly and she had only brought two inside. She was lit from either side of the bed, her messy curls aflame on one side and her turned-up nose lit delicately from above on the other.

Etta slid her pants down and whipped her shirt up over her head. She drew back Alice's patchwork quilt and crept into the low, down-filled bed.

Alice stirred. "Toine?"

"No." Etta kept her voice low and slipped an arm around Alice's waist.

"Sylvia?"

"What?" Etta's surprise brought her voice back into her normal register.

"Oh shit, Etta! How are you back already?" Alice flipped neatly over in bed and hugged her.

Etta pushed her away slightly to look at her face in the weird greenish light. "Sylvia?"

Alice rolled her eyes and sat up slightly. She reached and fumbled for a glass of water, found it, and slurped. "Oh, don't be so shocked. You've never been jealous before."

Etta held her breath. She had never been jealous of Alice's Hive. This was different.

"You want a drink?" Alice's face was all innocence.

"Hmph." Etta gave Alice the eye for a few more beats and then took the water.

"Really, though, why are you back so soon?"

Etta put the glass down when it was empty. "Nobody is just happy to see me, I guess."

Alice tucked the blanket under her arms to cover her freckled breasts and pressed her lips together. "That's not what I said. I'm just curious. I thought you'd be gone all summer."

Etta sighed tiredly and reached down to the floor to retrieve her shirt. Pulling it back on, she spoke without looking at Alice's concerned face. "I found a little girl. Too little to travel with me. So I came home. And I missed you."

Alice smiled on one side and put a hand out on the muscle at the outside of Etta's thigh. "That's sweet."

Etta shifted away, ending their contact. "Guess you didn't miss me, though. Not if Sylvia's already the one you're expecting to show up in the middle of the night."

Alice glanced up at the windows. "Hardly the middle, love. The sun's just down. You know the hours I keep."

Etta sulked. "You start seeing her the day I left?"

Alice stood, breathtaking in any light, and stared down at Etta. "What I do is my business. What you do is your business. If you came here to pout like a child who has to share her toys, I'm already bored." She crossed her arms.

Etta looked up at her and then looked away. "I just thought . . ."

"You thought what? That I'm yours? That we'll tell our mothers and you'll move in and my Hive will sweep the floors for us?"

Etta had her pants back on. "Forget it. I came here for some comfort, but I see that's not something I can get here anymore."

Alice strode through the beaded curtain and came back as Etta was lacing her boots.

"Here. This is what you came here for. Something that's only for you." She held out a small box filled with vials. Each had a cork waxed into the open end.

Etta stared at it, hands still on her boots.

"Oh, you don't want it? Fine, I can just sell it to—"

"I want it. Thank you." Etta took the box from Alice's thin fingers, touching her short nails and suddenly feeling very sorry for herself. She held one of Alice's hands and kissed her knuckles.

"This . . . This isn't what I came for. I came for you." Her eyes were a plea that she couldn't say.

Don't want to leave, but I can't take back what I said. Can't help how I feel.

Alice sighed. "Yeah. But you want too big a piece. Next time, you knock."

Etta slipped the vials out of the box and into the inner pocket of her leather jacket. She picked up her pack and left noiselessly. Alice was silent as she went out the door.

The moon was rising. Etta looked up and down the little Nowhere streets. Up in the guard tower, she saw a red glow and rising smoke.

She snorted and climbed the ladder.

When she knocked on the hatch, she could hear them scramble to their feet and get their guns.

"Who—who is it? Who's there?"

"Oh shit. Oh shit."

"Relax, Rob. It's Etta. Let me in."

Rob, son of Marcia, unlatched the door and Etta climbed through. She threw her pack down and hugged him. "Have you got enough to share?"

Rob looked guiltily to the corner of the room where his joint was smoking still. He scratched the back of his head. "Yeah, we do. You won't tell?"

"Shit, no. Who's this?" She popped her chin to indicate the other man in the tower.

"This is Aaron, son of Lisa."

Aaron was too tall for the tower room and had to stoop a little. Etta nodded up at him and he nodded back. The three of them found comfortable ways to sit.

Rob got the mashed joint lit again and passed it to Etta. She hit it hard and passed it to Aaron. Both of them had been carefully trained not to stare, though they might go days without sitting and talking with a woman. They looked at the smoke, at each other.

"So, how's night duty?" Etta held the smoke in while she spoke, a croaky whisper.

Aaron took a long, deep hit and looked at Rob.

"Boring," Rob said, looking over the half wall at his back. "We haven't had a wanderer in moons. And all the raiders are out. Well, except for you." He added this last hastily, watching Etta exhale a cloud of smoke dense enough to hide her face from him.

"Did anyone come back after the thaw?" Etta watched the joint as it passed back to Rob.

"Elliot came back before the thaw," Aaron said hoarsely. "He had skis or something. Anyhow, he shot a boar and dragged it in on a sledge. They roasted it that night. We had a great party."

Etta nodded. "Elliot is a good raider. I bet he brought back some good stuff."

"Mostly news," Aaron said. "He met traders to the south who have a safe road to the gulf. There's a city there now, more than a thousand people."

"Bullshit," Etta said flatly.

"That's what Elliot said, but the traders were fat and had good clothes. He said they told him a thousand people, more than a hundred women, and five babies last year."

There were always stories like this. Towns where there were almost as many women as there were men, where the plague had not wiped out the old-world way of living together in the riches and freedom of babies born easily to women who were free to roam everywhere, common as dandelion fluff.

"Five babies a year, my ass." Etta could feel herself starting to float. She declined the joint when Rob tried to pass it back to her.

"A hundred women, though." Rob looked dreamy. "Of course they told Elliot they don't take in men."

"Of course." Etta laughed a little. "Those Hives are full."

"That's the thing," Aaron said. "The traders said no Hives. He said the women just take trade when they feel like it. Men bring in fish and furs and whatever, and the women come to the market to choose."

"Huh," Etta said.

"Have you ever been anyplace like that?" Rob looked at Etta expectantly, as a child looks when awaiting a bedtime story.

"No, not like that," she said quickly. "Most people I meet are travelers. In twos and threes. Not many cities to speak of."

"Oh." They both said it, disappointed.

After a little silence and another hit, Rob was ready to try again. "What's Estiel like?"

Etta looked above the half wall and saw the gibbous moon on its way up. "I don't want to talk about it. Rob, can I sleep at your place? Since you're up here anyway?"

"Of course! The bed's not real clean, but the room is empty. Amy likes everyone to sleep together, until high summer and then she can't stand us. She says either us or the bugs have to go." He laughed a little.

Etta was already opening the trap. "Tell her to get bug repellent from Alice. It works. I should know."

Rob fastened it behind her and Aaron started to snore. Softly, to no one, he said, "She knows where to get it. She just hates the smell."

Not real clean was an understatement. Etta was glad she was stoned. She fell face-first into the stink of a man and wondered for the thousandth time why the smell was disgusting and comforting all at once.

The smell of men is the smell of danger.

She drifted to sleep and jerked when she dreamed of the black-and-silver arch that brooded over Estiel. She did not wake until dawn.

Etta's pack was ready; she had been prepared to be gone all summer before her early return. Nevertheless, she observed the raider's ritual, learned from Errol and Ricardo when she was just a girl.

A raider must be prepared, Ricardo's voice lisped in memory. *You must carry always enough, but never too much.*

Think about what you know you can't replace, Errol added, whispering across time. How long ago had it been? Etta missed them sorely; they were like brothers to her.

Know everything in your pack by feel, know your inventory by heart.

She made Rob's bed and spread out her belongings on the blank space of his wool blanket. Her clothes were rolled tight, and she concentrated on extra socks. She knew socks were the success or failure of a long walk.

Beside those, she laid her leather journal and a small roll of pencils and a pen. These she scarcely looked at, remembering her mother's hands on the blank pages. She had loose-leaf paper, as well, in case she needed to leave messages.

Etta carried a few items from the old world. All of them were very costly, and most she had collected on her travels. Anything of value from the before was useful as payment for invaluable services, or as trade for something a person could die without. She laid these things beside each other, marveling, as always, at their smoothness and perfection.

One silicone menstrual cup, in perfect shape and boiled scrupulously clean. Etta had found a case of these on her very first raid and had brought them back to a hero's welcome. She had hated the rags and pads that women made and soaked in cold water by night. She had opened the case totally perplexed and unfolded an ancient, yellowing, folded paper that explained their purpose with helpful diagrams. Each in its plastic clamshell was pristine, forgotten in the storeroom of an old infirmary. She had carried it out past a chair with rusted stirrups, shouldering by it without a look. She didn't know what the chair was for and didn't spare it a thought.

When she had brought these back to Nowhere, her bag bursting with the small packages, Mother Ina had convinced her to give the moon-blood cups away rather than trade them. With the pliant little gift in her hand, Ina had quoted from the Book and pointed out that Etta was doing the work of the Unnamed.

Etta was sixteen and believed in the story of a hero. So she had agreed.

Beside her moon-blood cup, she laid her set of stainless-steel silverware and a metal bowl. These were plentiful, but good metalwork was always costly. Next to that, she laid her three sharp knives, all meticulously cleaned and maintained. They were always within her reach. Her machete next, with its rusty spots on the hilt but sharp as ever, in its black case that slung across her back.

In the bottom of her pack she kept a cunningly made wooden box full of tiny compartments. Into one of these, she rolled the vials that Alice had given her. Poison and cures and palliatives clinked and rumbled in the drawers, all sealed with wax or wrapped in bundles.

Nothing was labeled. Without an explanation, a thief would stake his life on trial and error.

The most valuable and dangerous item was her gun. It was a revolver that had been handed down in Nowhere for over a century. It had been maintained by every owner, and when there were no longer bullets for it, Brandon, son of Bronwen, had figured out how to make more. This process was long and difficult, and the smiths said it was very dangerous. Etta had thirty-six of them—six in the cylinder and enough to load it twice more. No one knew that number except her smith, Jaden, son of Janet. She paid him in lead weights and copper wire to keep her supplied and keep his mouth shut.

The gun itself had been a gift from her mother. It was given to Ina by a Hive whose Mother had died in childbirth, for Ina's help with their surviving daughter. Ina had passed it to Etta on the day the girl got her first blood and chose her path.

Ina told her that the gun had once belonged to the Unnamed. The first Midwife in Nowhere, who had come from far out west and knew what had killed the women of the old world. The one who had dressed as a man and shot slavers and handed out magic pills that could prevent deadly pregnancy. Ina, never one for superstition, even said that it would give her luck.

Etta knew her mother had expected her to become a Midwife. It wasn't until years later that she realized her mother had had this gift ready for her, instead of one of the traditional Midwife gifts. She might not be the daughter her mother wanted, but she was evidently exactly what Ina had expected.

Daughter Etta stroked the gun's oily surface before wrapping it again in the chamois cloth that kept it safe and dry.

Last, she stacked her maps of the old roads, her water bottles, and her stash of food. She decided to visit the storehouse again before heading back out. She had credit there and could get more buffalo jerky and oats. Maybe there would be fresh bread for breakfast.

She packed back up, everything in order, everything accounted for. The storehouse boys were happy to see her and filled her pack to bursting. She got fresh bread with butter and even some early berries on the sly, because they were happy to see her. She got venison and buffalo jerky and a good cake of salt, and considered herself richly provisioned.

Their requests were always the same: cuttings of live herb or vegetable plants that they lacked.

Green beans and wild mushrooms. What they really want me to bring back they'll never say.

Etta returned to her mother's house and found it crawling with men from Ina's Hive. They were pouring steaming pots of water through Ina's white sheets and scrubbing her bathtub.

Julian, son of Carla, wiped his sweating forehead with his shoulder as he looked up at her. He was almost as young as Etta herself. "Mother Ina went to work, Miss Etta."

"Thank you, father." Etta felt supremely uncomfortable and left immediately. She did not go to the schoolhouse where her mother worked. She didn't want to interrupt class, and she didn't know what she would say.

She went instead to the shrine of the Unnamed, as she always did before leaving Nowhere. She did not kneel and she lit no candles. She picked up the scribed copy of the Book and opened it to her favorite part, following the neat and even lines with the tip of one finger.

May I be brave where she was brave, she thought.

"Did you bring her an offering this time?"

All her bravery suddenly snuffed, Etta turned to face her mother.

She was surprised to see Sylvia there, too. Behind the two of them lurked Ani, holding the hands of both Belle and Chloe.

"I did." Etta shouldered her pack. "Come to see me off?"

"Yes, my living daughter, we did."

Ina took Etta's half-willing hand and led her outside.

Sylvia hugged her quickly, fiercely. "Alice wanted to be here, but she's growing a culture."

Etta raised her eyebrow. "Why would Alice see me off? I'm sure she has better things to do."

Sylvia smiled enigmatically and walked off. Ani brought the girls closer, and Etta crouched down to meet their eyes.

"Hello, Chloe."

The child looked much better this morning. Ani had bathed her and braided her hair to match Belle's. The girls looked like a set of salt and pepper shakers; Chloe, fully clean, was a towhead, and Belle was as black-haired as any girl Etta had ever seen.

"Etta!" Chloe hugged her around the neck. "This is Belle, she's gonna be my sister!" The child was beaming as she reached back for Belle's hand.

"I never thought I'd have a sister. Two girls in one house!" Belle grinned, and Etta smiled back at them both.

"You'll be the most popular house in town." She kissed Chloe on her forehead and touched Belle briefly on the shoulder, as she did not know the child well.

Standing, she spoke to Ani. "Thank you for accepting her into your house."

"Accepting? You brought me a healthy little girl! I am going to make you a set of new underwear while you're gone to thank *you*." Ani hugged Etta long and hard. Her braids smelled like the girls' braids—clean, fresh, and lovely. Etta breathed in deep.

The smell of women is the smell of home.

Her mother came to her last. "Come home safe, child. That's all I ask for."

Etta nodded, trying to swallow the unwelcome lump in her throat. She wanted to tell her mother she was sorry they'd fought, or that she was sorry she wasn't who she was supposed to be. She said nothing. She hugged her mother and felt the wooden baby belly push against her abdomen, hard and all hers.

"I'll come back."

Etta waved to the guard tower, where they gave the signal for the boys to open the gate. She stepped out into the seedling pines that crept closer to Nowhere every year.

When she was deep in the trees and could see nothing of the village, she stopped and stripped to the waist. She pulled from her back pockets two long, precious linen winding bandages, and slowly and carefully bound down her breasts.

Eddy stepped out onto the road and headed north.

The Book of Etta
Year 104 in the Nowhere Codex
Early Spring

Walked all day. Headed to old capital. Saw no one.

Early Spring

Walked all day. Found eggs in a nest. Saw no one.

Early Spring

Saw no one.

Eddy wrote in his diary first thing in the morning, to get it out of the way. He wasn't trying to please Ina, really. More just to prove her wrong. He remembered Errol's journal, the binding as soft as cooked celery, the pages stuffed with dried flowers and scraps of old-world paper. Errol liked to keep examples rather than describe them.

Ricardo's journal held maps and drawings, alongside page after page of counts. Every city he saw, he counted men, women, and children. He did sums and averages, trying to figure out if things were better east or west of Nowhere. If anyone had a secret. He had showed Etta the way he used the symbols that the Unnamed had used, turning words into math and math into words. Etta had watched, nodded, and written nothing for herself.

On the road, Eddy made oatmeal and sometimes had a little jerky. Water ran clear in the streams along the road, and he boiled it every night to make sure it was safe. He avoided all signs of fire and human habitation. According to the old maps, the capital was about a week's walk away.

He took his time. When he came to the Osage River, he consulted the map.

I wonder if people used to say Oh-sage or Oh-soggy.

He crossed the river. Its name didn't matter at all. He wrote nothing down.

After eight uneventful and nearly silent days on the road, Eddy heard sounds in the distance.

The old capital had been called Jefferson City. It was Eddy's experience that places were not often called by their old names, but it was a place to start.

Eddy checked and rechecked his gear. All three knives were hidden on his person. His gun was tucked into the back of his pants. His underwear strained around a pair of worn wool socks that gave him the desired bulge. He was dirty. He had waded across the river, not really bathing.

He strained to hear the far-off sounds again. He was pretty sure he was hearing music. It was a strange, booming kind of music unlike any he had ever heard.

Still, music is a good sign. People making music aren't starving. Do slavers make music?

Eddy didn't know if people could be too many things at once. The slavers he had met seemed to do very little else.

He approached the city openly, on a main road. Anyone could have spotted him. He waited to be called out.

As he drew closer to the outskirts, he saw that most of the old buildings were vacant, their roofs fallen in and walls sagging. He assumed there would be a center of some kind, where people clustered together. He followed the sound of music and his instinct. It seemed to Eddy that people drew one another as honey drew ants.

So I'll let myself be drawn a little.

He knew when he began seeing small household gardens that he had come to the right place. The town looked orderly, even cheery. Window boxes held flowers, and houses had curtains that were whole or well mended.

He was standing and admiring when he got that feeling that people were near. He laid a casual hand against the butt of his gun and waited.

Out of the door of a house not far from where Eddy was standing came a young woman with a little girl. The child was new to walking, chubby-legged and unsteady. They wore matching simple dresses of dark-green homespun. As they came closer, Eddy could tell there were good weavers here.

The woman and child looked alike. They also looked well fed and walked without fear. He let go of his gun and held up his hands, calling out.

"Good woman? Good Mother? I am a traveler from far away who means you no harm." Eddy smiled.

The woman tightened her grip on the child and then pulled the little girl up onto her hip. Eddy saw a flash of the little girl's bare butt as her skirt rode up.

That's just so the child can pee, he thought. *Doesn't mean anything but convenience.*

Despite the protective gesture, the woman came closer. Eddy could see that her skin was clear and moisturized and her teeth looked strong.

They do well here.

"My name is Eddy, son of Ina, and I'm from a place far, far south of here. I am traveling and trading, and I wanted to know if you folks trade, too."

Under her green bonnet, the woman had calm brown eyes and a square jaw. Her straight brown hair was bushy and came around her shoulders, getting caught up in her bonnet strings.

"My name is Deborah," she said slowly. "This is my daughter, Myles. We . . . you're on the wrong side of town for trade. But we don't see many travelers."

I can't believe I met two women first.

"Good Mother, I would be happy to talk with the men of your village and not waste any more of your precious time. I'm sure you have many things to do."

Deborah stiffened her neck slightly, but she seemed amused by Eddy's careful approach. She looked Eddy up and down.

"Can you behave yourself? Are you an outcast?" Deborah pursed her lips.

Eddy held out his hands and pushed up his sleeves. He smiled.

"Look me over, good Mother. No lost fingers, and no big scars. If I'm an outcast, I have no mark of it, right? If I'm dangerous, I've never gotten hurt, see?"

She looked over his skin and teeth. She drilled him straight in the eyes. Eddy knew that as a man he should drop his gaze in deference, but she seemed to be searching them. He held contact for as long as she looked.

"Alright," Deborah said with a shrug. "I'll take you to the square."

She gestured for Eddy to walk beside her and she put the chubby toddler back down.

"What do you trade?" Deborah's voice was light, curious.

"Goods from the before. Books. Anything you need, really. I'm a raider."

"I see." The child distracted her a moment and she looked away. "No, Myles, you cannot eat that stick." She turned back to Eddy, sighing. "And what do you want?"

"Metals. Vegetables and herbs that we don't have. Information. Skilled tradesmen, if they want to move on."

"Women?" Deborah was looking straight at him, her head turned full to the side.

"Only those who wish to come, or are in need of rescue, good Mother," Eddy said humbly. "I am no slaver, and I do not steal girls."

"Good." Deborah pulled up on Myles's arm when the child tried to crouch to the ground. "Do you have to potty? If you don't have to potty, we need to keep going. Oh. Alright then."

They waited while Myles relieved herself. Eddy looked carefully away.

They walked a while in silence. When the sound of music grew louder, Eddy asked, "What is that?"

"It's the pipe organ in the old church. It's a waste of work, but some of the ladies wanted to hear it. So they worked on it and cleaned the pipes out. It's a beautiful thing, but they left off their spinning for nearly a year to do it."

Eddy listened to the sound, alien yet appealing. "You make cloth here, I take it? Spinning and weaving?"

"Yes, it's one of our best enterprises. The trade we do is mostly in yardage."

Eddy didn't know that last word but extrapolated its meaning from context. "May I touch your sleeve, to get a feel of the work?"

Deborah smiled somewhat wickedly. "You were brought up right. Yes, you may."

She offered the arm that was not attached to the child. Eddy fingered the tight green weave.

"That's very good. I would like to see how this is made."

"I'm sure that can be arranged. Here's the square. I'll introduce you to someone in charge."

Eddy looked up from the cloth and blinked hard.

The square is full of women.

The space was wide and flat, with green lawns spreading out around a very old domed building, supported by columns. Eddy walked into the square, taking note that the lawns were planted with new tomato and strawberry plants. Everywhere he looked he saw signs of irrigation and constant maintenance.

Everywhere he looked, he saw women. He had never seen so many women at once in his life. Most of them dressed the way Deborah did: a long dress of homespun in brown or green and a bonnet. A few of them played with children of various ages, all of whom were girls.

How in the hell . . .

An older woman in a short-sleeved green dress crossed the square on the cracked paved path, shielding her eyes from the sun.

"Deborah? Who's that you've got with you?"

Deborah set down her child and reached out as the older woman drew near. They held each other's forearms at a distance for a few seconds. Eddy noted it, thinking it was their greeting. When they dropped arms, Deborah put her arm around the white-haired woman and gestured to Eddy.

"This is Eddy. He's a trader from the south."

"Hello, Eddy."

She held out a long, spotted arm. Eddy reached back, uncertain. She gripped him briefly above the elbow and he clumsily tried to return the gesture.

One arm for me. Two for Deborah.

"Hello."

She looked him up and down with blue-gray eyes, squinting. "I'm Thea. Where are you from?"

"South. Far, far south of here. Another city." Eddy shifted his weight from one foot to the other.

"I see. I can't blame you for keeping a few secrets. So, what are you looking for?" She watched him carefully.

"I didn't know there were people here until today. I'm out raiding, this trip—that is, in the old cities. Not in fine, lived-in places like this. And it's always good to find . . . people." His eyes darted around the open area and he struggled to make sense of what he was seeing.

If I ask right away, it'll scare them. But they have to know how weird this is, right?

"I can tell you have questions," Thea said. "I may or may not be able to answer them for you. We don't get many strangers here. You should have come in on the east side." She and Deborah exchanged a look.

"I'm not from Estiel." The name of the place tasted bad.

Deborah picked up Myles. "Well, we have to be on our way. Good luck, traveler."

"Thank you, good Mother." Eddy bowed his head to her as she left. He turned back to Thea. They stared at each other a minute.

"I have an idea," Thea said slowly. "Why don't you come inside?"

Eddy nodded, and they walked into the building with the huge columns. Up close, it felt to Eddy like the open door was a mouth behind giant tusks, and he was being swallowed up into the dark space within. He shifted his pack so that it ground his gun against the small of his back.

I have that, at least.

Inside, the space was lit by candles that smelled of tallow. Eddy immediately thought of the larger buildings in Nowhere and their day-time gloom. They had this same smell.

Thea led him into a smaller room, behind a heavy wooden door. He could hear voices on the other side.

As they came in, a man was drawing on a chalkboard on one wall.

"If we move composting to the east end of the airfield, we'll be able to—" He looked back at Thea and then did a double take.

"Who's this?"

Around the table, heads turned. Five men and two women. The man standing at the chalkboard was wearing a pleated skirt and a loose, open tunic. The other men appeared to be dressed the same, including a black man with an enormous beard. Eddy breathed a small sigh of relief.

Not another all-white town. Old women still prospering, not dead in childbirth. Thea is as old as Mother.

"We have a traveler from the south, everyone. This is Eddy."

Eddy nodded to greet them. A few nodded back, but mostly they stared.

Thea went on lightly, as though everything were under control. "I thought we could all ask Eddy to tell us about his city." She turned back to him. "Nothing too specific, I can tell you're squirrely about revealing its location. But we have questions. Don't we?"

People around the table looked at each other. Eddy looked at the windows, patched and broken.

"We do." It was the black man with the beard who spoke. He stood up at his chair and his belly rose huge and round above the table. "I'm Wilson. Will you sit and talk with us, Eddy? Have some water?" He gestured to an empty chair.

Thea slid into a chair and looked excited, as though anticipating a treat of some kind.

Eddy read the room.

They're shocked to see me. But nobody's tense. If I walked out right now, nobody would stop me. They'd be mystified, but a little relieved.

Safe enough.

He took his pack off slowly and hung it on the back of a chair. He pulled it out and sat.

"Alright. What can I tell you?"

Three voices spoke at once, and there was a small titter. Eddy smiled.

One of the women spoke up first. She had long hair pulled back in a ponytail and big black eyes. "I'm Athena. I'm in charge of schools here. I used to be a teacher."

"My mother is a teacher," Eddy said.

She smiled. "How many years of schooling do your children get?"

Eddy shrugged. "It depends. We all go to school until we can read and write and keep ourselves safe. Then there's apprentices, scribe training, people learn to work metal or chop wood. I became a raider at fifteen, so I went straight into training in the woods."

"What do you do, as a raider?" This was another man, with yellowed skin and cloudy eyes.

Sick. Probably dying.

"And you are?"

"I was the only doctor in this city, until I trained my replacements. My name is Bill."

"Well, Bill. I search for valuable things, from the before. Good tools and useful metal and machine parts. Sometimes other things. Books. You know how it goes. You get surprised by what you find."

Bill nodded and swallowed like it hurt him. Eddy figured he could ask whatever he liked, so he did. "Bill, are you sick? You look to be sick. Do you folks keep sick people working?"

Bill grimaced and Athena reached over and took his hand. "Bill has cancer. We can't do much to help him, and he wanted to keep working."

"Oh. I've seen a few old folks die of cancer. I'm sorry. Do you all make pain drugs?"

Athena nodded. "Are you comfortable, Bill?"

He smiled. "As comfortable as I can be and still keep my wits."

Eddy nodded. "We do, too. We have growers and chemists who make good stuff, sophisticated stuff. Better than most places I've seen on the road."

Nobody else has Alice.

Well, Sylvia does.

Stop that.

"How do you govern?" That was from Wilson.

Eddy sighed. "We have a council that's mostly Midwives and Mothers. Most of them are older, since that's when they have the time. The council has thirty representatives, all men, who handle contact with outsiders and peacekeeping."

"Do you have a lot of trouble keeping the peace?" Wilson's eyebrow was up.

"Every once in a while. A fight breaks out in a Hive, or something gets stolen. For the most part—"

"I'm sorry, a Hive?" Eyebrow still up.

"Yes, a Hive of men?" Eddy looked around the table and gauged puzzled faces. "You all don't have Hives here, do you?"

Here it comes.

Eddy began slowly. "So, in most places there aren't as many women as you all have here." He glanced up and then looked down at the table. "And Hives are a way for a woman to keep a number of men. So they work for her and take care of things for her, and she takes care of them. You understand?"

He felt rather than saw a number of them shift in their seats. There was some silence.

Thea broke it. "Yes, that makes sense. But as you've seen here, we have quite a few women."

Oh, so we're just going to say that like it's normal.

"Yes. Yes, I see that." Outside the cloudy window, green and brown shapes passed by. "But how?"

"Just as you don't want us to know where your people are," Wilson said evenly, "we would rather not have anyone know what we have here. You follow?"

"I follow." Eddy exhaled long and hard through his nose. He felt very out of his element. "Well. Well, I'm planning to move on toward Estiel."

Bill gasped a little. Wilson's eyes went wide, but he did not look at Eddy.

Eddy continued. "I haven't been in the city in a long time, only near it. But every time I get near, I find someone in trouble. Sometimes it's someone I can help. But you all are closer here. Can any of you tell me anything about it? I'm after some things I know I won't find anywhere else."

"Don't go there, son." It was a man who hadn't spoken before. Eddy looked up to meet his eye and found that he was a middle-aged man, with bright-green eyes that were wide with fright. "I mean it. I came from there, seventeen years ago. I wandered out with nothing, and I was nearly dead when some people from Jeff City found me and brought me here. There's nothing good there. I . . . I meant to get much farther away than here, or die trying."

Breathe slow. You're safe. You're here, not there. It's now, not then. Eight in, eight out.

There's nothing good there.

"What happened?" Eddy asked. He watched carefully as the man struggled with the question.

"It's not a story I like to tell."

Wilson put a gentle hand on the man's shoulder and squeezed it. "It's alright, George. Tell him so he knows."

George took a deep breath. "I was born in Estiel. I never knew my mother, I was brought up with all boys. All the women there are . . . well, you hear stories. I never saw any. Not once. But every year we'd get a few new baby boys, so the women were somewhere. I apprenticed in electricity; they have some there based on old solar panels. Or at least they did then. But there were fires and killings and no kind of law. We'd fix something and it would just burn down or be stolen. I finally left after . . . I escaped. I was being held with a group of other boys who . . . we were all smaller. Feminine. I escaped. That's the important thing. It's the kind of place you can't just leave, you have to escape it. You follow?"

Yes I just have to escape I can run I'm free to run.

Here. Now. Eight in, eight out.

"I follow." Eddy watched George calm himself down slowly and tried to do the same. Wilson squeezed his shoulder regularly, and George put his hand on top of the other man's.

"Why would you go there?" Thea was watching him carefully. "What are you after?"

"Women." Eddy didn't hesitate. He knew by this point they must know that. "But only women or girls who need somewhere to go. I have no indication that anyone here needs rescuing. But someone in Estiel might."

"Have you had much success?" Athena looked skeptical.

"Yes." Eddy returned her gaze steadily.

"How long have you been doing it? Maybe four years?" Thea asked it with amusement.

"Seven years. Six women and two girls. Most of them made it."

"From where?"

"All over."

"From Estiel?" Thea's eyes were narrowing.

"From near there. Camps along the road, people trying to reach the city. I've seen the Arch."

"Mmm," Thea said noncommittally.

Eddy thought he saw George flinch.

Here, now. What can we turn the conversation to?

"So, I see that you make good cloth here. I don't have a wagon to take much back, but I'd like to see how it's made. That's something we struggle with. We have good leather and other things we could trade, if you all were interested."

The air cleared a little. Wilson took his hand off George. Athena rose.

"I can show you where the spinners and weavers work. The dyeing is done a little farther out, because the smell is so sharp. You can talk cloth with Arabella, she's the foreperson of the guild."

"That'd be great." Eddy rose as well.

"Stay with us, if you'd like." Thea spoke with her chin raised. "I can arrange for space for you, and give you a night or two off the road."

Eddy nodded. "That's very kind. I'm happy to help in any way I can and earn it."

"You're earning it already."

Athena led him out the door and back into the sunlight.

They came through a wide barn door into a darker room. Eddy's eyes took a moment to adjust. Forty spinning wheels whirled inside the large space. One woman was singing in a low, husky voice. The wheels were all different; some were raw wood while others were ancient-looking lacquered rigs. Some had clearly been made of scrap: bicycle tires suspended over pedals made of hunks of plastic. Beyond the wheels, five more people worked drop spindles, pushing them deftly down the insides of their thighs, bringing wool over their arms and down to fattening bunches of yarn. Eddy looked around, mesmerized.

"This is quite an operation."

Athena smiled. "There are three out sick. Today's quota is light."

"Where does your wool come from?"

"Outside the city, we operate farms. Sheep, goats, cattle, and horses."

Eddy nodded. He had seen all the same on the bigger farms in Nowhere, and wild examples besides. However, Nowhere had only a few who could use a drop spindle, and no spinning wheels at all. Scavenging cloth was hard and heavy work, so only those raiders who had trucks could really do it. Most clothes were like Eddy's: leather and meant for everyday wear. Weavers were scarce, as well. A wool blanket was a costly thing. He stared around in amazement at what he was seeing.

In the dusty yellow light, spun wool lay in white and black and gray-blue stacks on shelves that covered one wall. On the far side of the room, weavers sat at looms in the same condition as the spinning wheels, though not so many. Eddy watched the shuttles move at a distance, entranced.

Softer and better than anything I've seen. This city is rich for trade.

One woman caught his eye, sitting on the edge between the spinners and the weavers. She was singing along but absolutely focused on her work.

Eddy popped his chin in her direction. "What's that woman doing? Why does her yarn look different?"

Athena smiled. "Oh, that's Flora. She's throwing silk. Come with me and I'll show you where it comes from."

They walked again, out to a wooded part of town. Athena showed him the mulberry tree with its huge leaves, all covered in the soft, flightless moths that had once been silkworms. Empty cocoons littered the ground below.

"See, they're harmless. Sticky little feet and they can't even fly." She held one on the back of her hand, passing it over her cheek. "Silk is hard to make and we only have the one tree. We only use it for things that are very special." She pointed out the immature worms, who lifted their heads as if to greet him.

"Like what?" Eddy thought of the woman named Flora, her long eyelashes downcast as she pulled out the worm-wool.

"Weddings. New babies. Precious things. There are only four silk weavers. They tend the tree, as well." She put the moth back on its leaf with the utmost tenderness.

"Are there any new babies now? Do you have a nursery?"

Athena looked down, tucking a lost lock of her hair behind her ear. "Not now, no. Did you say your council is made up of Midwives?"

"Sure, yes. The women who don't have children, but help bring them. You know." In Eddy's mind was his image of the Unnamed, and of Nowhere. The offerings of honey and fresh meat people brought to Sylvia and the other Midwives. He had traveled enough to know that every place had its own heroes and stories, and that his were known nowhere else.

"Huh. We have doctors and a couple of nurses who do that. Do you have new babies back home?"

Eddy smiled. "There's always a couple. One born last winter—Alexa, daughter of Cassie—and two others last year while I was out in the summer. Our Midwives are great, and we have good survival rates. What about here?"

Athena smiled thinly. "We do okay. About one child a year."

That doesn't add up at all.

"One child? With this many women? Do you have a lot of infant mortality?" He saw the look on Athena's face and was chastened. "Forgive me. That's a lot to ask. I hope things get better."

"So do I."

A small unease was beginning to creep up Eddy's back. He wasn't sure he wanted to stay the night, but he had said he would.

There should be more children. This many women, they ought to be knee deep in babies. Unless they figured out birth control, but why would they?

Athena brought them back to Thea, who walked Eddy to a small house that was appointed for a man living alone.

"The pinkish house over there on the left," she said, pointing, "has invited you to breakfast. She says any time after daybreak."

"Thank you. I'll do that."

"Pleasant dreams, Eddy."

That was not a phrase Eddy had ever heard before. He slept fully clothed, hands on his gun. He did not dream.

He watched the day break. He washed his face and hands with the cold water left in a tub in the kitchen for him. When it was full light, he walked to the pink house, pinker in the dawn. He circled the house once, hearing nothing. He circled again and heard sounds in the back.

He knocked at the back door.

Flora opened the door to the kitchen. She was tall, and much more striking up close than she had been at a distance, throwing silk. Her eyes were bright, glorious gray and she used some kind of ink to line them and make them stand out. Eddy had never seen that before. He had also never seen hair that was so dark red, almost purple. Everything about her looked careful. Her white apron worn over her green dress, her neat hands, her shy mouth.

So pretty.

"Good morning, good woman."

"I've got fresh eggs. Bread and some canned apples from last year. Sweet water from my own cistern and mint tea if you like it." Her voice was musical, tripping up and down the words like notes.

Eddy smiled, genuinely disarmed. "That sounds delicious, good woman. I am honored."

She laughed a little. "They told me you were very formal."

"Formal?"

She turned out of the doorway. "Please come in."

The eggs were boiled and still hot, sitting up in ceramic cups. Eddy sliced the heads off his and dove into the yolk with shreds of toast. He was hungry, and as Flora was finishing her own eggs, she pushed a bowl of canned apples toward him. They were preserved in honey with a strange spiced taste.

"What's in that?"

"It's called sassafras. I bought it from a trader last year." She dimpled prettily. "He told me it grows all over. Do you like it?"

Eddy had a large mouthful when she asked. He grinned around it and nodded.

"I'm so glad you're enjoying it."

When he could speak, he asked, "Have you always made silk?"

"The worms make the silk. I just throw it and weave it." She dipped her head and drank a little milk.

She kidding me, or just being difficult?

"So have you always done that?"

"No, I started off in wool like everyone does. I made the neatest, most even yarn, and the silk guild chose me."

"Can you show me what you make? I can't imagine what worm-wool must feel like."

Tell me you're wearing it and let me touch. He stared at her throat.

"Here." She rose from the table and left the room. She came back with a square of pale-white cloth that fit in her palm. She held it out. "May I?"

He nodded, looking up at her.

She pressed it to his cheek and rubbed it downward, slowly. It felt cool and impossibly soft against his face. He put his hand to it and touched hers.

"That's so soft," he said.

What an obvious thing to say. I am so good at this.

She smiled again, this time teeth and all.

"It took me a long time to get it this smooth and fine."

He smiled back. "So what would it take to get you to trade some?"

"Have you ever seen a running car?"

More than I'd like to.

Eddy shrugged. "We have a couple of trucks that still run. Making gas is hard and it stinks, but some of our guys use them to haul big stuff in and out of the village."

"That's what I want. I will trade whole bolts of silk for one of those."

Eddy sighed. "You want a lot."

"You have no idea."

Flora walked Eddy back to the town square. He didn't know what he was going to do. He figured it was about time to move on, but he wasn't sure he had established enough of a contact to ensure future trade. When they reached the center of town, he turned to her.

"What are you going to do today?"

"Work, like I do most days. Trying to get as much silk thrown as possible before the first berries come in. I'd like to do some dyeing this year."

"How old were you when you picked that up?"

She looked down. "I started spinning right after I came here. It was my first job."

"Oh, you weren't born here in Jeff City? Sorry, I just kind of assumed. Were you on the road?"

In Nowhere, travelers told their stories to the librarian, who edited them and gave them to the scribes. Knowing she had been a traveler sparked him to respect. Most of the people he met in safe places like this had never left home.

"I was, yes. As a child. I don't remember much." She wouldn't look at him.

"Did you come with your parents? Or with a group of people? Did raiders find you?"

"I came by myself."

Eddy let that hang for a moment. A little girl on the road alone was unheard of. He assumed Flora must have been sold to Jeff City, or escaped slavers on her own.

Fuck, I am never gonna find out unless I ask. Just ask.

"Does . . . Does Jeff City pay for girls? Buy them from slavers?"

"Um. I don't know." Eddy tried hard to meet her eyes, dropping his head to intersect her gaze. She looked away, at the floor, anywhere else.

"You don't know? Do you ever get new people in? Travelers?"

"It's been a long time." She pushed her dark-red hair behind her ears on both sides and smiled suddenly, bright and fake. "Mandel would know! Let's go talk to her."

Eddy felt that same uneasiness wash over him. Across the square, women walked carrying baskets and balls of yarn. Little girls wore bright bonnets to keep the sun off their faces. Two women stood consulting about ingredients for lotion, and the sound of their voices made Eddy feel a sweet and sad sort of envy.

Discussions between women only were rare and precious back home. Relished in talk between Mothers and Midwives, at first-blood parties and moments of privacy. Here, with so many women around, it was commonplace.

He wasn't paying attention to where they were going. When he turned his head back to match the direction of his feet, he saw that they must be headed into their infirmary. The sign above the door used the same symbol as the one in Nowhere: a red cross on a white background. Eddy had seen it a few times in his travels and knew it must be a symbol from the before.

Inside, the tallest woman Eddy had ever seen was wrapping a bandage around a man's forearm.

"Next time, just let it fall. Don't dive after it. You're not a young man anymore, Eamon. Your back won't carry you forever."

"Yes, Mandel. Thank you. I'll bring your house some good dry wood for this."

"That'll be fine."

Mandel turned around and Eddy watched with his mouth open. She was two heads taller than him, with rippling blue-black braids that hung shining to her waist. She dipped her hands into a basin and dried them on a cloth before speaking to them.

"Flora, so lovely to see you! Not sick, I hope?" Her mouth was kind and quick, and she looked Eddy up and down as she spoke.

"No, Mandel. Thank you, I'm well. This is Eddy, he's a traveler from the south."

"Good to see a new face, Eddy!" She reached out and gave him the same one-armed grip he had received before.

That must be the way a woman greets a man. Two women do it with both arms, woman and man with one. Or is it just one for outsiders?

"New faces is actually what I came to talk to you about," Eddy said. "Do you have some free time?"

"Never," she said with a small laugh. "But we can talk anyhow."

He nodded, remembering Sylvia and the other Midwives, the way they always seemed to be working. Sylvia had told her that they had to force each other to take breaks, just to keep morale up.

Mandel picked up a tray of instruments and began dropping them into a pot to boil. "So, what can I tell you?"

"How do you handle newcomers to Jeff City?"

"We don't have many." Her back was turned, but it didn't sound like a lie.

"Yes, I've heard that." Eddy forced his voice to stay even, not too eager. "But when you do get them?"

"It depends. On their attitude and why they came. What they want, you know."

"Do you accept new people, if they want to join you?"

"Sure, if they want to work and not make trouble."

"Men, too?"

Mandel was silent for a moment, putting the pot on a hook that held it over a fire in the far corner of the room.

She turned around and looked at him cautiously. "Yes, men, too. Do you need to leave your own town and join us here?"

"No," he said impatiently. "What do you do with slavers? With men who show up in the town square with a pregnant little girl and ask you what they can get for her?"

"Oh." Mandel tossed her head a little, and a black braid slipped over her shoulder. "As I said, that doesn't happen often. But when it does, we buy the girl."

Eddy worked his jaw for a few moments, unable to speak.

"Why?"

The tall woman looked at Flora and sighed. "To end her misery. To get them to leave without trouble. To keep the peace and keep the child."

"So you have repeat sellers? Men who steal girls from their people and drag them for miles to bring them here for . . . for what? How do you pay for them?"

"Doctoring, mostly. Men who live on the road live with running infections and bad teeth and unset broken bones. Sometimes just drugs, though we don't have much."

Eddy was hot all over, but somehow his heart was like ice. "You help them. You encourage the slave trade, and you keep slavers healthy?"

Mandel looked exasperated. "We didn't make the world, Eddy. We just have to live in it. They're going to do it anyway, at least they know they can bring them here."

He couldn't speak.

"Eddy," Flora almost whispered. "What do your people do?"

Eddy laughed shortly. "We kill them. For fuck's sake. Of course we kill them. We hang them up outside our gates with a sign that explains what we did. We take any women or children they have, and it ends there. It ends."

Maybe they just don't have the weaponry. Maybe they didn't have someone like the Unnamed to tell them how it had been on the road, how it would be.

"How barbaric," Flora said, looking at Mandel.

The tall woman clucked her tongue. "Dead men don't learn anything. Changed men change the world."

"Men don't change," Eddy said automatically. "They never have."

"If you say so," Mandel said with a hint of amusement. She turned her back on them without saying good-bye.

Outside, Eddy turned on Flora. "Is that what happened to you? Were you bought?"

"Not exactly."

"Well, what, then?"

"I was . . ." Her gray eyes darted for a moment. "I wasn't a slaver. But I was an apprentice to one. I was so young. They gave me the chance to stay and make a change. So I took it."

What does a slaver's apprentice do? Run down the little ones? Hold them while he sharpens the knife?

It must have showed on his face, because Flora looked like she knew herself judged.

"There's a lot here you don't understand," she said. "That you're never going to understand. Because you only see one solution."

She walked away and left him there.

Eddy wanted to leave town immediately, stomping out still burning with rage. He made himself wait.

Instead, he walked to the marketplace. He could see what Thea had meant; this edge of Jeff City was clearly the face they showed to outsiders. Huge reinforced gates blocked the main road in, patrolled by sentries carrying bows. The ratio of men to women on this side of the city looked right to Eddy. He saw only two or three women in the streets and stalls, mingled among thirty or forty men.

Everyone in the market was clearly armed. Mostly knives and machetes. A man walked just in front of Eddy, and he had a moment to admire the workmanship of the man's bow, smooth and curved like a tender upper lip. It was nearly as long as the man himself, Eddy saw as the other man strode away.

Pulling his hood back, Eddy approached the nearest stalls to examine the goods for sale. It was still fairly early in the day; bushels were full and the cool air was kind to the butchers. He passed by fruits and vegetables, noticing that their drying and canning looked expert. He fingered cloth of all types, though silk was kept away from customers' hands. At a dairy stall he bought a lump of soft cheese wrapped in a scrap of cloth and took a small bite. It was well worth the clay pot of toothache remedy he had traded for it. The cheese was smooth and salty, better than any he had had in Nowhere. He knew people back home would be eager to trade here.

The bowyer's stall was deserted when Eddy arrived. He carefully wiped his fingers and pocketed the cloth before laying his hands on the merchandise.

The bows on display were carved from ash and hickory, he saw. They were strung with sinew, and a bag of spares sat just out of Eddy's reach on the far side of the table. Behind it, ten bows were piled unstrung on top of a cowhide. He picked up one of the displays, an ash bow. He held it before him, testing the weight of it.

Through the purple curtains at the rear of the stall came a short man with a heavy belly that hung over his pleated skirt. His head shone bald in the center, ringed around the back with thick black hair. His eyes were as small and intelligent as a wild boar's.

"A beauty, isn't it?" He held his hand out for the ash bow and Eddy handed it over. The short man pulled the bowstring in profile, muscles suddenly clear in his inelegant limbs.

"A beauty, yes. Are you the maker?"

"Oh, I'm the bowyer, if that's what you mean. One of three here in Jeff City. Name's Fletcher, if you can believe that." He grinned, tiny teeth in a heavy gum line.

Eddy had never met a bowyer or a fletcher and didn't get the joke, but he knew from the man's tone that he had meant to be funny. He smiled and laid his hands on the bow's hickory twin.

"How did you learn?"

Fletcher laid down the ash bow and took up the hickory, seeming to need to take whatever Eddy had his hands on. "From my father, of course. It's the family trade. You a hunter? Named Hunter, maybe?"

Why do you have to talk so fast? Nobody is behind me.

"No, I'm a raider. Name is Eddy. I do hunt, though. Mostly for myself, but even then I could use one of these."

There were bows in Nowhere, most of them scavenged and preserved from the before. He had never seen a newly made bow.

"What do you shoot?" Fletcher grinned a little, ready to show off.

Men.

"Deer are probably the biggest thing. Birds. Whatever I can find and butcher."

The short man tapped both of his smart, square hands on the table and whirled around. He took two bows off the pile and held them up, gauging Eddy's height with squinted eyes. He made a quick decision and deftly strung a new bow. He pushed back through the side curtains and came around to hand it to Eddy.

Eddy took it, feeling the soft leather on the grip. He held it up and pulled the string back.

"You've shot one before?" Fletcher cocked an eyebrow and stood back.

"Yes . . . just. Well, a very old one. But I learned as a kid, before I got my apprenticeship."

The skin on Eddy's back crawled as Fletcher came close. "Here, let me—"

Eddy wheeled and stepped back, lowering the bow. "No, thank you. I got it. What will you take for this?"

Fletcher shrugged and leaned back against his own table. "I usually trade for meat. Antelope and buffalo are my favorite, but I see more deer. But you're not a hunter."

"I'm not." Eddy slid his pack down off his shoulders and knelt beside it. "But I bet I have something that you'll like." He felt down in the bottom of the pack and brought out a carved wooden box.

Eddy hardly ever got out the whole box. He knew by feel each tiny drawer and compartment, every secret catch. Fletcher was immediately interested.

"That box is a fine piece of carpentry."

"It is, yes. That's not what I'm offering, though." He sprung a couple of doors and drawers open. "I'm offering the best of what my village has to offer, which is mainly drugs. I have drugs here for toothaches. Earaches. Pain. For sleep, for itch, and for being blocked up. You name it, I've got it."

"Ha. You're like the horsewomen."

"The what?"

Fletcher shrugged it off. "Have you got anything that works on itchweed?"

Eddy pulled out one of the low drawers and brought out a long glass vial stopped with a cork. Within, bluish-white paste moved like a slug.

He stood up, holding the paste to the light. "You probably run into itchweed all the time, searching for the right wood. This here can be diluted in ten times as much water, or twenty times as much oil if you've got it. This will work on anything that itches, even musky bites. But save it for when you really need it, because unless you want to walk south for a while, it'll be hard to get more."

Eddy held it out to the man, who was rubbing his bald head thoughtfully. "I can surely use that," he said earnestly. "But a bow is a costly thing. Takes time to make right, and mine are the best. No disrespect to your trade, but what else can you offer me?"

Back in the kit, Eddy's slender black hands pulled out a small black ceramic pot stopped with red wax. He pulled out a second white pot of toothache remedy, just like the one he had traded for cheese. He palmed that one and then produced a tiny vial of clear liquid.

Holding up the white ceramic pot, he said, "This one is for toothaches. Rub it on or pack it into the hole and it feels a whole lot better. This black one is for itchweed, you can dilute it and use it a long time." He held up the glass vial. "This one is just pain relief. Hard pain, like a broken bone. Or to ease someone you love out of their misery. One drop is enough for a grown man." He fanned out his hands, offering all three.

Fletcher nodded decisively. "That's worth a bow and a string, plus a few arrowheads. You know how to fashion a shaft?"

They talked for a few minutes about how Eddy could manage the half dozen broadheads Fletcher slipped into his hand. The big man clapped Eddy on his narrow back and the younger man tried to smile rather than flinch. He strapped the bow on his back and turned around to show the bowyer.

"Look alright?"

Fletcher stepped in close behind Eddy too quickly and put his hands to the back of Eddy's waistband. Eddy pulled his sharp, curved knife and whipped around, his hand clamped on the back of the short man's neck, pointing the tip of the knife beneath his chin.

Fletcher held both hands up, eyes looking straight into Eddy's.

"I can see your gun. I can see it. That's all. I was going to fix it for you. The bow caught on your shirt."

Eddy let go of the man, who stood up straight and looked around. Eddy reached back and rearranged his clothes, pulling the bottom of the bow closer to his right side. He tested with his left to see if the top was in a position to pull.

Breathe. Slow and even. Eight in, eight out. Where are you right now?

He spoke to Fletcher without looking back.

"Don't close in on somebody like that. You ought to know better."

Fletcher walked back behind his table, wariness in his frame. "Yes, I suppose I ought to. I only meant to—"

Eddy came to stand at the opposite edge of the table. "Look. You and me did a trade. A good and honest one, and both of us got something. If you saw something you shouldn't have, you don't need to mention it to anyone. Right?"

Fletcher leaned forward, hands flat on the table. He spoke softly, his eyes watching people pass through the market. "I have one, too. A good one. I understand you don't want to have to defend it. We don't have a bullet maker, but I am trying to get the blacksmith to learn with me. Do you have one in your town?"

"No." Eddy set his jaw and rocked back on his heels, looking over his shoulder.

Shake it off. He didn't mean to spook you like that.

"Estiel," Eddy said. "There are bullet makers in Estiel." He looked at the purple tent curtains behind Fletcher.

The bowyer sighed. "So much for that."

Eddy took a step back and nodded curtly before walking away.

CHAPTER 3

There were bullet makers in Estiel. Too numerous to count. There were armorers of all kinds, bowyers and shield makers. Smiths and engineers, coopers and explosives men. There were tinkerers who harvested the plastic gadgets of the before and tried to electrify them back to life. There were teams devoted to solar power, to wind turbines. There was a melancholy gaggle of men who tried to clean the rust and rot out of airplanes and get their engines to choke up and start again.

Most of the airplanes in Estiel were used as drying sheds for vegetables and game after their engine parts had been scavenged.

Raiders from Estiel traveled so far north that they wore bearskins for the snow. They traveled south into the sweltering tropical heat until they reached the ocean. They knew the roads and the bigger towns better than most.

These raiding parties usually consisted of four men each. They had specific instructions about what to seek out, what to pay for, and what to take.

They were never to pay for anything they could take. They were never to transport people or goods that were not destined for Estiel, despite the wonders and rarities people offered for a chance to ride in one of their roaring trucks.

The Lion of Estiel wanted things in their order of importance. First: guns. Guns of any age, in any shape. Second: the components of black powder. The first raiders to find the great northern potassium mines were lucky until they weren't; three of the first four died in a cave-in. The last man returned and claimed the entire prize for himself.

After guns and powder, the Lion wanted metal. Brass and copper first, but iron and steel were just as important. The raiders were taught basic metallurgy to refine their eye toward what they could use.

Paws of the Lion raided in all seasons except the winter. Each man wore a claw on a leather thong around his neck, given to him by the Lion when he received his commission. In many towns and villages, people shut their gates at the sign of the claw. In others, they opened up and traded.

Jeff City welcomed these raiders at the eastern gates with some regularity.

The raiders of Estiel did not concern themselves with curiosities from the before. They only rarely sought books, and traded for food only for themselves. They did not represent the interests of their city in anything but arms. The Lion instructed them to report back if they found a town or village that produced arms of its own, used electric lights, or had a working machine capable of flight. Toward the bottom of the list were instructions in case they found a village of drug makers.

The last standing order was for the delivery of any and all females of any age and in any condition.

CHAPTER 4

On Eddy's last day in Jeff City, Flora couldn't seem to leave his side. She had seen him every day, making breakfast for the two of them and somehow finding him after she was done with work.

Sometimes when they spoke, Flora would lay her light, silky fingers on the soft underbelly of his forearm. He knew what she wanted.

He had finished packing to leave. He had chosen his route out of town. He had gotten up at dawn and skipped out on her for breakfast.

He went to the market on the east side of town and traded once more for food for the road. He bought dry oats and cracked wheat for porridge, plus a little salt. He knew he could forage for meat and fruits this time of year.

Coming to the eastern gates, Eddy was blinded by the sun rising over the tall walls of wood and iron that enclosed the market on that side.

Those dark glasses the old woman had, he thought, remembering the old woman with Chloe. *Got to find a pair.*

The gates were swinging open ahead and Eddy heard a far-off roaring. The sound cut off, and four men were admitted through the gate. Eddy knew from the way they walked that they were armed.

He drifted off to the right, as if he had meant all along to visit the final stall in the market rather than leave. It was a cloth stall, hard-woven material for sacks or overalls. He fingered the folds of the dark-blue stack in front of him and waited.

The four men walked straight to a central booth run by Deborah, the woman Eddy had met on his first day in Jeff City. She sold fruits and vegetables, and today her table was covered in bushels of chokeberries. She stepped up and offered the men sweet well water in glass jars.

They took them and drank, making conversation with her and bartering for their breakfast. One of them bought two big handfuls of chokeberries for a tallow candle, which Deborah accepted with delight.

At the sound of her mother's happy exclamations, Myles crawled out from under the table. Like any toddler, she held out her chubby hands and demanded the short yellow taper, wanting to hold it herself.

Deborah handed it over and adjusted the child's bonnet.

They were a little too far-off for Eddy to hear them, but he caught a few words.

". . . checked?"

"Yeah, she's a horsewoman."

What the hell is a horsewoman? Eddy drifted closer, head down, pretending to shop.

"Not her, the child." The leader of the four men was the tallest one, with long, sun-bleached curls. He pointed with his right hand and Eddy saw a scar running down his forearm that looked like the slit in the top of a loaf of bread, as if his arm had grown too fast and simply split the skin. Its edges were clean.

Knife cut, Eddy thought, and moved closer still. *Outcast?*

A shorter man with a black beard pulled at his claw necklace, adjusting it. "Probably the same. They all are here, I told you."

The blond leader dismissed him with a low gesture. "Deborah, is it? May I see the child?"

Deborah looked down and spread her hands nervously over Myles's head, indicating a field around the toddler's body. "She just pooped. It's disgusting, really." She made a sound she intended to be a laugh, but it croaked out of her, as flat a pronouncement of panic as a scream.

The blond raider leaned over the table and snatched Myles by one arm. He brought the child up and sat her on the table.

"No," Deborah said, clearly begging. "Please, no."

The fair hair on the backs of his hands shone in the early-morning light. He lifted up the child's green dress and peered under.

"Female," he said as he picked Myles up and handed her to the youngest of the four. The young man looked confused.

"What am I supposed to do with this?"

"Hold it, idiot. We'll put it on the truck and run it back to Estiel."

The young man held the child like he'd never seen one before.

Deborah tore her way out of the stall and went to the child, who was beginning to look distressed. "Please. Please, she's so little. You don't know how to take care of her. She's very . . . She's delicate. Sickly. Probably won't last through the winter. Please leave her with me."

The young man looked up at his blond leader, uncertain. Eddy sidled closer, coming up behind the tall man, sizing him up.

His hairy blond hand reached out again and pinched the deep rolls of fat on Myles's leg. "It'll live through the winter. Say good-bye."

Deborah was already crying so hard she could barely breathe. "Please. Please don't take her. Please don't."

All around, the market had come to a standstill. It was only merchants and their helpers this early in the day, but no one moved or spoke.

"You know the deal, horsewoman. Are you going to let us have it, or do we have to convince you?" One of his big hands disappeared inside his leather jacket and waited there.

Deborah stroked the child's face and the two of them cried piteously, Deborah because she understood and Myles because she did not.

"Sweet baby, I love you. I love you so much. Be good and be quiet. Be safe. Alright? Be safe. I love you. Mommy loves you."

The black-haired man pulled Deborah away and pressed something into her shaking hands. She let it fall to the dirt and Eddy saw that it was a bullet, small caliber and handmade.

Deborah fell after it, sobbing into her hands.

The tall man led them back toward the gates, the youngest struggling to carry the screaming Myles.

Eddy didn't fully understand what he had seen. *Why would they just stand there and let that happen? Don't they fight to keep their own? Who'd take one bullet for a living girl child?*

He looked down at Deborah, reduced to an animal in grief. He looked around at the merchants, who were all very busy at finding something else to do. A few of them were hiding tears.

Fuck this.

He stepped into the middle of the road, lining them up with his eye. The sun blinded him again.

"Hey!"

The four of them turned, surprised. The blond one walked forward and blocked the others.

"What?"

Eddy's mouth went dry. *Four bullets in. I'd have to hit all of them and miss the baby and not lose a single shot. And fast enough that they couldn't shoot back.*

He started to speak and a whisper came out. He cleared his throat. "You can't just take a child. There aren't many of those in the world, you know."

The tall blond man flexed his scarred arms and squared his stance. "This child is the rightful property of the Lion of Estiel. You have a problem, I suggest you take it up with him."

Something passed between them. Some wordless measurement was taken. The blond turned his back when he realized Eddy was no threat, just a young man brave enough to yell but not dumb enough to shoot.

Fuck me.

Eddy realized too late that no one was going to stop them. He hadn't moved fast enough, and the people of Jeff City hadn't moved at all.

Myles's wailing could be heard until the roar of the truck returned and then faded. Eddy could hear people coming to console Deborah, who was keening high and endless now. He stared into the direction of the rising sun for a long time, until his forehead was hot and his soul was sick.

Should have shot them should have shot them I should have at least tried and shot them. I should have died for her.

Where are you right now?

It was the question he always asked. It brought him back to the present moment.

He fought for breath. He wanted badly to touch his gun but settled for touching his bow.

He walked out of Jeff City and didn't look back.

The Book of Etta
Year 104 in the Nowhere Codex
Spring

Just left Jeff City. They make good cloth there. Bought a bow. Saw a girl stolen by raiders wearing claws. Seems like the mark of the Lion. Reminds me of something, but I don't know what. Walked all day, headed east.

Walked all day.

Walked all day. Made arrows and shot a rabbit.

The moon was a little fatter than new. Eddy figured it would be full when he was close to Estiel. The roads between Jeff City and Estiel were deserted. Eddy saw no blackened campfires, no telltale piles of shit to show that people traveled this way on foot.

By truck, though. Maybe.

He didn't look at the map. He followed the broken black of the old highway and knew from every map study he had ever done that this road, like all roads, headed into the old city with the Arch.

He did not think of the city.

He walked late into the day, tired but wanting to make up miles he had lost on a fruitless bird hunt in the morning. He was hungry but hadn't caught or found anything good in two days. He had decided to make wheat porridge tonight as soon as he found a good place to camp, but made himself continue until something sheltered came along. The wind had the sharp, cold tang of an incoming storm. He wanted a roof.

Up ahead, the road humped up and over the remains of a gas station, and a smaller road led north toward a cluster of houses. Eddy quickened his step as the houses came into view; almost none of them looked burned.

As he climbed up the overpass, he scoped out the old structures. He pulled from his pack a tiny pair of binoculars. They were bright-yellow plastic, made for a child. But they worked better than his own eyes, so he treated them carefully and used them with respect.

He scanned over the chimneys that still stood. Most of them lay in piles of crumbled brick, but a few leaned mostly upright. No smoke hung in the windless evening air. He swept judiciously from side to side, looking for any signs of life or trouble. Nothing stirred.

A sound caught his attention, and he peered anxiously down at the houses.

No, not there. Behind you.

He lowered the binocs and squinted back down the road.

The sound was horses. Eddy did not know horses well; very few people in Nowhere kept them. He had seen them wild on the plains more than once—huge, hoof-pounding herds that thundered terrifyingly, even at a distance.

A rider on the road was approaching fast, pulling a second horse behind them. Eddy lowered the glasses and looked around.

I'm above them, he assessed quickly. *I've already been seen. I won't outrun them. They'll probably pass right by me.*

He backed off the road and stood in the dirt at the edge. Yellow dandelions formed a line behind him. He watched as the rider slowed and came closer. He reached back and put his hand on his gun.

The rider was tall in the saddle, but completely covered. A long garment draped over their entire body, with a window at the eyes. Strips were tied at the rider's forehead and shoulders to keep the drapery straight. The cloth was periwinkle blue, streaming back in the wind on all sides as though it were light as air. The sight took Eddy's breath away for a moment. He shook off the awe and looked at the saddlebags, at the rider's hips.

Not armed. Why they stopping?

The horse pulled up and the second one stepped forward, reining in slower. The rider tied the reins of the second to the horn of the saddle and reached down to haul their long clothes up.

Eddy tensed.

The figure looped the yards of fabric off her face and around her shoulders. Flora smiled and pushed her red-purple hair out of her eyes.

"So glad I found you!" She worked for a minute to catch her breath. "Why did you come this way? Don't you know they're looking for you?"

"Who is?"

You know who is.

"Those raiders from Estiel. The Lion's men. What happened? I've heard you tried to kill one of them."

Eddy shook his head, looking back down the road. "What are you doing here?"

"I couldn't stand the idea of them finding you out here all alone. I came to bring you back."

Eddy pulled up his hood and pointed over the road. "I'm going to make camp in one of those houses. And then in the morning, I'm going to head into Estiel. I am not going back to Jeff City, now or ever."

Flora slid off her horse and landed pretty lightly. She hauled her cover all the way off and threw it over the animal. The horse was dark brown and seemed tired. Eddy looked nervously at its huge black eye.

"Then I'm going with you." Flora pulled at the reins and started to walk. "We can talk about it in the morning."

I hate horses.

As if she'd heard him, Flora popped her chin at the brown horse first. "This is Apples. And that one," she said, nodding to the cream-spotted smaller horse, "is Star. See the star on her head?"

"Sure." Eddy didn't follow. He was happy to see Flora, but he was put off by her assumption that he would just accept her coming along.

"I've got squirrels in my saddlebag. And some arrowhead potatoes." She looked back over her shoulder. "You hungry?"

Grudging, grumbling, Eddy walked forward.

They found a faded blue house that looked safe enough. Eddy climbed through one of the long-gone windows and kicked out the rusty door from the inside. There was a garage attached where they could keep the horses out of the rain that was now imminent in the heavy, scented air and the electric crackle in everything they touched. The space had no door, only a huge, empty hole where one might have been.

Thunder rumbled and bashed right on top of flashes of green lightning. Eddy walked around inside the house, trying to find the most intact part of the roof. One of the back bedrooms seemed best. The room smelled of rats, but there was a small fireplace they could use.

They were nearly an hour in making it habitable, and by then the rain had begun in earnest. They pushed an old wardrobe in front of the window, then argued about using the bed to block the door.

"If anyone wants to bust in on us, they'll come through the window," Flora said, exasperated.

"You don't know that." Eddy stared around the room, trying to come up with a compromise. He stalked into the house's kitchen. It looked like every other kitchen he had ever seen: picked clean and looted for anything that might hold value. He pried open a warped cabinet door under the old sink and found two plastic trash bins.

"Here," he said. He shook one of them out on the floor. It was full of rusty cans, made of cheap metal that smiths in Nowhere never seemed to want. "Gather these up."

As they walked back to the bedroom, they laid the cans everywhere so that an intruder would be sure to knock more than a few down as they made their way in.

"The storm should cover our smoke," Eddy said. His teeth were chattering. The front rooms of the house leaked in odd spots. The back bedroom had one good-size leak in the farthest corner from the hearth. That was luck. He turned himself to their kindling and rummaged in his pack for his flint and steel.

"So did you? Try to kill the Lion's men?" Flora fidgeted, wrapped in her cloak and still freezing.

He concentrated on the fire. "Better question would be why all of us didn't stop them from taking that baby. Myles. Everybody just stood there and let them take her."

"Violence isn't the only—" Flora began.

"Oh, bullshit. You said that before, and I get it. But there wasn't *any* resistance. So you all didn't want to kill them. Alright. But you could have just blocked them, just taken her away from them. She's as good as dead, you know. Maybe not tonight, but someday soon. They won't wait. She'll be serving before she gets her blood and pregnant right after."

"You don't know that."

"I do."

Smoke poured out of the blocked chimney into the room.

"Shit." Eddy felt for the lever of the flue, wrenching at the corroded metal. It wouldn't budge. He pulled out one of his knives and used the haft of it to pound at the handle until it screeched and gave. Hot air rushed upward and he yanked his hand back.

He fed the fire without speaking until it leapt and crackled. He pulled off his leather boots and put his socked feet in front of the heat. Flora scooted up and joined him.

"It's not our way," she said quietly. "It just makes things worse. And the Lion's men . . . They could make things much harder on us. We made a deal with them."

"What is that deal?"

Flora shook her head and Eddy saw tiny droplets of water caught in the fine baby hairs around her face. "I don't know all of it. But I know they take girls. And I know we let them."

"Always babies? They can't even wait until they get their blood?"

Flora shrugged. "They're looking for a particular kind of girl."

Eddy remembered something they had said. "They don't take horse-women, is that right? Like you?"

He watched her. She was sitting with her knees drawn up to her chin. She turned her head away from him and set it on her shoulder. "Yes, like me. They're not interested in us."

That doesn't make any sense.

"Nothing I saw in Jeff City makes any sense."

She didn't answer him.

They fell asleep three feet apart, shivering in front of the fire. Eddy woke up twice, when the wind knocked over a can and when it howled. He did what he could to keep the hearth hot.

Dawn was cold and wet. He woke up to Flora banking the coals and tucking eggs into the ashes.

"These'll only take a minute."

They ate breakfast in silence. When Eddy was done, he brushed off his hands and stood up.

"Well. I'm going to keep moving toward the city. You should probably head home."

Flora stood and adjusted her cloak. "I told you, I'm coming with you. We really shouldn't go to Estiel. Is there something you need there?"

"I don't want you to come with me. I don't want company, and I don't want a horse. I especially don't want a coward. Alright? Now go on home."

Flora looked down at her boots. "I thought . . . I thought that you liked me. I thought you might stay." She looked up at him with her stormy gray eyes. The ink she used around them was smudged and she was puffy with sleep. It was easy to say no.

"I don't know what you thought," Eddy said shortly, "but that isn't possible."

She huffed a little air and smoothed her hair out. "Why? Because we think about things differently? Because I don't believe—"

He shouldered his pack and went to turn away from her. "I don't care where you go. Just don't follow me."

"I don't care," Flora said simply. "What we believe doesn't matter to me. Only what we do. I want you, Eddy!"

She called out to him as he tried to walk away. "I want you. I want to follow you. I left my home to follow you. I want . . . I want something different." She sighed as she struggled to put words to her desire. "I want to be different than I am at home."

Eddy stopped in the doorway. He heard himself echoed back, that need to escape not just home but the ghost of himself who lived there.

He did not turn. He did not take her hand. But she was watching him carefully, and he let his shoulders settle down just the smallest bit.

"Fine. Let's see to the horses."

Apples and Star trotted out of the garage the minute they were untied from the old pipes. They looked to be in much better spirits than their human companions this morning. Apples began eating the tall grass and wild wheat immediately, while Star lowered her head to drink from a deep puddle.

Eddy watched them dispassionately.

Never even tried to ride one of these things.

"How much faster do you go as a horsewoman than if you're walking?" he asked.

Flora gave him a funny look. "On horseback it's four, maybe five days to Estiel. Much faster. But you have to be careful not to push them too hard." She reached over and stroked Apples's side.

Eddy's stomach contracted. *I don't want to be there that soon.* Memory flashed Estiel's black rainbow at him again. He took a deep breath.

"I've never ridden before. I've seen it done, but I really don't know how."

Flora nodded, patting Apples. "That's why I brought Star. She's a training horse for little ones who are just learning. She's very gentle. Patient."

She gives these things too much credit.

"I see."

Eddy was unsteadily mounted and cantering onto the road not long after that. Flora set an easy pace, but he could immediately feel that he would be saddle-sore later.

"How do you keep from . . ." He indicated his crotch and thighs with his free hand. "It hurts like I'm going to be sore later."

Flora laughed a little. "You get used to it. Nothing to be done."

"I see." Eddy spent the next few minutes trying to adjust his seat. "So you were a slaver's apprentice? I never did get the story."

Flora sighed, looking off into the distance. She rearranged the folds of her cloak. Eddy was grateful that she did not wear the huge covering tent she had worn the day before.

She thought a long time before speaking. "I don't remember most of that time. I was very young. But yes, I worked for a slaver. His name was Archie. He was old, and he used to tell people he remembered the before."

"He couldn't have been that old." Eddy adjusted again, feeling punched in his vulva.

"No, it was just something he said. He made up all kinds of stories. He said he had flown in an airplane. That he saw one of the great glass cities while it was still standing. He said he had known a king in Florda. That's who I'm named for. Flora, the king of Florda. That's where he found me."

"Where's Florda?" Eddy was sure he had seen that name on a map somewhere.

"Far from here. It's warm there all the time, and wet. There were huge monsters there that slid up out of the water and ate men. I remember. You don't forget a thing like that."

"Monsters?" Eddy lifted an eyebrow, but she wasn't looking.

"Yes. Green and bumpy, with huge mouths and rows of teeth. They change their shape and color to look like logs floating in the water, and then they spring."

Flora spread her arms wide in front of her, miming the snapping of enormous jaws with one arm above and one below. "They could swallow you whole. I still have nightmares about it."

Eddy tried to picture it.

Like the dinosaurs in my old schoolbooks. But they said those were extinct a long time ago.

Then again, those books don't know anything.

Flora cleared her throat. "Anyway, Archie said he wasn't the one who cut me, he said I came that way. I don't remember that at all, I must have been a baby."

Eddy pulled the reins hopelessly, trying to bring Star over closer but failing to communicate with the animal. "I'm so sorry that happened to you. I know some people who are cut. That's hard, and I'm sorry."

Flora shrugged. "I don't know any different. So I don't feel like I lost much. But I watched Archie do it to the kids he sold, and a lot of them were old enough to know what they were losing."

They rode in silence awhile.

"And somebody bought you in Jeff City? Who was it? Your mother?"

"My father," Flora said, wistfully. "He's gone now. Died in a twister seven summers ago. It didn't come close enough to hurt the city much, but a flying piece of wood hit him in the head. He was a good man. He made dyes so rich and so bright. He was the best man in town for it. But I was a woman by then, and already learning my trade. I missed him, but I could get along on my own."

"So, no man in your life? No Hive, right?"

Flora shook her head and smiled thinly at Eddy. "I've heard about Hives. Sounds like a good time, but we don't have them in Jeff City. I've been with some men and some women. But nobody like you."

"Men *and* women? Really?"

Flora's smile got shy. "Sure, why not?"

"No reason," Eddy said, trying to sound uninterested. *Like the Unnamed.*

The smile widened and warmed. "What about you? Men? Women? A Hive back home?"

"Not part of a Hive. A couple of women that I like to be with. But we can't . . . It isn't a permanent arrangement." Eddy stared off, pretending to watch the road.

They trotted forward.

Eddy said, "I guess that might be easier where you're from. Since there are so many women."

"Easier? How do you mean?"

"Like no one . . . No one stops you. If you want to be with a woman." Eddy was looking at the horse's mane.

"Stops you how? Like someone would stop you from stealing?"

"No," Eddy said, struggling for the words. "Not like that. Just, you know. Pressure. Disapproving. Making you feel like you don't belong."

Flora shrugged, then clicked to Apples, who had begun to slow down. "Why would they? What business is it of theirs?"

"I don't know. Just wanting all women to be Mothers, I guess."

"But all women can't," Flora said quickly. "Some won't even try. Does someone make them, in your city? Is breeding forced there?"

"No, nothing like that. It's just . . . complicated." Eddy thought about Nowhere, and the respect that women were showed. More than respect; often something like worship. But only if they were being the right kind of woman.

He remembered a couple of women who had lived together when he was small, the way people had subtly left them out of things, forgetting to invite them or just not talking with them. He remembered the elder Sylvia and Carla, in particular, being cold toward them. Alice had been even younger; had she seen the way her mother acted? Did she learn her stealth that long ago?

In the end, the two women had started a Hive they could share. As soon as they made the change, everything had turned around. It was as if some pressure had been eased, and all of Nowhere could breathe easier. They had both died in childbirth, a few years apart.

Eddy realized Flora was staring at him, waiting for him to speak. He thought about the town square in Jeff City, all the women in their shady bonnets.

"Why aren't there more children in Jeff City?"

"What?" Flora was unscrewing the lid of her plastic canteen to get a drink. She held it out to Eddy.

"With that many women, there should be a lot more children. Did the Lion's men take them away?"

"No." Flora drank and put her canteen back. She took a moment to collect her thoughts. "None of the horsewomen can have children, of course."

Of course?

"So, I don't know what it's like where you come from. Where do you come from, anyway?"

Eddy let the matter of horsewomen drop for the time being.

"I'm from Nowhere. It's a few days' walk south of Jeff City. Soldiers lived there, in the before."

"So, in Nowhere. Do you have a lot of children?"

Eddy sighed, trying again to ease the horse closer to Flora's. They seemed to be drifting apart. "Not as many as we'd like. The Midwives do all they can, but . . . most pregnant women get the fever. A lot of them die, and most of the girl children do, too. They're all born with it. We get one or two a year."

"We got one last year," Flora said with a sigh. "Maynard. And the last one before that was Myles."

At the sound of the lost child's name, Eddy clenched his jaw.

"They just let them take her. I let them. Cowards, all of us."

Flora snorted, low and short like her horse. "It's not a simple question, Eddy. The Lion's men burned down a whole town to get one fifteen-year-old girl. That was a few summers ago, the refugees came into Jeff City. They had tried to fight. Instead of that one girl, they lost every girl they had. Hundreds died, and the town burned all the way out to the woods. It's a terrible cost, but we pay it."

"Would *you* pay it?" Eddy looked at her sidelong. He wanted her to give the right answer.

"I can't have children. I'm cut. So it doesn't matter. Can't be mine."

Eddy had never heard of someone being cut so badly that the Midwife told them children would be impossible. However, he knew plenty of women who decided for one reason or another never to try. He didn't ask.

"They're all yours. They're all mine. They're you and they're me. Imagine if nobody fought to keep you."

"For all I know, nobody did." Flora clicked her tongue and her horse sped up, out of earshot.

They crossed small towns that were completely burned out. Some of them had burned a long time ago. Others were fresher and still had the acrid stink of burned plastic, livestock, people.

They camped in a rusty steel shed less than a day's ride from Estiel. Eddy got more and more nervous as the city became inevitable. His hands shook and he spooked Star. They tied the horses up outside, and Flora brushed them down and cleaned their hooves. Eddy sat with his journal.

The Book of Etta
Year 104 in the Nowhere Codex
Spring

Almost to Estiel. Traveling with Flora from Jeff City. She has horses.

He sat with his pen hovering over the page. His ink was made thick, so it never dripped or ran. He watched it hang over the edge of the nib, full and round as a pregnant belly. He tried to make himself write.

I could write the Arch. I could write the moon-blood-cups closet. I could write the chair.

The hand holding the pen went rigid and the nib twitched. Ink as thick as cold blood spattered on the page and his right hand. He cleaned it and put it away, his mind a perfect and studied blank.

Where are you right now? You're cleaning a pen. Hold the pen.

Flora yanked the balky steel door sideways in its dirt-clotted track. She had put on her head-to-toe garment again. "There were muskies out there big enough to suck me dry." She pulled the blue cloth over her head and laid down the two sets of saddlebags.

"So, tell me about Estiel." Flora settled in like she was expecting a long story.

"No." Eddy said it like a reflex, not meaning to speak at all.

"What?" Flora's face was concerned. "Are you mad at me?"

"No. No, sorry. I don't know the city well. I know there are smiths and metalworkers. You can smell it when you get close. The city is partially walled off, but not everywhere. I usually come in from the south, so we should get a look at the west side this time." Eddy's voice trembled.

"Are you alright?" Flora put that same soft hand on the inside of his arm. His skin erupted all over in the puckers and bumps of gooseflesh, and he shivered.

"I'm fine." He closed his eyes as soon as he knew she was going to kiss him.

Her kiss was patient, like she anticipated a century in which she'd get to know him. Like a first raid, just a look-and-see. She pulled back, smiling.

"I really wanted to do that."

He smiled back, he couldn't help it. "It's nice to kiss somebody I didn't grow up with," he admitted.

"Right?" She leaned forward and kissed him again, harder this time.

Eddy let himself be kindled. The blood rose in his face and neck and his whole body thrummed like a plucked string. He raised one hand and put it to the side of her face.

Outside, the horses whinnied and stomped. Flora looked in their direction a moment, but Eddy reached for her and she sighed, both of them forgetting the sound.

Just in the moment that they began to burn as one flame, they heard the terrible, baying howl.

Flora jumped to her feet with a short scream. "What the hell? What is that?"

Eddy had his gun in his hands. "Wolves."

He pried the door open a little way and saw that it was too late.

Eddy, unused to horses, hadn't thought about whether they'd be safe outside. When Flora heard the sound of the struggle, she tried to push past him. He held her back.

They were not truly wolves, not all of them. Many were wild dogs, but the species were well on their way to remerging into a single one.

Apples, being the bigger horse, reared up and kicked at the predators. Her hooves crushed one wolf-dog's skull, splattering its brains in the dirt.

Star twitched back and forth, snorting, working to free herself. A wolf leapt at her throat and buried its teeth in her flesh, hanging on to drag her down. Another wolf joined the first and Star went down, her creamy spots reddening.

Apples had sustained a few scratches when she slipped her rope. She ran wildly, disappearing into the night. Star went down and the wolves swarmed over her, snapping and yanking on every side of her body.

The sound of killing teeth on the horse's bones pierced the night and seemed to go on and on before the animals slept. Flora cried gently after her yelps of grief subsided. She crawled, as entitled as a child, into Eddy's arms. He held her as it got dark, but they could not sleep.

"I hope Apples ran home."

"Where else would she go?" Eddy did not know whether wild herds of horses would accept an outsider. Would they look at her shoes and know she had been property?

"Do you know any songs?" Flora was sniffling, shaking.

"Sure, we sing in Nowhere."

"Can you sing me something?" They were wrapped together in cloak and blanket, shivering more from horror than the cold.

Eddy sang low, trying to keep the dogs' keen ears well out of it.

Pack up all my care and woe
Here I go, singing low
Bye bye blackbird

Flora snuggled down into his arms, but it was no good. Outside the shed, the wolf-dogs began again to howl.

CHAPTER 5

In the morning, they avoided the slick red mess that was all that remained of the dead horse. They walked east, following the same road toward Estiel.

Flora's face was swollen from crying. As the sun broke free of the morning gray, she pulled on her all-over cover.

"What do you call that thing?" Eddy was annoyed by it. He felt like he was talking to a bedsheet.

"A veil. Women who left Jeff City said to wear one everywhere to be safe."

Eddy laughed a little.

It's not a secret there's a woman under there. It's like a wrapped-up present.

"You'd go safer as a man. It wouldn't be diff—"

"No." Flora cut him off, her voice hard and low.

"What?" He wanted to see her face. He couldn't fathom why this would upset her, as little as it meant.

"I will never, ever wear the clothes or the guise of a man." Eddy imagined her jaw flexing, the soft white of her neck blotching red.

"Why not? It's not worth it, looking like a woman. It's like showing raw, bleeding meat to a dog." Eddy remembered the horses and wished he had thought about it a moment longer. "I mean . . . you know. Men are just . . . You know how they are. They see a woman or a girl and they just lose all their other feelings. Like when they took Myles."

"So you'd rather be like them? The hunter, rather than the hunted?" Flora's voice simmered with anger.

"That's not the point." Eddy felt himself getting angry in response. "I'd dress like a tree if I thought I could get away with it. I don't want to be a hunter. A slaver. I could never do that."

"You don't know what you could do."

A few moments passed; the only sound was their shoes grinding in the broken remains of the old road.

"Being a woman is sacred." Flora's voice was prim, like a child reciting catechism.

Eddy snorted.

"In the before, people didn't know that, because we were everywhere. The plague came so that we'd understand."

Eddy laughed out loud. "Before the plague, women were rulers and peacekeepers and cooks and dancers and whatever they wanted to be. And they had medicine that made it impossible to get pregnant. They were free. And now they're property almost everywhere, raped to death and sold to monsters by monsters. But I'm so glad they're sacred now. Thank you, Plague God." He stood with his hands on his hips.

Flora turned to him, stopping in her tracks. She hauled the veil up and he saw that her face was red and her teeth were bared. "Is that what they think where you're from?"

He had stopped to face her out of instinct, but he tried to pass it off as a momentary hitch. He kept walking, his back to her.

"Nope. Where I come from, people think women should be having babies or catching babies, and that's all there is to it."

"Being a Mother is how a woman saves this world. It's how we restore the balance," Flora called from behind, not catching up.

"Or fatten a slaver," Eddy called back, not slowing down. "You save the world. I'll just clean it up."

The sun was high overhead and the days were getting warmer. Flora thought for a long moment, then stuffed her veil into her pack and walked slowly, tiredly, after Eddy.

It took her a little while to catch up.

"Do you ever wish you were a woman?" She was quieter now, chastened.

Eddy held his breath a second, wondering if Flora knew.

Is that why she's asking me all this?

He glanced at her out of the corner of his eye. She didn't seem to be judging him.

"I wish I was neither. I wish nobody cared." Eddy pointed to a clutch of trees. "Let's eat, okay? I'm starved."

Eddy knocked a nest out of a tree and roasted four small eggs on the fire they hastily made. No bird returned to the tree to mourn.

They reached the outskirts of the city in the evening. They smelled it first, the stink of sewage suddenly strong as the wind shifted.

"We must be coming in close to their dump site. Or their pits." Eddy rummaged in his case of wonders and came up with another small ceramic pot. "Here." He held it out to Flora.

"What's this?"

"Mint and pine sap and a couple of other things," he said. "Smear it on your veil where you're breathing and it'll cover the smell." He was pulling out a long strip of cloth and doing the same for himself, binding it over the lower half of his face.

"Will it stain?" Flora looked uncertainly at her finger.

"Probably, yeah." His voice was muffled.

She pulled her hand in under her veil and moved to put the salve on her skin instead.

"I wouldn't do that," Eddy warned.

"This is all silk," Flora said shortly. "I'm not going to—*ohhh.*" She moaned in sudden sharp pain. "It's burning," she whined, wiping at her face. "Cold and burning."

Eddy grinned. "No use now. You'll have to just wait it out. You'll have a red spot for a day or two. Don't," he added as she pulled in her canteen.

Too late.

She cried out sharply as the water only intensified the pain.

Eddy laughed low, but Flora could see him.

"It isn't funny! It hurts so bad!"

He laughed harder and saw that Flora was starting to laugh, too. Her eyes were red and streaming with pain, and it was all so ridiculous.

Estiel was surrounded on all sides by suburbs, which grew steadily into the leaning and crumbling taller buildings that were the foothills before the mountains of the city itself. Eddy heard his own laughter bouncing off the brick walls just a moment too late.

A signal. A whistle into cupped hands that wavered high and then came low again before cutting off. Meant to sound like a bird, but Eddy was used to this kind of subterfuge.

"Cover your face." His voice had dropped to a growl.

"What?"

He yanked his hood up and pulled the mask up off his neck to cover everything but his eyes. He wanted badly to touch his gun, but he reached up and pulled out his machete. The edge was murderously sharp; he honed it himself every chance he got. He held it in a two-handed grip as he squinted, looking for the spotter.

"Eddy, what?"

He shushed her with a warning gesture, hand held low. He listened, every sense as keen as the knife.

The same call came again. And a third time.

Eddy's head whipped to the right and he felt a tiny *crick* in his spine under the rigid pressure of his neck muscles. The sound had come from two or three blocks away. He wasn't sure they'd been seen.

Walking backward, he crowded Flora into the shelter of a half-fallen brick chimney. She had covered her face as he had ordered.

"Why don't we just go to the trading gate?" Flora was whispering, barely making a sound.

"Because they'll take you. Do you want to get taken?" He spoke rumblingly, in his lowest register, eyes still scanning above them.

Rooftops aren't stable. Maybe they're in a tree?

She laid her light hand on his shoulder. "They won't take me." She stepped closer. "I've done business with traders from Estiel. They know what I am."

The men came at ground level, so stealthily that Eddy didn't see them soon enough. Three of them, so similar in looks that they could only be brothers. Each of them wearing a claw around his neck.

Eddy tensed up with the machete. Flora strode around him in her gray-blue silk veil, formless and without tension. She held up both hands.

"Paws of the Lion? Lion of Estiel?"

The men showed no weapons and looked at her with aloofness.

The tallest man spoke first. "I am Eric, Sheriff of Estiel. These are my deputies, Anric and Alric. Yes, we are Paws of the Lion." He put both thumbs under his wide leather belt, waiting.

Flora pulled the veil off, lifting it with both hands. Eddy quivered like a bowstring.

"I am Flora, a silk thrower from Jeff City. Horsewoman. Do you know my kind?"

Eric squinted, but Anric came forward. "I know your kind. I know your work." He had the same close-cut black stubble as the others, but blue eyes instead of brown. All three were deeply tanned. "Who's your man?"

Flora reached back and Eddy transferred the machete into his left hand, keeping it loose and easy. "This is Eddy, also from Jeff City. He's a hunter."

Alric crossed his arms. "What's your business in Estiel? Come to trade?"

"Yes," Flora said evenly.

Eric nodded to their meager packs. "Trade what, horsewoman?"

Flora spread her hands wide and smiled nervously. "Dogs got our horses and we lost some gear. I have silk for trade in my bag. And Eddy here has drugs."

Eddy swallowed hard.

Shit. In for it now.

Bright interest showed on all three faces as the brothers looked at one another. "What kind of drugs?"

Eddy cleared his throat, shook his head. He took a deep breath and cleared it again.

Deep. Stay deep.

"A selection. Infection stops. Sleeps. Toadstool tea."

The three men began to smile.

"Eddy, did you say?" Eric smiled pleasantly at him.

"Eddy, yes."

"Are you the maker?"

"No, but I know the maker. West of here." His face was still covered, somewhat muffled by the balaclava.

It's the distance, he thought wildly. *The distance between the nose and mouth. That's what Alice said. Shorter for women. That's the giveaway. Breathe. Eight in, eight out. Where are you right now?*

Eric was walking toward him. This was the moment. Eddy pulled down his mask and looked up at the man, his mouth set in a straight line, lips pulled in.

"Do you want to see what I've got?"

"No," Eric said. He didn't seem to have noticed anything unusual in Eddy's face. "We have strict instructions to bring drug traders to the Lion. He'll give you a very good price for them."

"The Lion?" Flora's face was blank with confusion. "Really? The Lion himself?"

"It's your lucky day." Alric said it, offering Flora his arm.

Eddy was grateful to walk alone.

Young men, all wearing claw necklaces, scurried to and fro in front of the old hotel. They carried baskets and boxes; they swept the paved areas and hoisted pulleys to raise suspended parcels to the upper floors. They all had a sense of purpose and an air of organization that Eddy had never seen before. He watched, fascinated.

Eric, Anric, and Alric fell into single file as they passed through the main doors. Alric gently took his arm from Flora and directed her to follow him. Eddy brought up the rear.

Despite the cleanliness of the place, inside and out, Eddy could smell waste. The smell they had picked up on the wind turned out to be a dump site. Eddy pulled his mask back up, seeing that deer had been gutted here, and waste like fish tails intermingled with unidentifiable junk to create the terrible stench.

"Let them try the oil," Flora suggested.

"What oil?" asked Eric.

Eddy tried to kill Flora with his eyes. He still had it in his front pocket. He drew it out and told them slowly and carefully how to put a drop on their handkerchiefs or any bit of cloth they had.

"But not your skin," he added. "See how Flora's face is all red?"

Alric looked over and laughed and Eddy saw that he was missing a good number of his teeth on one side. "Oil can't burn you! What did you do, set it on fire?"

Flora laughed a little back, settling into the easy game of getting along with men. "No, truly! It's very strong, like itchweed or a wasp sting. Be careful!"

The men laughed a bit more, but they were cautious.

"The smell is almost covered," Anric exclaimed. "What is this oil?"

"It comes from a couple of green plants," Eddy said. "And then carefully purified. I don't really know, I just know that it's better than the smell of shit or carcasses."

"That's the truth," Alric said.

Past the trash dumps they walked through a deserted section of town, which was beginning to look more and more like a city to Eddy. After a few streets, they began to hear the sounds of children at play.

Is this really Estiel? Where are you right now?

Eddy struggled, caught up in the memory of freezing black water and the slick of kerosene that slid above it. The Arch creaking in the windy night. He shook it off.

A group of boys were playing a game up ahead. They had a large leather ball and they were shooting it toward a high metal ring on a pole. They ran and shouted, working in teams. They grew quieter as the party drew near.

Eddy could see that the boys were all thin and dressed in skirts. They seemed tall for their babylike faces. Most wore their hair long, but there was no mistaking them for girls. They watched the sheriff and deputies surreptitiously, the game becoming a show.

"Carry on, boys." Eric waved to them before bringing out a pouch full of dried brown leaves. He began to roll the leaves together with paper, spitting on his hands to make it all stick.

The boys didn't move.

Eddy looked at them, making eye contact with the one holding the ball. "Is this a school group?" He returned his gaze to Eric, who was examining what he had rolled together.

"It's the catamites. They don't go to school."

Alric whistled at the boys, long and low. They tittered and milled together, the pretense of the game dropped. They were clearly nervous, but not really afraid.

The boys' eyes were drawn to the flame as Alric lit his cigarette. One of them came forward and smiled at the sheriff.

Eddy watched carefully, seeing the way the boy thrust his hips forward and pursed his lips. He saw the child put a hand on his slim waist and pop his chin toward the man.

Eddy knew at once what a catamite was.

Eric put the roll of dry leaves in his mouth and brought the flame to the end of it, his big hand cupped around the fire. He inhaled through it with a suck and draw, the way Eddy smoked joints with the boys in Nowhere. The brown leaves caught and smoldered. The smell was heavy and unpleasant.

It looks like a joint, but it isn't cannabis. Eddy knew the Latin names for the varieties of marijuana grown in Nowhere. It was a small crop, but a good one. Worth more when it was dried and stored in the winter. This smelled nothing like that.

The boy, who looked to be about eleven, spoke up. "If you put that in my mouth, I know what to do with it."

Eric laughed and chucked the kid under the chin. "I bet you do, pretty boy." He sucked again, exhaling a cloud of smoke. "But this cost me a lot of bullets. So I'll have to find some other way to see if you know what to do if I put it in your mouth."

The kid giggled and ran away, seeming like a kid again. Eddy's mouth was dry.

Flora made no sound, but Eddy saw her finding a way to look at anything but the boys.

"They are so pert at that age," Alric said, starting to walk again.

"And as pretty as a girl," Anric added. "Eric, can I have a drag?"

Eric sighed and handed the joint to his brother. "Eddy, you ever smoke the real stuff like this? Did your drug maker sell you any tobacco?"

"Tobacco," Eddy said, tasting the strange word as he inhaled its smoke. "No, I've never seen it before."

Eric sighed again and accepted his joint back. "This comes from the Republic of Charles. They grow it there."

Eddy nodded sagely as though he knew what that meant. "We smoke something else where I'm from."

"Skunkweed?" Alric asked this with some amusement.

Eddy weighed the sometimes skunky smell of cannabis in his mind and guessed that must be what they called it here. "Yes, good skunkweed. I have some of that to trade, as well."

The three brothers laughed and Flora shot him a look that he couldn't translate.

"We get that here," said Alric. "But the Lion's men don't smoke it. Addles the brains."

Eddy nodded and forced a grin as they laughed.

When the Arch first came into view, he had been readying himself to see it for a long time. It still took his breath away.

Flora stared up at it, openmouthed. "I've never seen it. I've just heard stories . . ."

The sheriff and his men puffed up with pride. "The Arch of Estiel," Eric said grandly. "Stealing metal from it is punishable by death. It's owned by the Lion."

Flora nodded vigorously. Eddy counted his breaths, eight in and eight out.

"You okay, man? Tired?" Anric was looking at him with concern.

"Yeah. Yeah, I'm fine. Sometimes I have the breathing sickness, is all."

Anric nodded. "Black men. Only guys I've known who have the breathing sickness are black. Must be something in your blood."

Eddy nodded, counting.

Eight in, eight out.

The ruined city of Estiel hulked above them. Steel skeletons sagged and buckled. Some of the older buildings stood gutted by fire. Most of the ancient city had burned, but people built along the sidewalks and held both sides of the river. New buildings made from logs and rough-planed lumber stood in between stalls thrown together with plastic pipe and fabric. They passed people selling gutted game and moonshine, stalls filled with the junk of the old world and the plain black ironwork of the local blacksmiths. Eddy's sight filled with knives and pokers and he struggled to count his long breaths.

When they passed two stalls in a row selling pin-lock manacles, Eddy crossed the sidewalk and pretended to be very interested in a man selling wild mushrooms.

The baskets were full of small brown and white buttons, interspersed with morels and even truffles. The mushroom man was fat and dirty.

Alice would pay this man good money, Eddy thought. *But only if he kept his eyes open for those red ones with the white spots. Amanitas.*

He was thinking of the day he had gotten his blood and become a woman; the woody, hateful taste of the mushroom in his mouth. The way the walls of his mother's house had flexed inwardly at him and how Ina's voice had seemed to come from everywhere at once. A voice that said—

"Eddy! You wandering off without us?"

Eddy's head jerked back toward the sound of Alric's voice.

Where are you right now?

"Sorry, I got distracted." He wiped his sweating palms on his pants and looked around, trying to see where they were headed.

The men and Flora had split toward a path that led gently uphill. Eddy jogged a few steps to catch them.

The Lion of Estiel lived in an enormous hotel that looked across the river, its back to the Arch. Eddy came up the stairs slowly, looking at the tall, wide building.

Hotels were popular everywhere Eddy had ever traveled. The ones in cities were often made with steel and had held up through the years. He could see that this one had once been mostly glass on the lower floors, with steel framing arranged for view rather than warmth or security. Board siding had been nailed up over much of it, but the wide doors and every third panel or so stayed open and empty. The place was scrubbed clean, whitewashed, and the front grounds were neatly kept.

Eddy caught a strong smell and it took a moment to place it. It was the smell of cats. People kept cats all over Nowhere and other towns he had seen; cats kept mice out of food stores and could be fed with the organs and scraps of a kill. Nevertheless, he hated cats. He hated their stink and their indolence; he hated the screams of their nighttime mating and daytime fighting. He had seen big cats in the wild as he traveled, the size of dogs but far more deadly. Their green flashing eyes in the night. He had awoken more than once to the shrieking of a rock cat, thinking he was hearing a woman on fire.

Their oily, sharp stink was in this place. He knew that once a cat claimed a place by piss, that smell would never leave it. He peered into the corners of the cavernous space, dusky even at midday, looking for the flash of cat eyes.

There must be hundreds of them, he thought, taking a deep whiff of the green oil on his balaclava. But he saw none.

"My three boys!" The voice boomed out of the shadow of a man, crossing into the room from the blinding light of an open window on the opposite side. Eddy looked up sharply and saw him, like the black shape of a man cut out of the blue sky and the river that they faced.

He was tall and broad, more giant than human. He held chains taut in both hands, but Eddy could not see where they led.

"Father!" All three chorused at once, leading the column out toward the patio where the man who could only be the Lion stood. Eddy followed a few paces behind, walking carefully. He tried to slow his breathing.

The sun blinded him momentarily when he emerged from the shaded darkness inside the hotel lobby. The light flashed off the water and the remaining silver scales on the Arch. He put up a hand to shade his eyes and tried to focus.

The Lion was so much taller than Eddy that he had to tilt his head back to look him in the eye. He was ruddy and tan, with permanent windburn and sunburn in the crescents beneath his eyes. His hair and beard were red gold, long and untamed, the mustache curling into the mouth. His shoulders were broad and massive, like a man who chopped wood or rowed a boat every day. Eddy looked down to check for weapons and saw that the man wore none. His boots were knee-high and made skillfully from good leather.

Eddy's eyes followed the chain in the Lion's right hand, and when he came to the end he blinked furiously, thinking he could not possibly be seeing what he was seeing.

At the end of the chain was a full-grown lion.

Not a rock cat, not one of the black or tawny wild things Eddy had seen in the hills or on the plains. This was a lion like Eddy had only seen in pictures: impossibly large, with a mane around its face like the corona of the sun. The animal was bored, lolling on its side on a warm patch of concrete.

Panicked, Eddy looked right and received a shock equal to the first: on the chain in the Lion's left hand was a tiger, just as large. The tiger sat on its haunches, and Eddy realized with his breath stuck in his throat that it was staring at him. Its posture was negligent, its golden eyes half-lidded. But it was looking directly at him. As it stared, the tiger yawned. Its mouth gaped, huge yellow teeth standing out like a series of silent threats. The tiger licked its lips after, smacking unhurriedly before returning to its princely state of closed-mouth repose.

Eddy didn't realize he was pissing his pants until his skin felt wet. He clamped those muscles down immediately, shutting off the flow.

They'll smell it, he thought in a panic.

He didn't know whether he was worried about the cats or the men.

Eddy remembered Flora and looked to her anxiously. She was staring at the tiger with her mouth open. She had taken more than a few steps backward.

The Lion was openly enjoying her discomfort. He did not speak, but stared her down like her fear was something he could eat or drink. The three brothers seemed to be waiting for him to finish.

Finally, the Lion looked at Eric. "So, what have my boys brought me today?"

"Father, we brought you Eddy, a traveler from the south. He is a drug maker." Eric bowed his head slightly.

Eddy stepped forward, masking his fear of the cats as best he could. "Not a maker, really. Just a trader. The maker back in my home village."

"And where is that?"

"South of the Black Mountains," lied Eddy.

"Black Mountains?" The Lion swiveled his head toward Alric.

"It's the name some people give to the Odarks, father." Alric pulled a pocket-size map out of his back pocket and put his finger to it. "Along the southerly route to the Republic of Charles, six or seven hours by truck."

The Lion nodded. "What manner of drugs do you make there?"

They already know too much. I told them too many things. Whatever it is he's looking for, I had better not have it.

Eddy cleared his throat. "I have some small amounts I can trade you. Sleeps. Toothache remedy. Some for pain, some for itch."

"Show me." The Lion sat in a low, curved-back chair and the cats sat beside him, spreading out lazily in the sun.

Eddy came as close as he dared before kneeling and sliding his pack off his back. He pulled the wooden case out and looked up.

The Lion's gaze was intent on him, but his body held almost no tension. He was completely at ease.

Eddy laid out his wares as a peddler does. He gave quick explanations for each vial and pot and tiny sack of powder. He glanced at the big cats every few seconds. When he looked up, the Lion's face was that same visage of relaxed interest.

Eddy pulled out all but the most hidden compartments where the most dangerous poisons and the essence of amanita were kept. He rifled through his bag and laid out one of his deerskin sacks of cannabis.

"I understand your men are forbidden this . . . uh, skunkweed. But in case you're interested . . ." He trailed off.

"Sir." The Lion finished.

"I'm sorry?" Eddy looked up, confused.

"In case you're interested, *sir*. I am not your Lion, so you need not call me father. But by strangers I am called sir. Don't you have a sir in your own village?"

Eddy thought of his mother.

"Yes, sir. But I do not call him that. However you wish to be called. Sir."

The Lion turned his head toward his right, regarding his lion on a leash. Eddy watched the small muscle that crossed from his jaw to his collarbone stand out under his tanned skin. He looked at the corded strength of the Lion, and he waited.

"Have you done much trading?" The Lion did not look back at Eddy.

"Yes, sir. A fair amount. I know what they're worth."

The Lion glanced at him sharply.

Too far. Don't anticipate his reasoning.

"I mean, I know you've got drug makers of your own, sir. Obviously. I meant these were quite valuable to people in places like Jeff City, where there's hardly a doctor to speak of."

I know you don't have any such thing. But let's play dumb.

"Yes, of course." The Lion jingled the big cats' chains. "Anric. Go upstairs and pick a handful. I'd like to trade with Eddy."

Anric went toward the staircase at a jog. They waited.

Flora grew bolder as they watched the tiger lick one of his paws.

"Sir . . . where did they come from?"

The Lion smiled and Eddy wondered if he filed his teeth; they looked sharper than the teeth of any man he had ever seen.

"Why, from right here, horsewoman."

Flora blushed a little. "I mean, sir, I've read about them in books. They come from far away."

"So they do. But you must have also read that in the old world, they were kept in cages for the amusement of children. Have you heard that?"

Flora nodded vaguely, looking between lion and Lion.

"Well, these were in Estiel in the old world. My great-great-grandfather was their keeper. In the time of the plague, he freed them and they followed him as their leader, sensing his greatness. In time, men sensed it, too. He was the first Lion of Estiel. The lion is the king among animals, you know."

"Yes, sir."

You would have agreed with him if he told you that that lion could play the fiddle, Eddy thought. But he didn't speak up.

"So my grandfathers and my father bred these cats as they bred their sons: with strong females and with a care that they could always lead. We bred for strength and size and intelligence, and we drowned the small and sickly. That's the way of Lions. The way to keep your line from becoming weak."

Flora nodded.

"You horsewomen in Jeff City, you're lucky. You came up with a good use for weakness. I have none."

Flora's face burned and Eddy stared at her.

Is he talking about the women they steal from Jeff City? Do the catamites come from there?

He thought of the boys who had sidled and giggled at them, ready to serve. Had they been born free? Bred here?

Anric came downstairs carrying Myles, the toddler who had been taken from Jeff City. Behind him followed a short line of women and girls.

Eddy stared hard. He knew it was Myles; she wore the same simple garment, open at the bottom. The child looked tired, but alright.

Behind Alric, there came a girl of about seven with straight black hair. Then three teenagers, all pregnant. One woman of about twenty and another of about thirty. They were clean and clothed, but they shared a dull, downcast look of vacancy.

All slaves. Some of them born slaves.

Eddy could not look away.

The Lion did not spare them a glance. Alric put Myles down and the oldest woman picked her back up mechanically. The woman was short and generously proportioned. She wore a black dress and a strange kind of white bonnet, made of a fine material that Eddy couldn't place. He wondered where she was from.

The Lion was waiting when Eddy finally looked back at him. He had pulled the tiger in close and was absently stroking the cat's big furred ears. Eddy could hear the purring quite clearly.

"I won't pretend that these aren't worthy goods," the Lion began. "My offer is this: one truck with enough deez to take you almost anywhere. A map of places where you can get more from my men. And one of these. Your choice of females, from my own stock."

The Lion's lips lay together and the man was perfectly still. Eddy stared him down.

Flora stepped close to him and put her hand on his arm. She drew breath to say something and he moved her hand aside, taking a small step away.

Careful, now. Careful and slow.

I have never traded for a woman in my life.

Eddy glanced up to the ceiling, remembering the pulleys outside that carried goods to the upper floors.

How many women up there? How many girls?

He couldn't kill the men. He knew shooting his way out was a dream that ended in the nightmare of capture or maybe even being eaten by one of the Lion's dangerous pets.

But he couldn't refuse, either. He looked at the women, evaluating.

No good answer.

The woman in the bonnet was singing in some foreign tongue to Myles and rocking her slightly. He wondered what happened to the children she must have had since she got her blood. If she was still alive, she was probably a safe Mother. Maybe many times.

Don't use the baby's name.

"I'll take the little one," Eddy said as evenly as he could. "And I want one more thing."

The Lion put up one red-gold eyebrow. "Well then, you had better offer one more thing."

Eddy pushed the catch on one of the secret drawers, kneeling before the box. He stood up, holding a vial of Alice's best painkiller. "I want bullets. I know they're made here."

Alric, Eric, and Anric all shifted, somewhere between discomfort and fright.

"You have a gun?"

It was a gamble, letting them know that he was carrying. He had Jaden back home, but Jaden's bullets often didn't fire at all. There was an opportunity here to get more and better ammunition than he had ever had. Eddy also guessed that this might raise his status in this place. If they didn't rob him of it immediately.

Eddy nodded, eyes on the Lion.

"Let me see it."

"Once our deal is struck," Eddy said, his face like stone.

The Lion gestured with his hand, a little clutching as if to say *Give it to me.*

Eddy strode forward and put the vial in the Lion's hand. Both of the big cats stiffened, lax muscles suddenly turning to steel beneath the skin. Eddy did not retreat.

"That's the best painkiller we can make. It comes from the pods of a flower, and it looks like milk. It's called—"

"Opium." The Lion turned the vial over in his hand.

"Somniferum," Eddy finished softly. "Som."

The Lion stood up and towered over Eddy.

"Do you have more of this?" His eyes were like those green cats' eyes Eddy had seen in the night.

Shit. That's the thing he wants.

"Two more vials. Sir."

"Get them."

Eddie sprung the same catch again, feeling the Lion's eyes on the back of his neck as he bent to the task. He cleared the compartment, bringing out the other two glass vials.

He handed them over and the Lion took them ungently, snatching them from Eddy's outstretched hand.

The line of women was quietly disappearing. The woman who had been holding Myles looked over her shoulder forlornly before vanishing around a corner.

"I need more of this. Much more. I can send men to your village to get it, or I can trade you for a drug maker to come here. I am rich for trade, you will find."

Eddy shook his head. "This can only be made where the flowers grow, and they're difficult to transplant. Picky. I can send traders to you with more, as soon as I return home. We do no trade with strangers who come to us. Security, you know. Sir."

The Lion looked at him and Eddy knew he was being measured. He looked back without flinching.

"Bullets and females, every time you send me opium. You understand?"

The Unnamed would free every woman you're holding here. She'd find a way.

"I'll find a way."

The Lion held out his hand to Eddy, who stared at it, not knowing what custom he was being asked to participate in. The Lion saw that and enveloped Eddy's small hand in his two huge paws, still holding the chains. He pressed Eddy's hand between hot skin and cold metal and pumped it up and down.

"Then we have a contract." The Lion snapped his fingers at Anric, who was at his side in an instant. He dug into a pouch at his waist and pulled out one of the claws on a leather thong and held it out to Eddy.

Eddy stared at it.

"Put it on," the Lion said. "It will open doors to you, wherever you go."

Eddy took the piece of jewelry into his hand, willing it not to shake. Not taking his eyes off the Lion, he said, "Flora, collect the girl. We're going to get my bullets and my truck and be on our way."

The Lion nodded, his sharpened smile returning. "Eric, see that he gets his goods."

Eddy made Eric leave the room while he showed his gun to the bullet maker. The man was old and leathery and handled the gun like an expert. He gave Eddy a rough wooden box filled with two hundred bullets.

"Not all will fire," said the man in a quavering voice. "But most will."

Eddy had never had so much ammunition in his life. He thanked the old man and left, totting up in his head the number of bullets he had just seen. He couldn't count high enough to explain it to Flora.

The truck was much harder. Eric took them to a warehouse where armed men guarded dozens of trucks. The one that Eric showed him was mostly rust-colored. The cab was roomy, and a wooden bench ran the length of it. Eric showed Eddy how to crank-start the engine and made as if to leave before Eddy stopped him.

"I don't know how to drive it," Eddy said desperately. He looked at the stick that shifted the gears, the wooden pedals that controlled the fuel, with terrible dread. Eric looked at him blankly.

Flora stepped between them, Myles asleep on her shoulder. "I do. We're all set here, Eric."

Eric nodded and walked away, explaining to the guards that the trio would soon be on their way.

"Sit inside with the baby," Flora said. "I'll be in in just a minute."

Flora restarted the truck with the crank, and then the door gave a metallic groan as she wrenched it open. She slid onto the buckboard and shifted the truck into gear.

"How did you learn this?" Eddy asked her.

"I learned as a child. On the road." Flora had been quiet nearly the whole time they had been in Estiel. Eddy thought it was possible that Flora was more afraid of the place than he was.

"Oh." Eddy held Myles on his lap. The child was quiet, too. She seemed sleepy all the time.

The truck drove noisily, bumpily, and getting out of Estiel was slow and tiresome going. More than once the raw chopping noise of the engine cut out and Flora had to restart it with the crank. The motion and the smell of the fuel made Eddy feel sick, but Myles stayed as deeply and easily asleep as if she were in a soft bed.

Once they made it to the open road, Flora asked to see the map.

"We can get back to Jeff City and take Myles to her mother." She looked at Eddy, suddenly unsure. "That's what you wanted, isn't it?"

What else would I want?

"Yes." Eddy laid a tentative, gentle hand on the sleeping child. "Of course that's what I wanted."

"And after that?"

Eddy thought about it. "Do you still want to come with me?"

Flora smiled as Estiel faded behind them.

"You're going to need a driver."

CHAPTER 6

They made Jeff City in the middle of the night. The main gates were closed and manned by archers, and Flora climbed out of the still-running truck to give the password. By the time they found Deborah's house, it was dead quiet through the whole town. Flora shut off the chugging engine near the market and they walked, Myles asleep on Eddy's shoulder.

They stood on the doorstep for a moment before knocking.

"Listen." Flora stood with her head inclined to the house's old wooden door. Her gray eyes caught the moonlight; all her careful ink and paint was gone. Eddy stared at her naked face and heard nothing.

"What?"

Flora clucked her tongue and whispered to him. "She's crying. I can hear her sobbing. Can't you hear it?"

Eddy shook his head and rapped smartly on the door. He hadn't known he was hearing the woman crying within, but he sensed something cutting off as heels pounded the wooden floor on their way to the door.

Deborah appeared, looking decades older than when they had last seen her. Her eyes clapped straight onto Myles's curved back as she slept, and instantly Deborah was on Eddy, clambering to take the child out of his arms.

Behind her, another woman appeared looking just as haggard. Eddy saw that her skin was unnaturally pale, as though she had never seen the sun.

"Myles!" Deborah cried. "Oh, my Myles, my baby! Oh, my baby! Oh, how did you find her? How did you get her back here? Oh, my Myles!" Deborah was clutching the baby and whimpering, crumpling to the floor with Myles held tight against her. The other woman joined them, fairly crushing the child between their bodies.

The other woman had the same face as Myles, Eddy could see. He looked back and forth between the three of them, the two adults distorted by their weeping relief, and the child still apparently too sleepy to react.

Flora gently got them to move inside to a sofa. Eddy followed and closed the door behind them.

"Eddy traded for her. With the Lion."

Deborah grew very still. The other woman looked over at her.

"The Lion himself had her?"

Flora nodded. "Whatever they were giving her hasn't worn off yet, she slept the whole way here." She inclined her head to the still-groggy child, now starting to make sleepy babble in her mother's ear.

Deborah patted Myles all over, as if checking for injuries. The other woman kissed the baby's plump cheeks.

"Gave her?" Eddy asked. "You mean drugs?"

"Of course." Flora was looking at the floor. "That's why he wanted your opium so badly. It's for the breeders, and for the girls just brought in. To keep them quiet and calm."

Eddy went hot and then cold all over. He sat in stunned silence.

"What can we do? What can we ever do to make it up to you?" The other mother was standing now, reaching out for Eddy.

Flora put a hand on the woman's shoulder. "I'm going to be gone awhile, traveling with Eddy. Look after my house for me? It's right next door, so you won't have to go far, Lily. Alright?"

Lily looked back at Deborah, as if seeking permission. Deborah nodded vigorously over Myles's head.

"Your house and your garden, as if they were my own. I swear it." Lily dropped her head and kissed Flora's hand. "I can never thank either one of you enough. Our baby is home. I'll never let her out again."

Eddy said nothing.

Flora moved toward the door. "Let's leave them alone," she said to Eddy. "Come on."

Eddy stood dumbly and moved toward the door as if in a dream.

As they walked to Flora's house, he found his tongue.

"How does Myles have two mothers?"

Flora looked straight ahead while she answered. "Deborah is a horsewoman. She's not cut, though. She can still have children."

Eddy shook his head, not understanding. "No, but how did it happen?"

"I wasn't in the room when they conceived the child. How should I know?" Flora sounded annoyed, distracted.

"Why isn't Lily allowed out of the house? Why did she have to ask for permission?" Eddy ground his teeth. He didn't understand anything he was hearing.

"Because it isn't safe. The Lion can take any woman his Paws see, so it's better not to be seen. She's right to keep the baby home from now on. It's better if every child in Jeff City is a boy. Hiding in plain sight is too risky."

At the mention of the Lion, Eddy grew hot again.

"We shouldn't have done that," he said through clenched teeth.

"We shouldn't have rescued a baby?" Flora's eyes were very wide.

"We shouldn't have done any *business*. You let me trade with him. I know I can never go home and tell them I paid for a slave, that I bought a girl and didn't kill the man who was selling her. But you let me trade him som, knowing he would use it on the others." He held fists at his sides and looked up at the moon.

Flora shrugged. "What will happen to them will always happen. They've probably been breeders all their lives. The opium just makes it easier on them."

Eddy couldn't answer. His throat felt closed. He wanted to scream.

"I told you," Flora said softly. "I told you there was more than one way to see this. It isn't simple."

The ring. The patch. The pill. Eddy turned them over in his mind, thinking of the casual, offhanded way they were written about in the history of Nowhere. He knew that the Unnamed had traded birth-control drugs sometimes when she couldn't save them. She had made it easier on them.

No. I am not a Midwife. I should never have . . .

He thought of Myles, returned to her mothers. The way the child, even through her haze, had curled with perfect trust into the two women's arms.

"It is simple," he said. "Working with people like the Lion is wrong."

In the corner of his peripheral vision, Flora shrugged. "It's all wrong. What we did, what you did, what the Lion does. Things can't be right again until the balance is restored."

The balance.

They didn't talk again. In Flora's little house, there was one bed. Eddy slept on the floor in the kitchen.

They did not rise until it was nearly noon.

◆ ◆ ◆

By the time they were preparing to leave, half the town had turned up to see them off. Eddy shifted his weight from one leg to the other, trying to look very concerned with his pack.

Thea and a handful of other women loaded bundles of cloth into the back of the truck, tying them to the pitted, rusty bed. People brought them dried food and water jugs, blankets and hats, warm clothes to suit them both. Eddy packed and repacked gear, waiting for Flora to say her good-byes.

People wanted to grip his arm, call him a hero, and thank him for returning Myles. He couldn't stand it at all, couldn't make any response. He endured it.

Yes, I'm a successful slave trader. I returned someone who should have never been stolen in the first place.

He climbed into the cab long before they were done speaking to him. The truck had holes where once glass windows had been; there was no barrier. People gripped his shoulder through the opening on his side, they spoke to him through the windshield. He was frantic to get away.

Finally, the crowd parted and three women approached Flora.

They wore their hair shaved on the sides and in braids in the centers of their heads and down their backs. All three of them had visible horse tattoos.

These must be the horsewomen, Eddy thought. He watched them carefully.

They all spoke quietly to Flora, and each of them gave her a ceramic pot stopped with wax. Flora took these and touched foreheads with the women to say thanks.

Eddy could hear them saying, "The balance, the balance." He rolled his eyes.

"Flora! Let's make some distance before nightfall?"

Flora nodded and came toward the crank. She got the truck roaring, and the small crowd cheered. She climbed into the cab, pushing her pack ahead of her.

"Let's go!" She was alight with happiness and adventure. Eddy remembered his first raid, his first time out of Nowhere. He had had that same feeling.

It had nearly gotten him killed.

"Let's go."

Eddy discovered he hated the truck. The board they rode on in the cab was hard, and nothing he put under his ass seemed to offer any padding. The roar of the engine was so loud that any conversation had to be shouted to be heard. The wooden wheels bumped over the terrain, sending up the shock and vibration of every rock and rut they rolled over. The deez was hot and stank sweetly, with rich exhaust seeming to pour off in every direction. The smell of it made Eddy's head swim, and he stuck his head as far out of the portals as he dared, holding on to the metal, desperately seeking fresh air.

"—to your village?" Flora was shouting over the rumble.

"What?"

"Do you want to tell me how to get to your village?"

Eddy bit his lips and settled his sore hindquarters back on the board. He didn't answer right away. The map was spread out against the wooden dashboard, pinned down with thin metal tacks. His eyes traced the routes that moved south out of Estiel, taking a long time to measure the distance between Nowhere and the nearest outpost of the Lion.

He put one finger to the map and shouted toward Flora. "We need to go to this fuel station here, and then we'll head for a place I know. I don't want to go home. I have work to do."

"What work?" Flora bellowed back.

"The same work I've always done."

They drove all day, refilling the deez tank from one of the plastic barrels the Lion's men had tied down in the truck bed. As the sun started to set, Eddy was desperate to stop the awful rocking and rolling and to just sit still. They slowly crossed a bridge of cracked and ruined asphalt, rolling in the dead center and looking ahead with trepidation. The bridge was whole but listing to the right. It would not stand forever.

On the other side, Eddy pointed out a stone cottage with an intact chimney. They parked the truck in the dirt and waited to see if anyone came out to see what made so much awful noise.

Nothing stirred, but the woods on either side of the river were deep and alive with the sounds of insects. No doubt that night they would hear dogs and wolves howling at the summer moon.

"Get the gear inside," Eddy said. "I'm going to sit out and see if there are any deer at dusk."

"Can you really use that thing?" Flora eyed him as he pulled his bow free of its bundle in the truck bed. He had managed to make three shafts, straight and slim.

Not many, but all I need is one.

Flora fought with the front door for a long time before dropping her bags and climbing through a window.

She came back out through the door of the cottage and got the rest of their gear inside.

"We're going to have to block some windows," she called out to him.

Eddy nodded back, standing in the open truck door. He waited for her to go back in and then climbed atop the roof of the cab.

He sat very still, absolutely silent. He held the claw around his neck and thought of the stink of cats.

The smell of a predator. Same everywhere.

Wonder what I smell like.

He dropped the claw and it made a tiny *slap* sound as it hit his skin. He didn't see the buck until it swiveled its head suddenly in that moment. It was a huge, full-grown deer with a wide-branching set of antlers. Its eyes were on him and he dared not move, not even to nock his arrow.

Take me all night to butcher it. No salt, no smokehouse. Most of it will rot.

Hungry, he clicked his tongue just loud enough to make the buck take a few leisurely steps back into the woods. The sound also scared a handful of fat brown rabbits out of the underbrush. Eddy was surprised, but he got an arrow loose in time to catch two of them. It wasn't a great shot; the rabbits screamed and suffered, scaring away everything within earshot. Eddy ran to the two small animals trapped together by the arrow that had gone through the flank of one and the neck of the other.

The rabbit shot in the neck had either bled out or died of fright before he reached them, and it lay silent. The other kept up its awful shriek until Eddy buried his best knife in its eye. He rose with his kill and turned toward the house.

Flora stood in the doorway with her hands over her ears. Eddy shrugged at her as he came closer.

"That's the sound they make. It's only death. There are worse things."

"It sounds like children screaming," she said quietly.

It did, Eddy knew. He said nothing.

By the time the rabbits were skinned, gutted, and spitted, Flora had recovered. She sniffed as fat ran off the meat into the fire.

"Can you make bread for tomorrow?" he asked.

Flora smiled. "I learned, when I was younger. I have no talent for it, but I make good cornbread. I trade for wheat bread, from someone who knows how and has a man who can knock down a beehive."

Eddy cut the rabbit, crunching through the backbone and laying it on Flora's tin plate. He did the same for his own and sat beside her on the stone hearth inside the cabin. Flora tucked in immediately, drawing sharp breath through her teeth as she realized the smoking carcass was still too hot to touch.

Eddy tipped his own plate to the side, draining off the still-liquid fat into a glass jar he had set on the floor.

"If we go back to Nowhere . . ." He stared at his rabbit, waiting to see if more grease would weep off the well-fed meat.

Flora looked up at him, licking her lips but forgetting her dinner.

Eddy did not look up, though he felt her eyes upon him. "It's south of here, along the route we're following. I'm not going to go there until I've found at least one woman or girl who needs help. That is what I've always done."

"Myles was—"

"Myles doesn't count." Eddy snapped the words, setting his plate down against the stones with a rattling clang. His head rang with the aftermath of the long, rough ride and its heady stink. "I shouldn't have had anything to do with that. I bought her. It doesn't matter if I gave her back to her mother, or ate her, or kept her as part of my own harem. I'm one of them, now. I'm . . ."

Flora smiled a little. "A slave trader? One of those men? A Paw of the Lion?"

He did look at her now, his brown eyes blazing. "How can you even say it? How can you . . . ?"

Eddy felt a searing in his eyes, the moisture there catching the day's sweat at the corners and stinging, blinding him. He fought for control.

"It's not a line," Flora said patiently. The nervous little smile still curled one side of her lips. "I don't understand why you act like it's a line. It's not as if there are slavers on this side and you and your righteous hero's life on the other. We're all a part of the same world, and living in it and trying to stay. We all have to do things we don't like."

Her smile was gone when he looked up. She had gotten back to the business of tearing her rabbit apart to eat it. A little blood showed where she cracked a joint and buried her teeth in the flesh.

Where are you right now?

"We do. Yes we do."

I'm circling around it. I can't explain it to her. It is a line.

"There are things that are just wrong. There's white and black."

Flora swallowed a big bite and clearly didn't like waiting to take the next one. "You mean like you and me?"

"What? No. I mean like there's male and female."

"Like you and me," Flora said with her mouth full.

Eddy looked quickly down and drained a little more fat off his plate and into the jar. He pulled thin meat off his own rabbit's ribs.

"There is a line. A line I won't cross. There's a line that separates things from their opposites."

"Like killing people." Flora had given up on breaking the rabbit's little bones and was gnawing, the whole roasted body lifted to her mouth. "That's a line many people won't cross."

Dead people.

"That's just doing what you have to do," he said aloud. "Sometimes there's no other way."

"What if there were no other choice than to work with slavers?"

"There's always a choice." Eddy's hunger was in him somewhere. He swallowed bites of meat, hoping they met somewhere in his hollow middle.

"Yes, there is."

Eddy looked at her and saw his own mother in her raised eyebrow.

He sighed.

"Anyway. I don't want to go back to Nowhere just now. I want to show you a secret. Once you've seen it, you can tell me where you want to go."

"A secret? What kind?" Flora's forehead was uncreased and serene. Nothing seemed to bother her; she always bounced back to some kind of internal peace.

Still angry at her, still frustrated. She can't see it at all.

Want to kiss her, even so.

"A forgotten place," he said. "It's strange and beautiful. I've been there many times."

She nodded, her eyes on the bones of her rabbit. "Alright. That sounds like an adventure." She licked her fingers and crossed the room to rummage in her bag. She returned with a small iron pot.

"When you're done, put your bones in this. Tomorrow, we'll have some soup."

Eddy nodded. "Good thought." He tossed his bones in when they were clean. He took the jar with its tiny runoff of rabbit fat and found a similar sized jar in his bag. He pulled out the lotion Alice had made him and stuck two fingers into the thick, white preparation.

The smell of rendered fat was improved significantly by the fresh mint Alice had infused into the grease. Eddy added his ration of dinner fat and worked the two together between his hands. He rubbed the fat into his arms, lingering on his gray, dry elbows. He rolled up the legs of his leather pants and petted downward, his oily hands taming his curly leg hairs into arrows that rained down toward his ankles. He applied it to his face last, spreading it thinly across his cheeks and forehead.

Flora had wiped down their plates and kept herself busy, but when Eddy opened his eyes she was there.

"Do you need help with your back?" She smiled and he was glad he was sitting down.

Yes.

"No. Thank you, but no. I have to use it pretty slowly or I'll be out before I get home. Unless I shoot something with more fat on it."

Flora looked a little disappointed, but she nodded.

"I'm gonna walk the riverbank and see if I can get lucky elsewhere, then," Flora said.

Eddy missed the hint in his eagerness to bluster. "Do you have a knife?"

"Of course I do," she shot over her shoulder as she passed through the door. "Work on that window."

Eddy pushed the boards that had been pried out back into place, hammering with a rock he found in the yard. The rabbit bones boiled in the pot Flora had hung over the fire in the hearth, and just the addition of what little salt they had made it smell even better than the meat had.

It was full dark and the moon was rising over the trees. Eddy laid out both their bedrolls and checked all the windows and doors. He tried sitting by the fire and found that he couldn't sit. He made an inventory of what was left in his apothecary. He paced and sat and rose to pace again.

Fine, I'll do it.

He pulled open the leather journal he had had since his first blood. He turned a third of the way in, looking determinedly away from the chunk of pages that had been torn out. He found his last entry and put his stylus into the ink.

The Book of Etta
Year 104 in the Nowhere Codex
Summer

Drove all day, in a truck from the Lion of Estiel. Runs on deez. Stinks. Shot two rabbits. Traveling with a woman from Jeff City. Flora, who throws silk. Returned one female child (Myles) to her mother in Jeff City. Got her from a slaver.

No details. No stories. No explanations and no apologies. Less than a third of the page was filled in, even with Eddy's large, childish handwriting.

Before he could put the book away, Flora opened the front door.

Eddy started, reaching for the knife in his boot. When he saw her, he sighed with relief.

Flora held up a muddy clump of weeds with muddier tubers dangling below. "Guess what I found!"

When washed, the tubers turned out to be arrowroot. According to Flora, their arrow-shaped leaves had been obvious in the moonlight.

Flora grinned over her find. "They're like potatoes. You grow potatoes in Nowhere?"

"Not me, but some of the farmers do. I love potatoes. Nothing makes you feel as full as they do."

Flora was nodding, breaking the greens off and throwing the peeled clean tubers into the pot. "This'll be breakfast stew. Plenty of food to get back on the road."

When she was done, she wiped her hands on the front of her skirt. "So, you keep a diary?"

Eddy glanced over his shoulder to the purple book, still lying on the floor where he had left it.

"Yes. It's . . . it's kind of a tradition where I come from."

"Why?"

They lay down nearby each other, seeing slices of the starry sky through the cracks in the roof. Eddy told the story of the Unnamed as best he could, explaining how her book was the first, the book that became the history of Nowhere.

"So now everybody does it," he said, pausing to yawn. "To record births and deaths and harvests and raids. We all write our stories so that the people who follow us know how we lived."

"Yours must be full of the stories of where you've traveled! I'd love to read some of it," Flora said.

"You can read?"

"Yes, I learned as a child," she said patiently.

"Why? Can most people in Jeff City read?" Eddy was surprised. Scribes and Midwives were always literate in Nowhere, the scribes being chosen from the boys who learned the quickest and the Midwives from the girls who were the most clever. A few others in specialized trades, like Alice or the other druggists, learned to read, as well. Many raiders could not read more than they had learned as children, spending their youth learning to fight and to navigate. They brought home books without knowing more than their titles.

Etta had been chosen early as a candidate for Midwife. She had read the Unnamed's whole canon, and the extra volumes besides, many times over. She had read the *Physicians' Desk Reference* that was her mother's constant companion. She had gotten her blood relatively late, not until her eleventh winter. The Mothers had come for her then, Mother Ursula, Mother Priya, and Mother Charlotte. They had taken her for three days to the red house. They had fed her red foods and told their stories of when they had gotten their blood, when they had chosen their Hives, and when they had borne their first living children.

Etta's stomach and back had ached. She could barely eat even the delicacies that were offered to her. She listened to the Mothers' stories and knew she never wanted any of that for herself.

They did not force her to decide. They put a necklace around her neck, a precious seashell brought from the south sea. She had walked into her own house and found Mother Ina sitting at the kitchen table.

"My living child," she had said, rising from her old wooden chair.

Etta had been shocked to see her mother without her wooden baby belly; she wore it almost all the time. Her mother's embrace was softer than usual, and Etta was closer to her body, closer to the place where she had been carried in her mother's womb than she could remember ever having been.

"Mother," she'd said softly. "I've decided—"

"Hush, now," Ina said, sitting back down. She pushed a cup of raspberry-leaf tea toward Etta. The taste was bitter. Ina's Hive kept honey in the house; she saw the face Etta made and brought her one of the short jars. As Etta stirred honey into the tea and began to drink, Ina spoke softly to her daughter.

"I have something for you, child. Before you say anything, I want you to have it. I want you to have what you want, even if it isn't what I would choose. But I want you to go after it with both hands, whatever it is. And leave something good behind you in this life. Do you hear me?"

"Yes, Mother."

There were three traditional gifts for a girl who would become a Midwife. One was a book. The books given to Midwives were precious, and many of them were shared. Ina's *Physicians' Desk Reference* had been swapped many times for *Spiritual Midwifery* and *Birthing From Within*.

Ina's closest friends were Midwives, not Mothers. The Midwives could not or would not have children; there was a law to make sure that no woman would be both. The law was old; sooner or later everyone chose. Most chose to try to have a child, no matter the risk.

Other Mothers made Ina angry, with their broods of two or three living children. Despite six pregnancies, Mother Ina would only ever have one. Her book did not answer her questions about why her other children had died, or why she had not died with them. The books she borrowed did not explain why others could have so many and she only one. They didn't hold the secret of why so many women had none at all, why so many women died with their first locked inside the casket of their body.

Mother Ina had seen two caesarean sections. One was disastrous, the other a miracle. Both were performed on dead women.

Ina knew there were worse things than dying that way.

Ina's final pregnancy, when she had seen nearly forty summers, brought her Etta, her one living child. It had almost bled her to death and cost her her womb, cut from her by their best Midwife and taking her weeks to recover. When Ina had awakened, weak and lost, to find Dana nursing a newborn beside her, she had assumed Dana was there to tell her that her own baby had died.

Instead, Dana had handed the rosy bundle over to her, saying she was glad to have enough milk to spare.

Ina could barely raise her arms to take the child. She didn't dare believe the baby was real, really there, really hers.

Eventually, she would nurse the child herself. Eventually, she would understand that her training to be a Midwife was at its end. Eventually, she would name the baby Etta in a ceremony attended by all the Mothers in Nowhere, all the people Ina had learned to ignore.

Mother Ina sat beside her living daughter, a package wrapped in soft deerskin in her hands.

"My living daughter, life doesn't ever hold what you wish it would. But it holds things you can't even dream of yet, because you haven't seen them. Do you understand me?"

Etta nodded, her hair in braids with bone beads at their ends that clicked when she moved.

"The Unnamed saw the whole world change, but it did not stop her from chasing after what she wanted to have."

She wanted to find her lover, Jack, Etta had thought with the thrill she always felt in this story. *She wanted to save women from slavers and bring them good drugs. She wanted to be a hero.*

Etta nodded at her mother.

Ina's hands unwrapped the package and she pushed the object toward Etta, who at first could only see the glints of candlelight that flicked across the smooth surface.

When it was before her, Etta saw that it was a revolver. A gun, a gift from the old world. She stared at it but did not touch.

"Where . . . ?"

Ina settled back in the chair, rubbing her neck where her wooden baby belly made her sore every day.

"It belonged to Bailey, the Midwife who brought you. She got it from Judith, who got it from Emily, the one who the Law is named for. Emily got it from Shayla. Shayla was willed it when Doc Jane died. Doc Jane was what they called—"

"The Unnamed," Etta breathed.

"Yes." Ina looked her daughter in the eyes. "This gun came across the world with her. It saved her. It's been owned by Mothers and Midwives both. Whatever you choose, it now belongs to you. It's been cleaned and oiled for almost a century, but not fired. The bullets were gone before even Shayla received it. But there are bullets in this world, and you will find them."

Eyes gleaming, Etta reached out and touched the cold steel of the cylinder. Ina put her hand on top of her daughter's.

"This is you," she said softly. Their eyes met again and Etta, tired and emotional from her first blood, could see nothing there but her mother's love. There was no control there, no guile. Just her mother's hand on hers and the words she would never forget. "This gun is blank and empty, and you can fill the cylinder with anything at all. You can pack it with dirt or fill it with bullets. You can change the world forever, depending on where you point it. You can leave behind terror or justice. You can be as important as the Unnamed, or as lost as any of the men she put down with it. You hear?"

Etta swallowed. "I hear." She took a breath and held it. "I'm going to be a raider."

The moment broke like a dropped clay pot. Ina sat back against her chair, sagging. "Child, you don't know what you're going to be."

Etta had wrapped up the revolver, sure that her mother was wrong.

The gun and the book. The tools of the Unnamed. Eddy was better with one than the other.

Flora was shaking her head. Eddy had his hand on his own book.

"No," Flora said. "Most of the people in Jeff City can't read. I learned before I came there."

"From the slaver you worked for?" Eddy asked.

"Yes. He taught me so that I could read to him. He liked having stories read to him by one of the children at night, so he could fall asleep."

"Why didn't you run while he was asleep?" Eddy asked, as if it were obvious.

"Because I didn't know where I would go, or how I would live on my own," Flora said with only a little edge in her voice. "I was only four or five, you know. I don't really know how old I am. But I know I was tiny then. Not big enough to make a run for it."

"How many years before you got your blood?"

"What?"

"Well, if it was six years before you got your blood, then you were probably four. I mean, it's not exact, but it would give you a range."

Flora was silent for a long time. "I don't remember."

Eddy was still staring up at the slice of stars. "Oh, come on, what about how 'being a woman is sacred' and all that nonsense? Wasn't it celebrated?"

Flora didn't answer. Eddy looked over and saw that she had turned her back to him.

Must have fallen asleep.

He wanted to get the story of her first blood. That was always a way to get to know a woman.

Maybe. Maybe I'll tell her. When we get to the cave.

The rabbit stew was everything Eddy had hoped. He ate two platefuls and asked Flora if he could drink the stock from the pot.

She held up a finger to him while she drank from it herself. She handed the cooled pot over to him when she was full enough. "Finish it off," she said.

They loaded their gear back into the truck and looked at the map. Flora pointed out the road that led south, all the way to Nowhere. Eddy stopped her, putting his hand over hers, stopping it about where he wanted to be.

"This place is kind of hidden," Eddy said. "But we're not far now."

He pulled his hand back slowly and she looked at him with a little smile. The heat that passed between them might have radiated from the truck, but he knew it hadn't.

"We'll be there before midday." Eddy looked away, hoping for the morning air to cool his cheeks. He looked at Flora as she pulled up her balaclava and cast her slitted eyes out on the road.

Flora nodded, squeezing her eyes shut and starting the truck. "More than anything, I wish we had goggles. My face hurts from holding this scowl all day."

"Mine too," Eddy said. But his words were lost in the roar.

The Unnamed told Jodi, the girl that she loved, the truth about what she was. I read that story over and over. She just took it off and showed her. Jodi didn't want her, but she might have. It could have worked out.

It could.

Beneath the balaclava, the curve of Flora's jaw was concealed. Eddy could see the glowy skin of her neck. Her right-side collarbone was showing above a sweep of her silk, and all he could think of was his mouth on it.

In the cave. I'll be able to tell her in the cave.

He itched beneath his binding.

They came around a corner past an old car wreck, seven or eight rusted-out hulks with moss grown over the whole mess.

"I know where we are," he yelled to her. "Turn left up here."

She nodded, excited. Her balaclava fell down and he could see her grinning.

The billboards still stood, but they'd been bleached blank long ago, only the broken frames remaining, outlining nothing. Behind them, a short brick building stood with an enormous brass sculpture of two men in strange hats, tarnished but bright in the sun.

Flora shut off the truck and they took their packs, leaving the rest in the vehicle. Eddy got out ahead of her and ran to the statue, smiling at it like it was an old friend.

She came up behind him after a minute and bent to the nameplate that sat before the two figures. Much of the writing was obscured by black and green tarnish, but Flora read the name aloud.

"Jesse James. Who is that?"

Eddy shook his head. "I read about him in a book once. A famous criminal in the old world."

"A slaver?" Flora turned to him, confusion on her face.

"No, he stole money."

"What's money?"

Eddy shrugged. "It was paper that people used to trade for food. My mother tried to explain it to me, and some of the other teachers tried, too. Nobody really understands it. It was like an idea that people fought over, and that made it valuable."

Flora shook her head. "That doesn't make any sense. Why wouldn't you just trade the food?"

"Like if you had to trade for a whole city," Eddy tried again. "You couldn't carry it all with you, so you'd carry the paper and the paper would be like a promise that they could turn in for the food."

Eddy reached forward and touched the knee of the kneeling, bearded man. "I came here on my first trip away from home with the raiders who trained me. I was just a kid, and I had no idea there was anything like this in the world."

"Who trained you?"

Eddy frowned. "Two men. Errol and Ricardo. They were sent out west a few years ago. Nobody has seen them since. They were good men."

Flora put a hand on his shoulder and there it was again. That same baking heat, and this time nothing to blame it on but the steadily rising sun. He reached out and cupped the side of her face. She was warm and smooth and the two of them inched closer to one another, like magnets.

"So is this what you wanted to show me?" Flora asked.

The moment broke again, and Eddy pulled his hand away. "No, this isn't it. It's this way."

He led her up the stairs toward the brick building. When he looked back, he saw her face was unsure. He reached out his hand and she took it. "Trust me."

Inside the building was darkness. Only a little light came through the windows, some of which still had crazed glass in them. The shelves inside were still filled with junk, and Flora dragged him toward a stack of rotted plastic bags that were furry with dust.

"There's cloth in these," she said as she ripped one apart and the gloom began to swarm with the gray particles.

Eddy coughed in response, but Flora was unfolding a cotton shirt. Even without much light, Eddy could read the words printed on the garment.

"Meramec . . . Caverns. Route 66."

"What is that?" Flora was rubbing the cloth between her fingers.

"Cavern is an old word for cave," Eddy said. "And Meramec was the name of this place. I don't know what it means."

"And the numbers?"

"It's what they called the big road. It's on the old maps, if you look close. In this shape, right here." He stepped in to point out the shield design that held the numbers.

"Why would a road have numbers instead of a name?"

"I think it's because they used to have so many," Eddy said.

"Well, there's a whole lot of these here. Before we leave, I want to load some up. Even if only for scraps, old-world fabric is always popular."

"Okay," Eddy said. He was busy pulling an old torch out of his pack. It still had enough oily cotton on it, he thought. He nicked flint and steel until his torch caught. Then he took her hand once again.

Eddy led them to the back of the building, where a staircase loomed in darkness below them. They groped their way to the bottom, feeling the temperature drop. Eddy lifted his torch. The light seemed to open up the recesses all around them but only illuminated a little. Flora flinched from the enormity, shrinking into herself and closer to Eddy.

"Whoa, what the hell? It feels like a big empty . . . something." She looked suddenly frightened.

Eddy grinned at her, the torch held high. "It's only a little scary," he assured her. "After that it's just really exciting."

She didn't look convinced, but she followed.

The path led down and down, and Flora gasped the first time she saw that the rock above their heads was hanging down in long, jagged spikes.

"It's going to fall!" Her voice was rough and high, not far from shrieking.

Eddy's hand gripped hers tight, keeping her from bolting into the blackness that surrounded them.

"No no no," he said. "It looks like it's falling, but look, see?" He pulled her to the side of the passageway where the spikes hung low and put his hand on one. "This is just the shape that the water made, by dripping for thousands and thousands of years. Errol told me. It's been here since the world was new. It'll be here long after us."

The cave smelled sharp and salty, and Flora's face was strained in the low light. When they finally came to a stop, they could feel that they were deep beneath the place where they had started.

"Sit down here," he told her, helping her lower herself to the rock floor. He trailed a fiery circle around the space with his torch, locating a few others and lighting them as well. They sat in a circle of firelight, and Flora looked around. Eddy saw her realize that they were on the edge of a blue-green pool. Flora put her fingers into the water and tasted it. Eddy knew it would be bitter and metallic on her tongue.

Eddy laughed a little. "We can swim if we want," he told her. "But it's no good to drink. There's a spring near here where we'll fill up on water. But drink from your canteen, if you're thirsty."

Flora took deep breaths. Eddy put a hand on top of hers, full of irrepressible good humor.

"Errol and Ricardo told me that caves are sacred places, especially for women. Because they're secrets hidden away, like a child in the womb. They said that in some places, a girl's first blood is celebrated in a cave like this, in the secret dark."

Flora looked away from him, her face stormy. He gently brought her back around to face him.

"It wasn't like that," Flora said.

She looks guilty. But why?

"What wasn't?"

Flora shook her head, pushing Eddy's hand away from her.

"It wasn't celebrated when I . . . My womanhood. We didn't . . ."

Eddy sighed, seeing the shine of firelight in Flora's eyes.

"So I brought you here to tell you something," Eddy began. "A secret. My secret. Because I like you and I want to be honest with you."

Flora shook her head again, tearing up.

"What's wrong?"

"I don't know. Nothing. Go on, tell me."

He smiled nervously. He pulled his shirt up over his head and showed her the long strips of bandages wound around his chest. He reached to his side and, with a long, practiced hand, untied the knot there. He unwound and pulled and worked until at last he could breathe, every inch of her skin exposed to the cool, wet cave air. Her nipples popped free of their flattening bind and peaked in the slight cold. She was nervous, but it felt right.

"I don't know how people in Jeff City feel about it," she began shyly. "But two women cannot live together in Nowhere. It's . . . People say it's a waste, that women need to form Hives and share their wealth, but I only . . . I've never . . . Flora, I feel for you. Something like love."

Etta knelt, leaning forward, and kissed her. Flora stiffened all over. Her face was wet and she trembled.

"What is it? Is it the cave? Is it me?" Etta drew back, worried.

Flora shook her head and lunged forward, kissing Etta hard and bringing both hands to her revealed breasts, squeezing them fiercely, petting her with pent-up hunger.

She pulled back only an inch, pressing her forehead to Etta's beneath her. "It's not love," she said heavily. "You don't know me well enough. But you do want me, and I want you, too." She bit Etta's lower lip and Etta felt herself tighten up all over, cramping in a hot rush of pleasurable agony. "But you don't understand, you don't understand." Flora was moaning against Etta's neck, nibbling and licking as she went.

"Have you ever been with a woman before?" Etta panted, pulling at the endless loops of silk draping that covered Flora.

"Yes. No. Kind of." Flora still sounded fearful, and Etta could not think why.

Just get it off and let me see you, I'll show you. I'll show you how.

She pulled again at Flora's infinite garment, finding nowhere that it began or ended. She gave up on pulling at her back and caught her beneath the armpits, hauling her up and throwing the weight of her leg over to reverse their positions. Flora turned breathless, and as she came face-up in the torchlight, Etta saw that she was still crying.

"Is this okay?" she asked, peering down into Flora's gray eyes. "I want you, but I can stop. Do you want me to stop?"

"Don't stop," Flora sobbed.

Etta dropped her mouth to that beloved collarbone and kissed her softly at first, then gathering intensity and biting her, trying to slide down and find her breasts in the curtains of silk.

"Eddy . . ." Flora barely breathed it.

"Etta," Etta said.

Flora said it over and over, tongue flicking fast.

"Help me," Etta murmured against Flora's skin. "Help me find you." She reached down and slid her hands up behind Flora's knees.

Here, she thought as she ran them both up Flora's legs, feeling her muscles jump below the skin. She brought her thumbs to the insides of Flora's thighs and stared her in the eye, licking her lips, knowing where she would go.

Here, I am. Here.

When Etta's hand first touched Flora's throbbing swell, confusion crossed her face. Horror quickly followed as she brought both hands swiftly to it, feeling out the whole of its shape, and understanding ran up her arms and reached her disbelieving mind.

She backed up off of Flora in a flash of silk, long expanses of fabric falling back over Flora's thighs, returning her modesty. Flora sat up, reaching for her.

"Wait! Wait, please. Wait." Flora was begging.

Etta found her shirt and put it back on, standing a few paces away.

"What the hell are you?" she asked, graceless and mean.

"I'm a horsewoman," Flora said, miserable. "I know you heard that word more than once. Do you really not know what it means?"

Etta crossed her arms. "How could you?"

Flora sniffed and tried to laugh. "You tell me, *Eddy*."

"That's not the same! I do it for survival."

Flora really did laugh that time. "It's *exactly* the same," she said. "I never saw your real self coming through, though. I have to say, you're very good at this."

"Yeah, that's because my life depends on it," Etta said as she gathered up her bindings.

Flora hitched a ragged breath. "Can we please talk about this?"

Etta laughed shortly. "I'm leaving. You can find your own way out of here."

Flora was on her feet and beside Etta in seconds. "A minute ago you were in love with me. Now you're abandoning me in a cave?" Her voice dripped with accusation, leaving rock spikes hanging from the ceiling of her mouth.

I turned him over in nothing flat. I could take him. I'm safe here. Where are you right now?

Etta took a second to get control of her breathing. "Alright, let's talk. But you do not touch me. Understand?"

Flora nodded, looking at the firelit cavern floor. She sat. Etta turned her back and began the slow business of binding once again.

"How long have you been doing this?"

"What do you mean?" Flora's voice was small.

"Pretending to be a woman." Etta was dropping her voice down again, as low as it would go.

"I'm not pretending," Flora said. "This is all I've ever been."

Eddy said nothing but kept his back to her.

Flora pulled a thick cloth bundle out of her bag and laid it in front of her. She waited. When Eddy turned, she gestured with both hands. "Can you sit with me, please?"

Eddy crossed his legs and sat, his hands in his lap.

Flora gestured to her kit. "I have a good razor and I keep hair under control. I use this rinse to keep the hair on my head this color red. I use this metal pincher to pluck out my eyebrows. I do everything I can to be beautiful."

"A beautiful *man*," Eddy said waspishly.

Flora bit her lip and tears returned to her eyes. Her voice shook as she went on.

"This pot is full of a special cream. The horsewomen who saw us off brought me as much of it as they could spare. It's made by pregnant mares. The women process it in big basins and mix it with fat and . . . I don't know. Most of it is secret. It's a remedy from the old world, for people who need help being womanly. Being women."

"You aren't a woman," Eddy said, flat as a stone. "What's your real name?"

Flora's eyes spilled tears now. "My name is Flora. It was given to me when I was free. Before that I had no name, I had nothing."

She took a minute to get control of her breath. "I was never a boy," she said. "I was sold and sold again as a girl. I was taught everything by a woman who trained other women to service men. But I hated it. I knew I was a girl, and I knew that I loved other girls. I wasn't like the girls or the boys. I was . . . something else."

I was something else, Eddy thought. *I knew that I loved other girls.*

Sympathy bloomed in him, small and fragile. He tried to stomp it out.

"I'm like one of the silkworms," Flora said miserably.

"What?"

"You saw them. Born as worms, eating leaves and raising up to your fingers when you touch them. That was me. I turned into something else. I got my wings, but I stayed blind. I can't fly, you know. I'll never really . . ." Flora cleared her throat and looked up at Eddy, focusing on his face. "You know?"

I turned into something else. Eddy remembered what Athena had shown him in the mulberry tree, the way that the little worms spun them and changed in their private darkness into something else.

Eddy thought of the chair and felt himself enclosed in a cocoon of rust and dirt and time.

I turned into something else.

"So you were broken. So you're not anything."

Flora drew herself up straight, anger cutting through heartbreak. "I'm *Flora*," she said, the roughness of a scream surfacing in her smooth, low voice. "I'm a weaver and a silk thrower. I'm as much something as you are, Eddy. *Etta*. Are you broken? Are you nothing?"

Eddy's chin pulled back as if she'd slapped him.

"No, I do this for survival. I do this like the Unnamed did. To stay alive on the road."

"I'm staying alive, too," Flora said, her voice hoarse but her eyes on his. "And I make it possible for the Lion's men to be unsure, to not round up every woman they see. I serve other women, and I love other women. And no, it's not acceptable in Jeff City. I haven't had a lover in years."

Her voice broke at the end of this sentence and the sound of her loneliness was bigger than that cave, than any cave on earth. She shouted down into it, hearing her own echo.

"I don't care if you don't want to fuck me," she said. "I don't care at all. But if you loved me even a little, you'd want to know me. I am overjoyed to see you unwrapped and know you."

Eddy's face burned as he watched Flora give herself over into sobbing, her face pressed into a double handful of her own silk.

It's not the same. It isn't.

I still want to kiss her.

Him. I cannot touch him.

Her.

It isn't the same. She's the same, but it isn't the same. We aren't the same.

They sat that way a long time. Flora cried herself dry and turned over on her side, curled up like a tiny child who wakes up and finds herself cold and alone.

Eight in, eight out.

Where are you right now?

Is that shame? Am I ashamed of this? I'm angry enough to kill her. Him. He lied to me.

I lied to her.

It isn't the same.

He looked at the curve of her back and felt uncertain rivulets of time and old hurts wash over him, dripping in him, shaping him.

The things we see give us our shape.

He looked at the stalagmites, remembering when Ricardo had taught him the word. The way they reached up with all their might, while the stalactites that hung down hung on tight. He had known, even then, that inside every man and woman there was a place like this, made of stone that changed slowly, shaped by the trickling of what they saw, heard, did.

Rage steamed out and pity dripped in. Pity drained out and longing washed in. Still he sat.

One of the torches went out, then another. Eddy looked around, deciding that one of them would keep burning if he slept awhile. He didn't want to wake up in total darkness.

He lay down behind her and slowly, slowly, crept to curl up behind her.

"I don't know what this means," he said, low in her ear.

"I don't know what anything means," she rasped back. "But I'd love you to hold me."

He held her, deep in that forgotten hole in the earth. They slept.

Outside it was high spring, and the world was waking up.

CHAPTER 7

Bees?

The thought woke Eddy with a start. He sat upright and shook Flora, whose face was swollen in the light of the last torch.

The sound bounced off the cavern walls, like the singing of a choir that was very small or very far away. It wasn't quite the buzzing of bees, but for Eddy it was close enough to frighten him.

Eddy had been stung more than once after shimmying up a tree or climbing into an old attic in search of honey. Nowhere had no good sugar-bearing crop; the surest way to make friends with a baker was to be good at bringing them honey. After the honey was traded for bread or a minuscule, precious cake, Alice would buy all the wax and propolis Eddy could harvest. Any drug maker would buy wax, just as any scribe and any brewer would.

But Eddy always chose Alice.

If that's bees, there's a swarm out there.

They got to their feet slowly, staying crouched. Eddy gestured to Flora to retrieve the torch and she did so quickly, avoiding the puddles and pools all around them. When she fell in behind him, he had drawn his gun.

They went back up the path and then the staircase that led to the squat brick building. The grayish light inside the building led them, and they put their torch out. When they drew near the windows, Eddy gestured silently with his free hand for her to stay behind.

Nowhere to go if it is bees. Get down deep and throw ourselves in the water.

He remembered Ricardo warning him against drinking the water here, describing it as salty and strange. Eddy's teachers hadn't known if it was dangerous, only that it was no good for drinking or bathing.

Can't shoot bees.

When he got to the windows, he saw that he wouldn't have to. He turned back to Flora, counting on his fingers.

"It's the damned cicadas," he said glumly. "I can't believe it's been seven springs."

Flora laughed. "That's nothing," she said.

Eddy looked back over his shoulder. "They're gonna make driving hard," he said. "We need goggles. Or face shields made out of something clear."

Flora was already tearing open more of the bags that held cotton shirts. "I've got it," she said. "We make basket masks in Jeff City, with holes big enough to see out of but not big enough for a bug to get in. It's no trick at all to do that with this cotton."

She was using her own small knife, cutting slits into the material, tearing it into long pieces. When she tied one on Eddy, he held up his hands in front of his face.

"I can only see what's in front of me," he complained.

"Like a blinkered horse," Flora said. She was tying on her own mask, then redistributing the yards of silk she wore to cover her more completely.

Eddy didn't know what it meant to be blinkered, but the mention of horses brought the echo of his earlier feeling of betrayal. He shrugged.

"I guess this will do."

Flora didn't move to leave. "Where are we going?"

He looked at her through the mesh of the mask she had made him. He couldn't see all of her at once. He had to sweep his head from side to side to get a sense of the room.

"Do you want to go back to Jeff City?"

She crossed her silk-draped arms. "Not just now. Do you want to take me back there?"

Eddy looked down for a second, deciding.

"No, I don't."

Flora nodded. "Look, I want us to promise that we won't hide anything else from each other. If we're going to be on the road together"—she looked up at Eddy, frustration clear on her face—"then we need to be able to trust each other. Do you agree with me?"

Eddy nodded.

"Do you still want me to call you Eddy?"

"On the road, I am Eddy. That's it."

Flora nodded, resolute. "Alright then."

She stepped forward, groping without peripheral vision, and took both of Eddy's hands. For a moment, she held him in the two-handed grip Eddy had seen pass between women. She dropped her right hand and held only his left.

They stepped out into the singing cloud of insects, still holding hands.

Eddy pointed on the map for the route Flora should follow. They were driving on a huge, wide road that Eddy had avoided when he was on foot. It was clotted in some places by the hulks of ancient cars, but they found their way through. The paving was cracked and crumbling at the edges, with wide swaths worn away by rain and floods. The truck's wooden wheels stood up to the rocks and debris they rolled over, Eddy noted when he checked them before refueling.

If it stops running, we'll just have to walk. Used to walking, anyhow. Quieter. And no matter what, we've gained all this distance so much faster than we would have otherwise.

They were heading west along that old-world interstate. As the sun started to appear before them rather than behind, Eddy knew they would have to make camp somewhere and try to find something to eat. Their stores of food had been meager to begin with and had just about run out.

He checked his bag. He had just enough cracked wheat to make them porridge one more time. He knew Flora still had a little salt and some dried fruit.

Through the slits in his mask, he scouted along the sides of the road, watching for patches of anything edible. He had always gone raiding in spring; he knew that fruits and vegetables would be small but ripe enough. Water would be plentiful. Game would be foolish, out in numbers at all hours, trying to reproduce.

He tapped her shoulder and indicated that they should stop soon. She nodded vigorously, pointing to her ass as she tilted it to the side.

Yeah, I'm sore, too.

Pulled over. They got out stiffly, shambling more than walking. They had been rolling almost uninterrupted all day.

"I'm going to try and find something we can eat," Eddy said.

Flora was pulling a knee to her chest as she stood, trying to stretch out her thigh muscles.

"I'm never sitting down again," she moaned. "I'll build a fire."

They had stopped on a desolate stretch of highway, without a building or a sign of human habitation in sight. Flora was not pleased about that—she hated sleeping in the open. But she was too glad to come to a stop to argue about it.

Slowly, bending like a much older woman, she stooped and gathered an armload of dry wood for a fire. On a flat spot beneath a flowering tree, she built a phalanx of sticks and put a little of the old cotton between them. With her flint and steel, she caught a small fire and shielded it from the wind with her body until it was big enough to live on its own.

She stretched and paced and fed the fire, singing a song in a low voice. She kept her eyes on the road, waiting.

On the other side of the old-world highway, Eddy was walking in the basin of an ancient flood. He found spoor and the leavings of acorns and was pretty sure there were wild pigs here somewhere.

He had seen great, hairy boars in the wild. He had also seen the tamer, smaller pigs that people kept in Nowhere. He kept still, waiting to see which lived here.

It was a small pig, barely more than a shoat, that decided to test him. That was just as well, Eddy knew, since they needed more salt than they had to cure the meat or keep any of it.

He nocked an arrow and managed to shoot it, but only in the deep muscle of its leg. He had to run it down and cut its throat. He bled it out before bringing it back.

Flora lent her inexpert help to butchering the small animal, and together they roasted it, eating the crackling fat and waiting for the larger, meatier pieces to get done.

"So," Eddy said. "I want to ask you about everything, but I'm sure you don't want to tell me everything tonight."

Flora wiped the grease away from her mouth, and her eyes flashed in the firelight. "I want to ask you quite a few things, too."

"Alright, you go first, then."

Flora had another small bite of meat halfway to her mouth and stopped. She looked at him again before looking into the fire.

"You've been to Estiel before."

"Yes."

"But you didn't know the Lion?"

Eddy shrugged. "I mostly kept out of the main part of town. I tried not to run into anybody."

Flora fidgeted. "It's just . . . the Lion's men are everywhere. There are more little towns like Jeff City. We all pay tribute. He's . . . He's everywhere."

Eddy stared her down. "Tribute? Is that what the kids are?"

"What? No! No, we pay mostly in yardage. The children . . . The girls are different. The Lion takes girls from everywhere. People who don't give up their girls end up dead."

"End up dead anyway. No girls, no women. No women, no children. Jeff City's fires go out."

Flora's head was turned away and Eddy's eyes traced the long muscle that ran from just below her ear to her collarbone.

Still pretty.

No point, but pretty.

"Unless there's some secret you horsewomen have," he said nonchalantly.

She faced him then, her eyes searching his.

"What?" he said.

"Nothing." She looked away again.

The wind picked up and blew smoke in Eddy's face. He got up and started gathering the bones of their meal to take them away from camp. He almost didn't hear Flora when she spoke again.

He turned back to her. "What?"

"Why didn't you ever come to Jeff City before? You said you've been doing this a few years. Rescuing women and girls. Why didn't you come to our town sooner?"

He walked back toward the fire, looking down. He didn't answer right away.

"I learned the route when I was apprenticed. Ricardo. He kept old maps. He showed me the road to follow. Errol taught me what to look for, how to tell if stuff was useful or not. I just . . . I never took a different route. I always go that way."

"Why?"

"I found good things along the way. Things I could trade or bring home. Lots of little towns on that road, with just enough people in them."

"But you could go anywhere. You could explore, see anything."

Eddy's breath came too fast and he worked to get a hold of himself.

"Yeah, I can go anywhere."

Where are you right now?

Eight in, eight out.

"So where have you gone?" Flora was excited just to ask.

Eddy stretched his legs out in front of him. "All over. South to the Odarks. East to Estiel. North to the Faces. But west . . . There's nothing out west. Errol said so."

"Where would you go, if you could?" Flora's eyes were bright.

"Where would *you* go? You sound like you've been planning this."

She blinked in surprise. "Oh, anywhere. Just being out here—" She gestured around them in the gathering twilight. "Somewhere that isn't Jeff City. It's incredible."

"You were in Florda, as a child. Where was that?"

She looked down, subdued. "South, I think. It was so hot. And the trees were so different. Leaves like huge fans, instead of like little waving hands. And there were fruits there, sweet and bright orange and full of juice. But I was so little, and so scared then. I hardly remember."

"You said you were sold as a girl," Eddy began. "How?"

"I was cut, and my hair grew long."

"You were—" Eddy stopped, feeling his throat close. He remembered her saying she couldn't have children because she'd been cut. He'd thought she had meant . . .

"Gelded," Flora said in a small voice. "All catamites are. It keeps us from becoming men, when the time comes."

"But you still—" The shock of the cave was back in his body, making his pulse quicken.

Eight in, eight out.

"Yes, I still rise. Wouldn't be much use in a catamite who didn't function. But I can't produce children. You know how this works, don't you? You've read books. Don't you have catamites in Nowhere?"

Eddy leaned back on his palms, trying very hard to seem relaxed. They always seemed to return to the same fight.

"No, we don't geld boys. We have Hives. We geld livestock, of course."

It was quiet between them for a moment. The wind picked up and Flora's dark-red hair blew in front of her avid face.

She's not angry at that. Good.

"In the codex, the book I was telling you about? Back in the time of the Unnamed, there was a man. Named Breezy. He . . . He and another man were together, and he dressed as a woman. It's in the book, in their own words."

Flora leaned forward, fascinated. "What happened to her? To them?"

Eddy laid his head on his shoulder, staring into the coals of the fire. "I don't know. The book never mentions them again. But he wasn't the only one. There are a few . . . of that type in Nowhere. They keep to themselves, mostly, like any of the closed couples do. Some of them look womanly, but nobody pretends they're women. They're not gelded, they grow beards and look like men."

"Like you?"

He lifted his head. "You see a beard?"

Flora ducked her chin a little. "No, I mean looking like a man. Like you do. You must have worked a long time to get so good."

"I can't be Eddy at home," he said shortly. "It would be a disgrace. My mother . . ."

"Wouldn't she understand?"

He puffed out both cheeks and leaned forward, hunching slightly. He thought of Ina's tired face, her constant talk of babies.

"No, she wouldn't. I'm Eddy on the road, and I'm Etta at home. I'm both."

"Is . . . Is this who you are? Are you always Eddy on the inside?"

He looked up at her, startled. He wanted to snap that it was none of her business who he was on the inside.

He thought for a long moment.

I'm more angry that I don't know the answer than that she asked.

"I want to read the story."

"What?" He had trouble remembering how they had gotten there. "What story?"

"Breezy. The Unnamed. The old world. The whole story."

"It's really long. You could read the short version, though. The one everybody reads. If we went back to Nowhere."

Flora's silks seemed to balloon around her as she sprang forward. "Yes! Take me to Nowhere, I'd love to see it!"

When Eddy didn't respond to her exuberance, Flora shrank a little. "Where are we going?"

Eddy looked steadily at the ground. "We're on the road toward Nowhere. But I wasn't planning to go there until I . . ."

"Until you've rescued a girl, right? You *did*. You rescued Myles."

"I'm supposed to bring them back to Nowhere. To where it's safe. Jeff City isn't safe."

"So you're taking me back."

"You're not—"

"In every way that matters, I am. What, you've never brought a woman back who couldn't or wouldn't have children?"

"That's not the point." Eddy knew he was losing. He felt his face growing hot.

"You mean you have to bring back prizes. Just like a Paw of the Lion."

"No, not like that. I don't steal anybody."

"No, you just get them by murder instead of by arrangement for tribute. How noble."

"That's rescue! There's a difference between taking a crying child away from its terrified mother and depriving a slaver of his wrongful property. If you can't see that, then we have nothing in common at all."

"We have plenty in common," Flora said in a voice like flint. "And you have plenty in common with *them*."

Eddy felt like his chest was filled with boiling heat, that if he spoke, his words might burn them both. "I couldn't take you to Nowhere, anyway. They'd see right through you, and they'd never accept it."

"You didn't."

Flora was closing the distance between them. Eddy found himself edging backward, sliding away from the fire.

Flora's voice was flat. "You didn't see me because you think there are only two kinds of things in the world. Men and women. Good and evil. Slavers and rescuers. You've seen more of the world than I have, but you know less about it. There's more in this world than you can even dream about, Eddy. You're only not seeing it because you won't."

She was outlined with the fire behind her. She was blacking out the stars. Too close. He hit her clumsily, warding her off more than trying to hurt her. It happened before he realized his hand had moved. He was out from under her and on his feet a moment after that.

Eddy spoke to her dark outline. "Don't. Touch. Me. I told you that. If you can't remember, then—"

"I know. I know. I just thought . . . I just . . ." Flora was blinking fast, trying not to cry.

"I'm going to sleep," Eddy said.

"Yeah, okay."

"In the morning, we'll head for Nowhere."

"If we go there, you don't need to tell them who you think I am." Flora's voice broke and Eddy knew she was crying.

"No, I don't."

They said nothing more.

CHAPTER 8

In the beginning, Nowhere had meant only the fort itself. When the Unnamed was alive, everyone lived within the walls and each household lived off its own garden. A century later, the town was surrounded on all sides by farmland. People kept sheep, goats, pigs, and a small number of cows and buffalo. Potatoes, corn, cotton, hemp, wheat, and sorghum stretched out on three sides. What herbs weren't grown on the grounds were semicultivated in the woods, and dedicated hunters brought down deer, turkeys, and geese in season. The approach to the town was paved with food and looked completely undefended.

Eddy knew that each farmhouse had its own guard. He knew the warren of tunnels, just wide enough for a man to crawl through, that ran under the network of meeting places under these farms. None of them had marks and there were no maps. Children were taught to navigate them from memory, in drills every summer until they were left alone with instructions to find the one door that was open to get out.

A few gave up and cried until someone came after them, but most found their way to the correct trapdoor.

If travelers or marauders saw these farms, they might steal and they might burn, but human casualties would be few.

During harvest, all other work was suspended and every man was dedicated to the work of bringing in the crops. Every woman who wasn't pregnant or bringing a child into the world worked in drying, canning, and preserving the harvest inside the fort.

No women worked outside the walls.

Eddy refueled the truck in motion, pouring deez through the tubing they'd been given, before coming back through the truck window. He pointed to an avenue between two tracts of land and Flora turned them onto the rough road. Clouds of hot dust kicked up behind the truck's wooden tires, and Eddy knew they'd be met. He reached up under his shirt and unwrapped his bindings quickly, deftly.

Through the blind of the old cotton shirt wrapped around his eyes, he saw three men in the road ahead of them. He reached over and patted Flora on the shoulder, pointing ahead. She eased up on the throttle and the truck coughed to a stop.

Eddy got out first, unwrapping his head. He held both hands up. The three men were not armed.

Rob, son of Marcia, was one of the men who met her.

"Etta? Is that you? How did you get a truck?"

For the benefit of the other two, she identified herself. "Etta, daughter of Ina. In the truck is Flora, from Jeff City. We came from Estiel."

Behind her, Flora slid off the board behind the steering wheel. "Eddy? Is it okay?"

Etta shot her a look over one shoulder.

"Etta?" Flora's voice was rising, unsure.

"It's fine, Flora. Welcome to Nowhere."

They drove the truck into town, past the House of Mothers. On her side, Flora saw a pregnant woman walking past them, and she watched the swollen woman's waddling swan's gait until Etta worried she would crash the truck. She reached over and patted Flora's arm.

"Shut it off. Park it."

People had begun to gather and stare at the vehicle. A line of young boys spilled out of the old school building, their hands all spotted with ink. Behind them, Mother Ina walked stately, her wooden belly carving out the air before her.

Etta saw Sylvia the Midwife, daughter of Sylvia the Mother, elbowing her way through the crowd. Sylvia was short, with very short brown hair. She was going gray in a few isolated spots, but she had a fierce face. She came close to the truck first.

"Etta! Who have you brought me this time?" Her smile was broad, and for a moment, Etta smiled back out of the simple pleasure of seeing familiar faces. Her smile faded as Alice appeared in the crowd.

"Where did the truck come from?" Alice was addressing herself to Etta, but looking Flora up and down in a frankly appraising way.

Etta held up both hands. "I'll answer questions at dinner, for anyone who wants to join me in the hall. Right now, I just want to get settled in. Okay?"

There were murmurs and grumbles, and Sylvia was not in the least dissuaded. She approached Flora, who offered her both arms after the custom of Jeff City. Sylvia, not understanding, gripped her hands and spread Flora's arms wide.

"You look good! Not like the starving little ones that Etta brings me sometimes. Full-grown, too."

Flora pulled her arms back and rearranged her silks. "I'm Flora."

Ina had closed in on them, after shooing the boys back inside. "Flora? Good woman, I am Mother Ina. Etta is my living daughter. I welcome you."

Ina held her arms wide and took Flora into them. Etta watched dispassionately.

Ina turned herself toward Etta. "You're back early. Again." Her brow was not wrinkled in concern, Etta saw. She thought there was something there like arch contempt. Still, when her mother held out her arms, Etta stepped in and pressed her belly against the wood.

"Mother."

"My living child."

They held each other for a long moment.

"I need to go to the bathers." She turned her face to Flora. "Do you want to come?"

Flora clutched reflexively at her clothes. "No, I'll do that myself."

Sylvia held out one arm as if to steer Flora. "You can wash at the clinic, after I've had a look at you."

Flora contracted like her whole body was a wound she was trying to bandage. "Look at me?"

Sylvia smiled. "I'm a Midwife. Etta will tell you, if you're worried. You can trust me. Tell her, Etta."

Flora looked at Etta with naked terror. Etta sighed.

"She won't examine you if you don't want her to, Flora." She turned to Sylvia's confused blue eyes. "She's alright. I didn't liberate her, she was free in Jeff City."

"Oh. Okay, then. I guess. No chance that you're pregnant, is there?"

Flora shook her head. "I'm not . . . I can't . . ."

"Oh, that's fine," Sylvia said in a hurried voice. "Don't worry about coming to see me, unless you're sick or hurt."

Flora relaxed visibly. "If someone will house me and feed me," she said, raising her voice to the crowd, "I have silk for trade."

"Silk?" It was Alice, her blonde hair and fair skin like a beacon in the sunshine.

Flora held a hand above her eyes to see. "Yes. Several yards, in my bag."

"That's a deal." Alice grinned and winked at Etta.

Oh shit. Alice moves fast.

The two of them disappeared arm in arm. Etta sighed and stalked away, muttering.

The bathers were surprised to see her again, but they said nothing. They had been trained never to speak to women who came to see them unless spoken to first. After Etta had been shaved and scrubbed for bugs, she was left alone with Tommy, one of the youngest men who worked in the bathhouse.

He rubbed her bare back with the minty lanolin preparation. Etta felt his long fingers on her skin, light and careful, and she turned around to face him.

Tommy was clean-shaven, with a face as pointed as a fox and red hair to match. He raised an eyebrow to her but did not speak.

"Tommy, can I ask you something?"

He put his sticky palms together and looked her studiedly in the eye. "Yes."

"You live with another man, don't you? With . . . I'm sorry, I don't know his name. He's tall and black and has that tattoo?"

He nodded carefully. "Yes, Heath. We live together."

"You never wanted to be part of a Hive?"

I'm scaring him. Pull back a little, find something to share.

"No, I never did. I don't know about Heath, but he doesn't want that now."

She held out an arm and he went back to his work, automatically and obviously grateful for something to focus on.

"Do you know Breezy? From the codex?"

He stifled a small laugh. "Of course I know Breezy."

"Why 'of course'? He's only in one little section."

He looked levelly at her. "Breezy means something to me that I don't think he means to you."

Easy now. Easy.

"I hear that. Do you . . . Have you ever?"

He switched arms and did not look at her. He waited for her to say it.

"You know how in the book, Breezy pretended—"

"Pretending is worthless. No man can be a Mother or a Midwife."

"Those aren't the only things a woman can do," she snapped at him.

He shrugged. "They're the only things that matter. Anyone can be a raider."

She drew back as if slapped.

Anybody can be a bather, too. You asshole.

I scared him. That's all it is.

"Hey, I'm not asking you because I want to accuse you of anything. I'm asking you because I met some people out there . . . People like Breezy, who pretend. You know?"

He didn't answer.

"And I wondered if there were any people here in Nowhere. People who have secrets. We all have secrets, you know. Tommy."

Tommy's foxlike brown eyes locked on hers, and for a second she felt as if he were challenging her. She stared back, trying to look harmless and interested. He looked away first, with something like embarrassment.

"We all have our secrets, yes. You're all set."

Etta went and lay down on a linen towel until her skin was dry enough to dress again.

I shouldn't have asked him that. If there are any like Breezy around, word will spread and I'll never know about it. I should have asked Flora . . .

She went home. Still thinking of Flora, she fell asleep.

She dreamed of the chair.

In her dream, the stirrups weren't rusty enough to break. In her dream, she strained and strained at it, but the exultant relief of her one free leg rising never came. She could not rise. She could not breathe.

She woke up tangled in the featherbed, wool blankets kicked to the floor. She was tearing air in and out of her lungs, a high whistling sound accompanying every breath. Both of her calves were knotted with cramps, toes curled in and thighs locked together. She tried to get out of bed and fell heavily to the floor, bouncing one high cheekbone off the wood there.

She struggled to pull her knees under her, screeching wordlessly. Finally she got her feet on the floor and began the shuddering struggle to bring her toes up to break the cramp. She slammed her palms against the wall, panting, forcing her right foot into the corner. Her left thigh seized in protest and her knees buckled.

Ina was there in a flash of candlelight. She helped Etta get one leg up on the bed frame, cupping her withered hand beneath her daughter's heel, pushing her foot back with the flat underside of her forearm. Etta cried out, sweat beading on her forehead. After a few minutes, the cramp subsided.

Mother Ina helped her back into bed and together they stretched Etta's legs, keeping her feet flexed. When the spasms had truly passed, Ina left the room and came back with a glass of water and a dish of cold spinach with congealed bacon grease flaked across the top.

Etta forked the dark-green food into her mouth tiredly, washing each bite down with a little water.

"You need potassium, child. What do you eat when you're on the road?"

Etta swallowed. "I eat what I can find, Mother."

Ina shook her head, as if no matter the answer it wouldn't be good enough. "You've been having these since that year you came back in the winter. Every time you're out, nightmares and cramps."

Etta swallowed an enormous bite and went back for more, her fork viciously stabbing the plate beneath the spinach. She said nothing.

"In the morning, I'll make some more greens with some mushrooms. And then at dinner we'll have yams. Where are you going tomorrow?"

She's talking past it. She'll let me forget it.

Relief washed through Etta when she realized her mother really only wanted to help, not to make much of her daughter's weakness. She softened, scooping the last of the spinach off the plate.

"Thank you, Mother. I'm going to speak to the council tomorrow."

Ina stood and picked up the empty glass, held her hand out for the plate. "Is something wrong? You know they'll find a home for that woman. Flora."

"It's not really about that," Etta said, trying not to think of Flora sleeping in Alice's low, wide bed. "I have news for them that I think they might need."

"Alright, child." As Ina lifted the candle and made to leave, Etta could see the lines in the old woman's face, like the paths marked on a map. She saw the way her eyes crinkled and the lids drooped. She reached out and put her hand on her mother's arm.

"Thank you. You're always taking care of me."

Their eyes met and Ina smiled just a little. "My living daughter. You were like a wrapped-up present. I didn't know what would be inside, but I wanted it so much."

Etta smiled back and settled down. She didn't dream again before dawn.

Nowhere's council was made up of five, and at least three had to be women. Individuals were nominated and voted on by current members. Those sustained held office until they wanted to be done.

The council that Etta knew was four women and one man. Bronwen, daughter of Judith, was the current head. She was the oldest woman in Nowhere, a mother and the head of a Hive that was rumored to include fifty men. Janet, daughter of the Road, was the youngest woman on the council and, the last Etta had known, was about four moons pregnant. She had been brought in by raiders, Julio and Chase, when Etta was a child. Janet had been barely a toddler when they discovered her, eating fallen apples and hardly able to speak. No one had known where she came from, and she remembered nothing. Carla, daughter of Petra, was a stately forty-year-old Mother and chemist. Jenn was the Mother of two living sons who both worked as guards. She believed she was not yet past childbearing and she kept a Hive of ten, trying every moon for a girl.

Emory was the only man on the council. He was a son of Judith, but nearly ten years younger than Bronwen. Emory was tall and strongly built after years of work as a lumberjack and carpenter. He had fourteen apprentices and they were regarded as some of the most skilled tradesmen in town. Emory had been part of four or five Hives in his life, and he privately believed that he had sired living children all over Nowhere. He couldn't claim paternity—no man in Nowhere had that right, even in monogamous families. Nevertheless, most of his apprentices had a certain resemblance, and a rumor persisted among the Mothers that children gotten by him were charmed with health and easy fertility of their own.

Etta knew each of them. Since her career as a raider had begun, the council had heard her reports of the wider world and applauded her successes. She was known as a singularly skilled seeker of particular goods and a reliable bringer of women. The council made things easy for her because of this, encouraging tradesmen to deal fairly or even preferentially with her, and reminding the people of Nowhere whenever possible that their female population was flourishing thanks to raiders like Etta, and Errol and Ricardo before her.

She knew where the council would be. She headed for their shared office, a single room dominated by a huge, wide table and ringed around with deep carved-wood chairs. Two young boys stood silently just outside the door, unmoving as Etta passed them. Though it was not long after dawn, she saw that the table was strewn with sheets of hemp paper and stacked with the hides of small animals on one side. Bronwen stood with her palms against the massive table, her forehead deeply furrowed.

"How hard is it to keep raccoons out of a corn silo? How many have they shot?"

Jenn gestured to the stack of animal skins. "They can't shoot enough of them. Rax said there's thousands of them. They're going to need poison." Jenn's voice was testy, as if she were being made to repeat herself.

Carla was shaking her head. Etta watched her, seeing Alice's features in a rougher, older face. Carla's hair was still golden and curled into wild ringlets like her daughter's. They had the same freckled, fair skin and the same strange eye color that broke mid-iris from brilliant blue to muddy greenish brown. Carla was going deaf and relied on an ear trumpet, forever cocked on her left side. When she shook her head, it wavered slightly.

"The last time we gave them free rein to use poison, we had people eating poisoned deer. They're irresponsible with it."

"Can't we just fortify the silo to keep the raccoons out?" Emory sat back in his chair, his long legs splayed out in front of him. He was strikingly handsome, as brown as a yearling deer with thick hair and a cropped beard. "We could build it up at the base, with metal bars that they can't get through or around, right?"

Janet spoke softly, her hand resting on the swell beneath her deer-hide dress. "They're too smart, that's the problem. You can't keep them out of anything."

Bronwen had spotted Etta by this time and was staring her down. "Can't keep you out, either, can we, child?" But she was smiling, showing her still-healthy teeth.

"Mother Bronwen. Mother Carla. Mother Jenn. Janet. Emory." Etta nodded to each of them in turn and they nodded back. Each smiled as well, except for Carla.

Emory rose smoothly, shocking Etta with his height as he always did.

The Lion was about that tall. Bigger, though. She looked him up and down before she accepted his proffered seat.

"Thank you, Emory. Mother Bronwen, you know I'm always looking to free women and girls."

"Of course, child." Bronwen's eyes were looking over the sheets of paper again. She was expecting a typical report.

Etta leaned forward and clamped her hands on the edge of the table. "Mother Bronwen, Mother Jenn, I have to tell you something. There is a man in Estiel who calls himself the Lion."

Bronwen looked up then, her cloudy brown eyes very focused. Carla rose, and Janet clutched her belly with both hands.

"He's holding a harem of women and girls, I don't know how many, but surely too many. I was able to take a child from him and return her home, but we left many more behind."

Carla put her mouth beside the ear of one of the young boys at the door, and moments later, the boy ran from his post. Etta knew the boys were runners, and Carla had probably sent him for tea. She ignored Carla and kept talking.

"They're all on the upper floors of a riverfront hotel. A group of armed raiders with a good-size boat could clean the place out. The trouble . . . The trouble is . . ."

Carla was standing with her freckled arms crossed, frowning at her.

She knows. She knows about me and Alice. That's why she's giving me this look.

Etta swallowed hard. "He's got a lot of men. And he's got . . . well, lions. That's how he got his name. Two, on chains. One lion, one tiger, and full-grown. Probably inbred as hell, but they still look deadly. I don't know how many, I just saw the two. But it's dangerous. I couldn't do it alone or I'd have done it already."

Bronwen was looking at Carla. Emory was staring at his boots. Etta realized that no one in the room would meet her eye.

What the hell?

The messenger boy returned, beaming. Behind him, Alice walked in. Flora followed right behind her.

Carla reached out and took her daughter's hand. "Alice came here yesterday, with our newcomer. They had something very similar to tell us, didn't they?"

Alice and Flora exchanged a glance.

Just set me on fire.

Carla waggled her ear trumpet. "What's that?"

Bronwen rolled her eyes. "Flora, you're from a city that's loyal to this Lion?"

Flora took a step forward and nodded warily. She looked clean and rested, and her eyes kept darting to Alice.

Nobody needs to set me on fire, I'll just burn from the inside out.

"Yes, in Jeff City. We pay him tribute in goods and women."

"Is he a slaver?" Janet looked uneasy.

Flora shrugged. "Not really. He keeps women, he doesn't sell them. And catamites."

"But they're not free to leave," Etta began, with a murderous edge in her voice. "Being held in slavery isn't better than being sold constantly."

"Nobody said it was, child." Bronwen's voice was maddeningly even and aloof. "But the situation is complicated." She gestured to Flora.

Flora found her voice slowly. "The Lion . . . he's heavily armed. There are more smiths and bullet makers in Estiel than in any other city I've heard of. All they do is make bullets and knives. And he's got thousands of men, easily. Then there are those cats to think about. I don't know that the women there are poorly treated. They're not starved and they look—"

"You don't—" Etta started, but Bronwen cut her off with a look.

"They look alright," Flora finished lamely.

Eight in, eight out.

Etta's nightmare stirred in the recesses of her conscious mind and she lifted her right foot slightly without knowing she was doing it.

Carla patted Alice's hand and let it drop. "You're trying to raise an army for a doomed rescue that doesn't even need to happen. Etta, there's no call for this kind of thing."

Alice looked guilty, but she agreed with her mother. "Didn't the Lion offer trade for som? Flora told me that he'd pay us very well, including trade in women. We could free them peacefully, without risking anyone."

Heads nodded around the room, and Etta realized she had lost this battle before she woke up this morning.

"Child, there's no call for this kind of fight. You'll see that when you're older." Carla crinkled her eyes, not smiling.

Etta's hands were clenched at her side, and Flora would not return her gaze.

"Good Mother, respectfully, you don't know what it's like out there. If we agree to trade with the Lion, then we're agreeing that women should be traded. We become just like them."

Janet shifted uncomfortably. Jenn began rolling up papers and moving them to the far sides of the table.

Etta took a step toward Bronwen, cutting both Alice and Flora out of her line of sight. "And sooner or later, the Paws of the Lion will reach Nowhere. They'll come here, and we'll lose to them, one way or the other. What I'm proposing is that we get ahead of that."

Bronwen was shaking her head. "That's not what we do here."

Oh, fuck this.

"It's what the Unnamed would have done."

Bronwen's thin lips disappeared altogether. When she spoke, it was as if she were biting off every word to spit it into Etta's face. "The

Unnamed left women behind all her life. She gave them drugs and hoped for the best, and she only killed when she had to. What you're doing is not what she would do, it's what a *man* would do. Go start a fight to die in, whether it's the right thing or not. Go take some women, whatever the cost. Maybe living on the road has made it hard for you to think like a rational woman. Maybe you should stay home for a while and think about that."

Etta's neck stiffened and she shot a glance at Emory. He was staring at his huge, empty hands.

When Etta looked at Flora, she didn't know what she expected to see there. Triumph, maybe. But Flora's gray eyes were full of pity. Alice held her head high and returned Etta's blazing gaze, and Etta realized that Alice had lined her eyes exactly as Flora did. Maybe with the very same tool, this morning.

Disgusted, she turned to leave.

"You could always become a Midwife," Bronwen called to her back. "When you're ready to settle into a woman's real work, and do as the Unnamed actually did."

Etta didn't answer but stalked out, too angry to speak. She heard jogging steps behind her and whirled, expecting an apologetic Alice or a tearful Flora. But it was Emory who stood there.

"I'd go with you," he said. "If that was the mission. I'd help you take down this Lion. For what it's worth, I think you're right."

Etta huffed a sigh.

"Men aren't rational, you know." He put his hands at his hips and leaned back a little. "It's not our fault, it just how we're made. We don't bleed like women, so we have to find ways to bleed like men. It leads us into foolhardy things. Like the wars of the old world. Or keeping lions on a leash." He smiled at her, ducking his head to seem smaller.

"It isn't foolhardy to take a heroic action," Etta said. "It's the things we do to change the world."

Emory shrugged, crossing his arms. "Maybe. But trading with him does seem more sensible than your way. My way. Our way, you know?"

Our way. Eddy's way.

She couldn't bring herself to thank Emory. She squinted up at him in the early sunlight. "What if I went without approval? Just on my own, maybe with a couple of raiders? Would you come with?"

He laughed a little. "I'm on the council because they think I'm not like other men." He looked back over his shoulder. "I just wanted to tell you that I know how you feel, not to encourage you. There are easier ways. Less violent ways. That's all."

He jogged back without saying good-bye.

When Alice and Flora returned to Alice's house, it was clear they had not expected to see Etta there.

She stood against the front door, one leg folded to put her foot flat against it, head down. When she heard them approaching, she did not look up.

"Etta?" Alice sounded a little worried.

"You told me I had to knock next time, so here I am." Etta looked at Flora, not at Alice.

Alice flushed beneath her freckles and moved toward the door. "Please come in, Etta."

The three of them went inside and Etta fought the urge to grab Alice by the shoulders and kiss her while staring Flora down.

Instead, she sat on the low couch in Alice's front room, just off her laboratory with a view of her greenhouse.

Flora stood against the wall with her hands clasped behind her.

If she could fade into the wall, she'd do it.

"I just wanted to come over and thank you for running straight to your mother with my report. Saved me some trouble."

Alice poured water into a tall glass. "Thirsty?"

Etta kept her eyes on Flora as she answered. "Yeah, I am. Every time I try to get a drink, someone else seems to get there first."

Flora blushed and looked away.

I don't believe this. I'm out of sight for less than a day and they're fucking.

She took the glass of water, and Alice sat across from her on a hassock. She motioned to Flora, who sat on the floor beside her.

"So, are you part of her Hive now?"

Flora would not meet her eyes.

Alice reached up calmly and snapped her fingers in Etta's face.

Etta was so shocked she nearly dropped her glass of water.

"You can't keep coming here and acting like a little boy, Etta. I won't have it. I don't owe you anything. And yes, I went to my mother with useful information. And yes, Flora is staying with me. Indefinitely."

"*I'm* a little boy? *I'm* acting like a man? How can you say that to me, when you're sleeping with a—"

Etta grasped for the words.

"Horsewoman?" Alice arched one perfect golden eyebrow. "Are you angry because everybody already knows your stories, or because you're not getting what you want?"

For a moment she could see herself clearly throwing the water in Alice's face. She gulped it down instead.

Flora spoke first, laying a hand on Alice's shoulder. "You'd never be able to take the Lion's harem, Etta." She said the name a little too hard, landing on the *t*'s like *d*'s, and Etta knew she had nearly called her Eddy again.

"You'll just make things worse," Flora continued. "Things can work as they are, and you can do good within it."

Etta clenched her jaw and counted her breaths.

Alice nodded her chin toward the greenhouse outside. "I can make you enough som to clean him out. You can have gallons of the stuff, more than you could carry. I never run short, and the bees are doing so well this year I have enough wax to seal up every bottle I've got. You can bring home all of them, and nobody gets hurt. Let me help you."

"It's not enough."

"Oh, Etta, it's never enough for you." Alice looked up at Flora. "We have so much more than most of the women in the world, and you don't appreciate it at all."

"She's not even a woman!" As soon as she said it, Etta was sorry.

Alice, as ever, rose above the bait. "I know exactly what she is. You're as narrow-minded as a monogamous man, you know that? We've always been outside of that, with our own secrets. Flora is just like us, but you're too closed off to see it. It's the same. Do you want to go after the Lion to stop him, or to take his place?"

Etta bolted up. Her voice shook. "I do want the som. As much as you can make. I'm going to come back with them, and I'm going to get their stories recorded. And then you'll get it. Everyone can tell me then that I'm a narrow-minded irrational man."

She turned on Flora. "You told me he wants the som for the breeders, is that right? To keep them calmed down, to take their children from them, is that it? Have you seen them up close? Have you seen how childbirth tears them apart? Have you drunk the milk of dead women?"

I'm not going back there with a trade for him, Etta thought with dead certainty. *Never again. I won't trade with him or anyone else.*

Flora had averted her face from Etta's. She was crying.

"I've seen things you couldn't understand," Flora said.

"You know it isn't better here, don't you? You can't be with Alice, not really. No one will let it happen."

"It is better here," Flora said, looking at the floor. "I know you can see that. You're not stupid."

"Better isn't good enough." Etta's throat closed up and she knew her voice would betray her if she spoke again.

Alice laughed a little, standing up. "Etta, what do you want? We're left alone. It's not like they'd haul us out into the street and kill us, sell us to men for doing what we do. It's just frowned on. You can't live with your mother raising an eyebrow?"

"It's not about that."

It's all the same thing, she wanted to scream. *Slaves and harems and my mother's eyebrows. We can't be what we are, because of how we were born.*

She said nothing.

"Etta, I think you'd better go." Alice's voice was cool but firm.

Swearing and shaking, Etta went.

The smell of Alice's house faded from her nostrils as she walked through the marketplace on her way back home.

The springtime stalls were full of first fruits and bright colors. Sweet corn was everywhere in bushels, ready to be practically given away. She stopped and traded a few old-world trinkets for some fresh berries with cream. She ate ravenously, still angry and feeling like she'd never be full. There would be a community dinner tonight, with spring lamb roasted for everyone. She'd have to be there.

She wanted to bind and change her voice and her walk. She wanted to be harder, simpler. Her own self.

I don't care what they call me. Fuck Alice. She doesn't know me.

Being Eddy doesn't solve it. Would moving in with Alice solve it?

She spun, unable to point to true north. She didn't know where to go with that feeling.

There was nowhere to go.

Ina's house was empty. Etta didn't want to go there but she didn't know what to do with herself. Alone in her bedroom, she finally pulled out her binder and put it on. She sat down with her book and pen and waited.

When it finally came, it was as if her hand moved without her volition.

The Book of Eddy

She stared at the name. It was the first time she had written it down.

Eddy

Eddy

Eddy

She wrote it a different way each time, trying out slightly different styles. She held the pen roughly and scratched the words down.

Eddy was born in the chair.

Once the words were written, her mind could not stop itself.

The chair the chair the chair the rust.

She slammed the purple book shut, knowing that the words hadn't dried and would be stamped in reverse on the opposite page.

She unbound herself, gasping for breath like she had come up from under water.

Eight in eight out.

Where are you right now?

But it was too late, she was in the chair.

It was over a hundred years old, and every move in it screeched like a caged bird. The rusty stirrups beneath her bare feet were like sharp crusty claws digging into her skin. She could smell everything, the dust of the place, the sweat of a stranger.

Etta vomited a splatter of berries and cream that looked like foamy blood across the floor. She wiped her face with the back of her hand and went and found Julian (son of Carla) and told him there was a mess in Ina's house she needed him to clean up. Julian scurried immediately and Etta watched him go. He had none of his mother's traits—not her white streak or the strange eyes that made Alice so unusual and beautiful. He was brown eyed and brown haired and so pleasantly normal that it calmed her to call him "father" and send him on his way.

An accident. A decision of who to sleep with and a risky stew of blood. You get blue eyes, you get brown eyes. You get light skin, you get dark. You're a boy and you're a girl.

Etta went to the shrine of the Unnamed and knelt there in the semidarkness until her legs went numb. She thought of Errol and Ricardo somehow finding and following her trail to the west, walking backward to the sea.

The dinner bell woke her and she rose gingerly, letting her legs warm up slowly. The memory of her cramps seemed very long ago but felt very near.

Ina waved to her the minute she walked into the hall, and she went dutifully to sit with her mother. She could smell roasting lamb with rosemary and sage, and her stomach growled. Men carried smoking trays of roast potatoes and green beans and corn out to the long tables, and bread followed with huge bowls of butter. Etta's mouth watered, and even Ina licked her lips.

Bronwen stood at the front of the room, flanked by Carla and Emory. She raised her hands and waited for quiet.

"I won't keep you all from eating while it's hot," she called across the room. "But before dessert, we will have some community announcements. Dig in!"

Etta filled her plate with piles of everything, including a huge joint of meat with marrow showing in the cut bone. She had essentially eaten nothing that day and felt starved. As she gnawed the bone, she saw Alice and Flora involved in animated discussion with Sylvia on the opposite side of the room. She watched them as she began to feel the stirrings of indigestion.

"That is a proper dinner," Ina said, wiping grease from her mouth. "I don't come to these things enough."

Etta nodded but didn't have anything to say. She was looking at the mural on the wall; this one was a tall, willowy pregnant woman with her hair caught like a flag in the wind. In the distance, children danced in rings on the hillsides and a foal ran alongside a fully grown roan.

When conversation had returned to a continuous buzz and the dishes had been cleared, Bronwen spoke again.

"Let's have announcements. Children born since the last community supper?"

Sylvia stood. "One boy, Kip, son of Druz. And one on the way, right, Janet?"

Janet waved shyly but did not speak.

"Refugees taken in?"

"One girl, Chloe, daughter of the Road, adopted by Ani."

Etta's eyes swept the hall until they landed on the little girl. Her cheeks had filled out and she looked like a different child entirely. Chloe did not see her.

"And one woman, Flora, daughter of the Road. Staying in the home of Alice, daughter of Carla."

Flora raised one hand briefly but did not rise.

"Both of them brought to us by Etta, the greatest raider of the last decade," Sylvia said indulgently.

Etta didn't know if that was true, but she rose half out of her seat to some applause.

Bronwen waited for the cheers to die down. "Trouble? Slavers?"

Rob rose and Etta could tell from there that he was stoned. "None since the last winter, Mother Bronwen. We've been very lucky." He swayed back down into his chair the way a feather drifts to the ground.

All over the room, people checked in. Crops were doing well, livestock was flourishing. The minutiae rolled on and the kitchen sent men out with bowls of fruits and cream.

Etta leaned close to her mother. "I'm too full for this. I'm going for a walk." Ina squeezed her hand in response and let her go.

Etta breezed past Flora and Alice without even attempting to eavesdrop. She stepped out into the wan light of a new moon and walked without a destination. She heard music and headed toward it without thinking what it might mean.

When she drew closer, she stopped in the street and tried to quiet her own breathing.

That's old-world music.

Old-world music was incredibly hard to come by. It existed mostly in recordings that could not be replayed, made for machines that had long been forgotten. Etta had heard it only a few times in her life, when someone could make an ancient machine work fitfully for a few seconds.

This music had that otherworldly depth, like a tiny orchestra was playing from inside a box. She followed the sound, being drawn to a house on the far end of Nowhere. She could see light spilling out of a storm-cellar window around the rear of the house. She crept toward it and lay on the ground, putting her eye to the tiny opening filled with yellow light.

She held perfectly still, listening to the song. The words were in another language, most of the time. She couldn't follow it but the sound was intoxicating. A woman with long, blonde hair swirled past her field of vision and she strained to see who it might be.

I thought I saw every woman in Nowhere at dinner, she thought rapidly. She would have missed anyone who wasn't there.

A deeper terror punctured her assurance for a moment.

What if someone is keeping captives right here? In my own city.

She pressed her face to the small section of glass, straining to see the blonde again.

No argument about it. I'll just break in right now.

She felt for the knife she kept in the back of her pants.

When the woman appeared again, her hair was in her face and she was laughing. Etta squinted, trying to place her.

Maybe it's someone I've never seen before. Maybe she's—

The woman was Tommy, the bather.

Breezy.

Tommy was lip-syncing with the song that was being played somehow in the basement. He was so drunk that he swayed on his feet. Etta realized that the redhead beside him was another man, some young thing in a wig. They danced together, pretending to sing the song.

Drunk as they were, they clearly knew the words. The nonsense lined up precisely with their slurred cadence, and Etta could eventually tell that some of their dancing was choreographed, after a fashion.

The song ended and another began. There was cackling laughter from the cellar, followed by a shushing. People had begun to trickle out of the hall and these hidden revelers must have known they couldn't count on hiding for much longer tonight. The music ended with a scratchy screech and Etta got up, dusting off her clothes.

What was that?

As she walked away, she couldn't help but look back.

Etta slept alone.

Outside the gates of Nowhere, walking away from the first light of dawn, Eddy tried to remember why he had returned home.

They were never going to come with me. They would never have attacked the Lion, even if Flora hadn't talked them out of it.

He walked with his hands wrapped around the straps of his bag, hunching away from it. He was carrying the short version of the Midwife's tale, but even the canon meant six books weighing down his bag.

Find the city. San Francisco. Just walk until I find the ocean. I'll find it. I'll walk her way, maybe take me a year. Do what she did, and read the book again. Know what she knew. Find what she found.

At once, Eddy regretted not taking the truck. He didn't know how to drive, and he would have run out of precious deez anyway. Still, as the sky lightened behind him, he compared the progress he was making to the way the distance had slid by outside the roaring truck just the other day.

Maybe find San Francisco by winter, at this rate. Wonder how cold it is there.

But before it got cold, he knew, he could make the most of the summer. He camped by the side of the road that night and roasted early wild corn for supper. For three days he traveled easily, catching fish in streams and gathering berries by the handful as he passed.

Maybe one more day before I come to country I've never seen before.

Eddy consulted the map. Errol and Ricardo had headed west on their last raid and not returned. Their notes on the fuzzed old paper grew sparse as the roads headed toward the sunset. The last places that had any notation were in the Rockies. Eddy squinted and saw that Errol had written the word *steep* in his slanting, left-handed print.

On the other side there will be Utah. California. The places she had come through before she came to Nowhere. When she was just herself.

He thought of the shrine, the candles. The hand-copied books, all full of her old-world words.

Will I become a book, too?

He slept in the open, arms crossed over the gun on his chest and bag under his head. He dreamed of the Lion and of Alice and Flora. He woke up not knowing where he was.

Almost nothing of the old world was left standing out here. The land was flat as far as the eye could see, the horizon the same green with the bowl of blue upended over it. A few rotted posts stuck up out of the ground and Eddy knew they had once held signs, but nothing remained.

In Eddy's life, he had seen twisters. Large and small, singles and sisters came every few years near and around Nowhere. Out here, he could see the way things had been torn apart and blown around with no one to rebuild anything. Out in a field, he saw the sun winking off an old bathtub, liberated from its home.

He walked all day, following the sun. He watched for a good place to sleep and found a low block building a little after nightfall.

He didn't see that there were bones in the room until after he'd lit his fire. A skull in the corner grinned, a gold tooth bright in the light. As the fire caught and bloomed, he saw there were maybe ten of them.

Eddy wasn't scared of human skeletons. Raiding old-world goods sometimes meant finding them—some dried-out and wearing rags of clothes, shut up in locked rooms for a century of forgotten time. Others, like these, were spread out in disorderly numberless pieces, with only what was left of their heads to remember them.

"What happened to you?"

The sound of his own voice surprised him. He touched the gold tooth and saw that another was wearing an old-world ring. He methodically picked through, pulling metal from the dust that used to be people, knowing that grave goods were valuable for trade. Long ago, Errol had told him about a time he and Ricardo had spent a summer digging among the fallen gravestones of an old-world cemetery.

He grinned, remembering Errol's long hair and his merry prankster's eyes.

"It was incredible. They buried people wearing shoes—good shoes! Gold, diamonds, little clocks on their wrists. And beads, all these beads with crosses on 'em. Find those all the time. Lots of work, but there's treasure every time."

Errol, where the hell are you now? West? I'm going west, too. Maybe I'll find you. Pick the gold off your bones.

One of the dead had worn a bracelet of polished metal—Eddy thought it was steel. He rubbed it with his fingers, seeing that it was engraved with words.

He spat a little, rubbing harder.

STERLING MANDELBROT

652-91-0004

DIABETIC

That must be a name. Sterling.

Is that a woman or a man?

In Eddy's mind, Errol's long black hair became the wig he had seen on Tommy the bather.

He stowed the treasure he had found and his hand touched his journal. He drew it out and sat with his back to the wall.

The last page he had written was badly blotted, but he knew what the words were there.

Eddy was born in the chair.

He found his pen and ink and began again.

The Book of Eddy
Spring Passing into Summer

I have decided to head out west. I am going to follow the Unnamed and watch for sign of Errol and Ricardo. Errol has long, beautiful hair, and Ricardo has pox scars. Someone might remember them, if I ask around.

He looked up and saw the words *Eddy was born in the chair* and had to count eight in, eight out.

He gripped the pen.

The Unnamed lost herself, too. She became a man, out on the road. The people who saw her believed. She could change. Like Flora. Like me.

So I'm going to do what she did. Go as far as—

Eight in, eight out.

It isn't a lie. Etta is a liar. I'm not.

Go as far as she always says I've gone.

My name is Eddy, son of the Road, and I've never been farther from home than Estiel. I've killed men. Etta always lies. She says she's been all over. She's been to the cavern and to Estiel and the roads between. Always the same way. She says she's killed dozens, but it was always me, and only a few. One with poison and two with my hands. Three or four with the gun.

Etta, daughter of Ina, wants Alice to want her, but only her. The two of them, together.

I know better than that. I know that women need more than one, and that it's a waste not to try and be a Mother. I know that a Hive is the most sensible solution.

Etta doesn't know anything.

I wasn't born in the chair. I was born when she was; I have always been with her. That's just when she let me out.

Eight in, eight out. The chair did not come clear in memory; it was only a separation between before and after.

I was with her before. Inside. Then, outside.

The metaphor was simple but Eddy resisted it, as he had all his life.

It isn't like birth. It's like splitting. Like in the books. Mitosis. Two splitting into one. Two lives, two books. I'll keep this journal, because I want to be like the Unnamed. I'll follow her road.

Eddy cleaned his pen. He was enormously calm, like the surface of a frozen lake. He cleaned his gun after that, and got comfortable.

Look at this bed of bones, he thought as he slipped into sleep.

The Book of Eddy

Spring Passing into Summer

If I'm reading this map right, and if I don't get into trouble, I can reach her city, San Francisco, by winter. I can find someplace to hole up and turn back after spring.

This part of the map is in bad shape, but I know I have to pass through some serious mountains to get there. I think if I swing north, I can avoid the worst of the part that's called ROCKY MTNS on the map. They look like trouble.

If I come to a place where I can trade for a horse, I'll do it. I don't know much about them, but I could learn.

I'm Eddy. I can do anything.

The Book of Eddy
Starting to Feel Like Summer

I am really good at shooting rabbits, so I'm not hungry.

I want to read the canon, but I'm waiting until I know I am somewhere that she was. Not much to do, but I think I'm going to start tanning skins off my kills. They're always useful.

CHAPTER 9

As Eddy was tanning a rabbit skin in the basement of an old house in what used to be Kansas, Alice was brewing som. She lined up rows and rows of glassware filled with the grain alcohol she'd bartered for all around town. Slowly, patiently, she cut the poppy pods and scraped their weeping milk into the grain alcohol. She distilled and packaged enough to fill a crate she would put in the back of Flora's truck.

Flora had woken up first, meaning to head over and see Etta. She wanted to apologize, to see if they could start over. She wanted to see Nowhere.

Alice was awake already, working in her lab. She saw Flora making her way toward the door.

"Etta?" Her voice held no accusation.

Flora sighed. "Yeah."

"Do you want to have something to eat first?"

Flora adjusted her bag. "Do you think she's not up yet?"

Alice shrugged. "She usually sleeps in when she's home. No rush, really." She set down the glass jars she was holding. "Come on."

Alice's kitchen looked like a different kind of lab, nothing like Flora's kitchen back home. She brewed strong tea made of toasted dandelion roots and set out a pretty loaf of brown bread with butter and honey. Flora ate a thick slice while she waited for the drink to cool.

"Who does she live with?" Flora chewed on one side of her mouth, where her good teeth were.

"Her mother, mostly. Ina."

Flora nodded, swallowing a too-large bite. "Why does Ina wear that black belly?"

"Because she's the Mother of a living child," Alice said patiently. "You'll see them on more women, out in town."

"What if you haven't ever had a living child? What do you wear then?"

Alice shrugged, pouring more of the steaming brown flower tea. "Just clothes, I guess."

"What do you do after your child grows up?"

Alice took a sip. Flora tried her cup again and found it still far too hot.

"Ina teaches the scribes," Alice said. "Some Mothers are on the council. Some work on the farms, or they spin wool. Different things. Mostly the men do that kind of work, though."

Flora nodded, blowing across the top of her cup. "What would I do, if I stayed here?"

Alice gulped again, impervious to the heat. "What you're best at, right? You should make silk here."

Flora laughed a little. "I'd have to bring the moths. And they have to have the right kind of tree. It's not as simple as that."

Alice thought that over. "Other cloth, then. We have few skilled weavers. You could teach boys to weave better cloth."

Flora nodded, taking another fingertip of honey on her tongue. "Only the boys."

"Probably, yes. Girls learn to be Mothers or Midwives. It's not really a good use of their time to learn things like weaving."

Flora cleared her throat. "So, will I have to explain to people that I can't be a Mother?"

Alice cut her own slice of bread and began to butter it. "No, at your age you'd know for sure. Many women cannot, and they stop trying."

"So they don't have Hives?"

Alice shifted in her seat. "Well, some Midwives have Hives, yes. But they count their moons and send them away when it might be their time. They try not to."

"What happens if they get pregnant by accident?"

Alice sighed. "There are things you can do."

Flora nodded. She took a sip of her tea. It was terribly bitter even after the honey. "So you do that here?"

Alice nodded, her cheeks coloring. "It . . . It's been part of Nowhere's laws since the Unnamed. She did it, too. But not everyone agrees with it. We . . . We don't talk about it. It's done very quietly, and the woman usually tells her people that it was a miscarriage."

They were quiet for a minute.

"Does . . . Do your people in Jeff City do it?"

Flora sipped, her gray eyes holding Alice's over the rim of the cup. "I've heard stories. But it's not allowed. The Lion says abortion can't be practiced in any tributary cities."

"Abortion." Alice said the word as though it were unfamiliar to her. "I haven't heard the word said in a long time. It's one of the lost words."

"Lost words?"

Alice nodded, chewing more bread. "A few years ago, the council at the time decided to remove some words from our books. Words that they said had destroyed the old world. I was really young, and I didn't understand. But I heard women talking about the word *abortion*. It's not really a lost word, because it's in the book."

She rose and went to a shelf in the other room, coming back with her copy of the Book of the Unnamed. She leafed through pages, looking for a specific section.

"Right here, in the Book of Roxanne. She's talking about Shawna, and she says that she knew about abortions. From the old world."

Flora set her cup down, craning her neck to see. "Eddy talked about that book. I wanted to read it."

"You mean Etta?"

Flora looked up at Alice, her eyes wide. "Yes. Etta."

Alice pushed the book toward Flora, still laid open. "You can read mine." She sighed, sitting back down. "So, I know there are other books with that word, but it's cut out of the page. Or the whole chapter is missing. There are other lost words. In stories about two women together, or about women who lived in slavery in the old world. I don't understand it."

Flora didn't either, but her eyes raked the page. "Cut out? Like how?"

"No, not from that book. Nobody has ever changed the Unnamed's book. But other books. Here."

Alice went back to her shelf and pulled four or five books out to free something that had been hidden behind them. She returned to the table with two books.

One of them was heavily damaged; really only part of the book had survived. No covers, and ragged pieces of pages were interspersed with whole sheets. Alice laid it on top of the diary Flora was reading.

"There's only parts of this," she said. "I found it when I was a teenager. It's about a girl named Molly and her lover, Carolyn. There's not much here, but you can tell they're in love. There were women together in the old world. There was a word for it, in the old world."

Flora held her breath. She waited.

"What's the word?" Flora asked.

Alice shrugged, gathering the books back up. "The people in the book are talking about a girl who might have had sex with another girl, at a school for girls in the old world. I don't know the word, but I know what they're asking. I asked my mother once about the lost words. She got really strange about it, saying she didn't agree with the council destroying any books, ever. But that was after she . . . she kind of found out about me. She was so disappointed."

Flora watched her go back to the other room.

"Do you think there was a word in the old world for what I am?"

Alice looked startled. "Oh, I don't think this happened back then. There were . . . There was an equal number of men and women. Why would it?"

Flora looked down at the Book of the Unnamed. She didn't answer.

"Do you know about Etta?"

Alice's smile returned and she slurped her cooling tea. "Of course I do. I've been with her, you know."

Flora looked up and then quickly back down. "No, I know that. I mean, did you know she's like me?"

Alice laughed a little and reached out to touch Flora's cheek, gently. "When I say I've been with her, I mean I've been inside her. She's not like you, my love."

Flora felt her blush spread across her chest. "No, I mean—"

"Come on, let's go see her." Alice was tidying up the table.

Flora got up and slipped the copy of the book into her satchel. "Alright, let's do that."

They walked across the open blocks of Nowhere, passing people as they went about their business. They saw Mother Ina, careworn and grim-faced, walking to the old schoolhouse.

They passed murals painted on patched walls. Pregnant women with long hair, full moons, and eggs seemed to appear in all of them. Flora felt a little more foreign than usual.

A woman with very short hair came right at them, carrying an armload of sheets. "Alice!"

"Sylvia!" The two hugged while Flora stood awkwardly, waiting. "I haven't seen you in a while!" She turned to Flora, looking her over. "How is our newcomer?"

"Fine, thank you. Fine." Flora tried to shrink, to turn away from Sylvia's invasive gaze.

"Well, we're on our way to see Etta," Alice said. Flora saw Sylvia's blue eyes flash, but her smile only widened.

"Of course you are. Well, don't let me keep you!" Flora watched Sylvia's blue eyes dart between the two of them as though she were searching for something.

Alice threaded her arm through Flora's and steered her away.

"What was that about?"

Alice rolled her eyes. "She's jealous. How do I always end up with the jealous ones?"

"Of me?" Flora swiveled her head over her shoulder to watch the short-haired woman go.

"Of you. Of Etta. Of anyone who's with me."

"Does she want to marry you? Or live with you?"

Alice snorted. "Yeah, I guess. Everybody wants something I can't give them. I make stuff no one else can make, you think that'd be enough."

Flora touched her own silk. "No, that isn't enough."

They came to Ina's house and knocked on the door. Alice called out to Etta a few times before they circled around to the back of the house. Alice could only see a tiny strip of the room, but she felt the emptiness. She thought of Ina's tired face.

"Shit. She's gone."

They both knew it was true.

Alice spent a few days showing Nowhere to Flora. They visited the log dorm where the boys lived, and Flora talked to a few of them.

After, Alice took her to see where the village had big dinners together and sneaked her a pickle.

"So the boys live all together, to learn their trades?"

Alice nodded, leading them back toward her place. "Yes, once they're big enough to leave home."

"How big is that?" Flora sucked her pickle, relishing the salt.

"Five years, sometimes six."

"Why don't they stay at home?"

"Well, Mothers have work to do. Many of them want to try and have another living child, as soon as they can. This way, the fathers can care for them and teach them, and women can do more important things."

"What about girl children?"

"They stay with their mothers, of course."

Flora digested that in silence, chasing it with a bite of pickle. "Until when?"

"Until they're ready. I moved out on my own in my fifteenth summer, but most stay longer. My mother . . . I love her, but we do not get along."

"Because she knows?"

Alice started, looking over her shoulders. "No. No, because she wants to control me. Pick out my Hive for me. I wanted to choose my own life. And by then I had already been studying so long. To be a Midwife, I mean."

Flora's brows knitted. "You're a Midwife?"

Alice cleared her throat. "Technically. Yes. Sylvia and I are both Midwives, though she's the head Midwife. I . . . I don't do much of the baby-catching. I'm more like what they used to call a doctor. I make drugs and see sick people more than I catch babies. But I know how. It just . . . It doesn't do for me what it does for them."

Flora watched Alice's face carefully, saw conflicting emotions cross it like the shadow of clouds on the ground.

"I've been to births where everyone is crying, just lost in it, either joy or sadness. It isn't like that for me. It's blood and shit and worry, and a lot of the time it's for nothing. Now, when I can break a fever or help set a bone . . . that's different. That's powerful. I'm just . . . I'm not like them."

Flora nodded. They walked the rest of the way in quiet understanding.

Flora waited a few more days before trying to tell Alice again.

"Where do you think Etta went?"

They were naked in Alice's big bed, the green glow of her night-paint creeping over their cheeks. Flora lay as uncovered as she dared, still shy about nudity.

Alice came up on one elbow and lazily dragged the backs of her nails over Flora's belly. "I don't think she'd go back to Estiel alone, do you? I mean, her plan depended on having help, didn't it?"

"I wish she would have just made the trade," Flora said, her insides squirming under the tickling sensation. "I would have helped her with that. We could have brought so many here."

Alice looked at Flora's eyes. "You're so different from her. You're like me. You see things from different sides."

Flora smiled and Alice kissed her.

Flora sighed. "I am like her, though. A little bit. She's like me. She's . . . She's someone else when she's on the road. Someone you don't know. Named Eddy."

"What?" Alice looked a little annoyed.

Flora took a deep breath. "When I met him, his name was Eddy. I didn't know he was a woman until much later. I've been reading, in the Book of the Unnamed, you know how she bound her breasts and pretended to be a man?"

Alice was following, but she didn't speak.

"Except I don't think it's like that, not exactly. I think she's more like me. I always knew I was a girl. I think Eddy's always been Eddy, but he just can't be himself here."

Alice looked down, and Flora brought in both hands to cover her sex, reflexively.

"I don't think that's true about Etta. I think it's just safety. Like, the Unnamed never did that again after she came to live here. Why would she? That would be like her saying that she wasn't safe here. Etta is safe here, just like she was. We all are. There's no other reason to dress like a man."

Flora didn't answer.

"The Unnamed did that. She was a raider. She did it to save women. And then she stayed here, to be a Midwife. Like I do, using medicine. The same work. Etta could have that, too. She just can't settle down, that's all. She's so stuck in her anger because we're a little different."

Alice looked away for a second, thinking.

"Anyway, dressing like a man here would mean giving away all of her power. Why would she want that?"

Flora couldn't pry her lips open.

Alice spread her arms wide, expansive and grinning. "I could do it. We don't need Etta. I could bind myself and go to the Lion with the som."

Flora searched Alice's face. "Are you sure you want to do that? I don't think you could look as much like a man as Eddy."

Alice scoffed. "Why, just because she's got muscles?" Alice curled a bicep and grinned at Flora, gloriously freckled in the green light.

Flora smiled in spite of herself. "Are you going to shave your head?" She reached out and touched Alice's gold curls. "There's an awful lot of binding to do here," she said, moving a hand to Alice's breasts.

Alice sprang like a cat and the conversation was lost for a while.

Later, Alice lay pressed against Flora's back, sighing as their sweat mingled.

Flora felt bolder, closer. She swept her red hair off her neck and smiled when Alice settled her lips on the spot she had exposed. "You could be like me."

"Hmm?"

"We could go to Estiel. And I could dress you in silks, and tell them you're a horsewoman. We could braid our hair alike. They've seen a lot of my kind before."

"Huh," Alice said. "That does seem more likely to work."

"We could trade som and come back carefully, so the Paws couldn't find Nowhere. Go every year, maybe."

"Are you planning to stay that long?"

Flora nestled into the warmth of Alice's arms. "I could stay here forever."

They planned for the next few days, looking over borrowed maps and talking about it only when they were alone. Alice packed away vial after vial of som, and even some seeds. She told Flora she didn't think they'd have any luck with growing it, but it might help them make a better deal.

They slowly planned the route by which they would drive into Estiel. The truck would likely be recognized by the Paws and they'd pass safely enough.

"We should have asked Etta for the claw necklace. She won't use it, and it might have helped us." Flora did not like using Etta's name. It felt funny in her mouth.

"Well, it's too late now," Alice told her. "We'll be alright. We'll be two horsewomen, bringing the Lion what he wants. Right? If Etta has done it all these years, how hard can it be? She always says there's hardly anyone out there. Right?"

Flora looked at Alice's guileless face and felt the first stirrings of doom. She could not say why, and so she could not say no. "Sure."

Flora taught Alice how to fuel the truck in motion. The smell of the rich exhaust made Alice ill, but she soldiered on. On the day they planned to leave, Flora dressed Alice and intricately braided her hair.

"There. You're just like me."

Alice laughed a little and grasped at her crotch as if to make a joke. Flora's smile faltered a little.

They stopped by to say hello to Carla, who sat bent over crop-rotation plans.

"Mother?" Alice crept up and tapped Carla on the shoulder.

"Oh!" Carla pulled her ear trumpet from beneath her papers. "Don't you look different!"

"Flora dressed me up! We're going to the woods to look for a tree that her moths can eat."

Carla's eyes narrowed slightly as she looked Flora's face over. "Not too far, I hope?"

"No, Mother."

"My living child." Carla put her trumpet in her pocket and embraced Alice. She nodded curtly to Flora. "You two be safe."

Flora nodded back.

The drive was bumpy and loud. Alice obviously hated it, but the feeling of adventure kept her spirits up awhile. On the second day, she was antsy.

"My mother will be worried by now," she said to Flora as they slept in the bed of the truck.

"I'm sure."

"Does your mother worry about you?"

"I never knew her."

The stars wheeled slowly overhead.

"This is the farthest I've ever been from home." Alice sounded very small.

"I've been all over. Like the Unnamed."

"Tell me about it?"

Flora told her about a swamp she remembered, where the trees stood up out of the water on roots like legs. Alice fell asleep.

They reached Estiel early the next day. As they predicted, they were taken straight to the Lion.

Alice seemed to thrum all over, like a string pulled tight.

"I'm considering taking a drop of my own cannabis oil to calm down."

"Don't," Flora said. "You're going to want to be sharp."

Paws walked them in through the front doors of the day-gloom hotel. Alice reached out for Flora's hand, but the other woman flinched away from her.

Alice had to crane her neck up to speak to the Lion, who towered over both of them. The big cats crept closer to her as she spoke, unnerving her until her voice was unsteady. Flora jumped in to help her, but quavered, too.

They told their story anyway. Alice pulled out tiny bottles of som with hands that shook, spilling the wax-sealed glass vessels to the floor. She picked them up and tried to control herself. She looked up and saw the tiger's nose twitching as it took in her scent. Its chain tinkled like the glass in the stillness.

The Lion held out his hand, chains wrapped around it. "Bring it to me."

Flora tried to take them from her, to step between her and the man with the cats.

"Not you. Her."

Alice held her head high. Her chin quivered but she stepped forward. She held out the som and tried to lay one in his hand.

His hand closed on hers and he pulled her close to him, between him and his cats.

"A lion knows its prey by scent." He took a long, deep whiff of her, crushing her into him. "My cats know what you are, and so do I."

Alice burst into tears, all courage gone.

"And you." He looked Flora over, appraising. "You're not the usual kind of thing I like to keep. But I think you'll be useful anyway."

Flora tried to dissuade the men who came to take them upstairs. In the end, Flora was dragged and Alice was carried, but they went. The cats' gold eyes watched them go.

Neither of them would ever return to Nowhere.

CHAPTER 10

Eddy knew all the stories. More importantly, his maps had once belonged to Errol, who had marked, not too long ago, every town that had any number of people in it.

The map that included the town of Topeka—Eddy tried all morning to figure out how to say that name—was one that he had not unfolded since it had been given to him. The bright greens and blues of the plasticky paper shocked him. There were black Xs at Topeka and then again at Manhattan, but the one at Topeka was beside a hastily drawn section of chain. That meant it was a slave-trading city and should be avoided. Manhattan had no other notation but the one that meant there was a town there, or at least there had been one the last time Errol and Ricardo had come through. Eddy planned to follow the road that cut south under Topeka, but would eventually lead him to the town that used to be called Manhattan, in the state of Kansas.

That'll take me north over the mountains, and then I can head southwest until I find her city.

Eddy foraged some eggs that day, tried hard to shoot a squirrel with his bow and missed it. He was beginning to think about getting up a tree and waiting for a deer. He should tan a deerhide or two in preparation for cold nights ahead.

Or something bigger than a deer, with real fur.

If there are deer, bigger things will follow.

But his bad luck continued, and he shot nothing at all. He could always find corn and early fruits, but it wasn't enough.

The Book of Eddy
Early Summer

On the road to Manhattan. The old raider's map says there's a safe town there. Maybe I can barter for some meat.

Far off, Eddy could hear wolves in the night. They howled and called to one another, keeping him awake. He had never had to fight wolves and didn't want to start now. On the road, he watched carefully for tracks and spoor, not knowing them like a hunter, but knowing enough to tell a prey animal from a predator.

He thought of Flora's horse and the red mess that had been left of her.

I wonder if they can smell me.

The Book of Eddy
Early summer

The Unnamed must have been light skinned. It's never been useful advice to me, rubbing dirt into my jaw to look like stubble. Still, a beard would be great.

I was going to wait until I was there to read the book, to be where she was. But I can always read it again.

She had a "compression vest," though. I get the idea. She didn't have to bind. I wonder if that was more comfortable. She says thank you to the "transman of yesteryear."

So there must have been others like her. Other people who needed to bind in order to survive. But she says that things weren't like this before the plague. Everybody says that before the fever, every woman could have children and they were all free. And the Unnamed had drugs that anyone could get, so they could decide when.

So why were there transmen in her yesteryear? Maybe they weren't really safe at all.

Like we say we're safe in Nowhere, but we really aren't. Everyone is much safer if we're all the same. So there's me and Alice and Sylvia and Miranda and the others, and there's Tommy in the basement and maybe Errol. There's Breezy, the girl toward the end of the book. Was she the first boy who became a girl? And the Unnamed when she was a man, and we're not safe, not really. Because if we're not the same, we're not really in and we might as well be out.

And out is slavers and the people who cut little girls. Out is the Lion and I bet every little city has a man like the Lion, someone who climbed to the top using women as the stairs.

And if the whole world is like that, then we're not really safe until we change it. We change it with poison and bullets.

Mother Ina thinks we change it with books and babies, but neither one of those can make it. I've seen them both get torn apart. It's not enough.

Even the Unnamed, she knew it wasn't enough. She asks herself over and over in her journal what is it for, and what does it matter, but I think she asked that question even before the old world ended. I think that question followed her, her whole life.

I think that when it changed, she was ready. I think that in the old world, women were slaves. Maybe not like they are now, but somebody needed that vest. Somebody needed her pills or her rings to keep from getting pregnant. Maybe slavery just looked nicer back then.

The old world made that chair.

He put the book down and breathed, eight in and eight out.

Where are you right now?

Who are you right now?

Eddy, son of the Road, was trying to decide. Writing in the light of a campfire he had built in the chimney of a long-gone house, he considered his memories.

The memories that were Etta's were his, too. They had to be. But they hadn't happened to him, just to her while he was there.

Like a silent twin brother.

A brother, even a twin brother, would not have been allowed at Etta's first blood. Still, Eddy thought of it as he lay down that night. He had terrible, low cramps across his back and he knew the morning would bring blood.

Etta's first blood had come too early for her and too late for everyone else. Mothers and Midwives talked long and often about how it used to come later in the old world. Women shared stories from their mothers and grandmothers, whose blood had come upon them at fourteen or even fifteen years. But girls in Nowhere were considered late bloomers if they reached twelve without having their passage. Etta had been eleven, nearly twelve, when her time came.

She had fought with Ina for weeks, over every little thing. Her mother had tripped on Etta's boots, left carelessly in a doorway. Instead of just apologizing, Etta had cried and raged that her mother was ascribing malice to what was really only laziness.

Ina had tried to offer her daughter strong tea and fresh venison for dinner to mend things between them, but Etta could hardly eat or drink. She had dreamed she was pregnant and she woke up in a cold sweat, knowing she would die in labor. She'd cried out in her sleep, the ghost of labor pains still in her.

When her mother had come in the door, her face soft with fear and concern in the candlelight, Etta had yelled at her to just leave.

Instead, Ina had put her palm down in the fresh blood on the sheets and held it up to the light.

For a sick, howling moment Etta worried that she really had been in labor, delivering the nightmare child into the world.

She knew what it was an instant later, but the terror had taken root in that dark bleeding secret place inside her. It would be with her always.

Ina had taken Etta to the baths, and the bathers had been dismissed. Word traveled door to door in the night. Mothers had bathed her and rubbed her body with rose oil. They told her stories of when they had gotten their blood and what it had meant to them. They told her how it would be and what to expect.

But I am not like them.

She didn't know Eddy's name yet. He was her secret self, her free self. He was the one who wanted to get out on the road, burning with rage, craving heroics. Other girls read the Unnamed and talked about birth and Hives and Motherhood. Etta read the Unnamed and thought about the way she practiced being something else. Talking lower. Staring slavers down. A ball of socks in her jeans.

Etta had a wad of clean cotton crammed between her labia, soaking up blood. It wasn't the same.

Later, when she was dressed in a red gown, the Mothers told her she could ask them any question and they were to tell her the truth. They sat in the House of Mothers and Etta thought hard, staring down at the floor between her bare brown feet.

"What's the worst thing about it?"

The Mothers had exchanged glances.

Mother Carla spoke first. "About bleeding, you mean?"

"About the whole thing."

Carla shrugged and Ina nodded to her. "Death is with you. He comes with the baby. You can feel him, like a stranger standing just off to your left, outside of your field of vision. He wants you, he wants the baby."

Ina smiled a little. "It makes you fight harder. At least, it did me."

Ina, the oldest woman in the room, seemed to have no patience for this part of the ritual. "Do you have any other questions, my living daughter?"

Etta shrugged. She didn't want to talk about blood or death anymore. She did not want to be someone different than she had been the day before, but that didn't seem to be up to her. She liked it better when Ina called her "living child." She couldn't say why.

Carla rose at Ina's silent prompting. She opened a tiny golden box and, inside, Etta saw a stack of dried mushrooms, cut into triangles. "When you eat these, you will see from outside yourself."

Etta had heard about this part from older girls, but they each said something different. Some of them said they'd been terrified and heard thunder rolling through their bloodstream. Others said they'd had beautiful dreams, seeing what their lives would be like, who they'd take into their Hives, what children they would have. More than one had just fallen asleep and awoken to a particularly bad stomachache.

Etta didn't know what she expected, but she ate the mushrooms. The Mothers left the room one by one, leaving her alone.

Etta felt nothing for what seemed like a long time. She tried to clench the muscles of her low belly each time her cramps rolled back around, curious if she could steel herself against them. It worked a little, but those muscles got sore quickly, as if she had never used them before.

She had been given a set of the cotton rags that most of the women of Nowhere used. One of them was folded in her underwear, but she knew it would be time for a new one soon. She clenched hard, her whole stomach seeming to fold in and draw up toward her. The pressure forced a torrent of blood out of her and she gasped at the sensation.

She looked around, preparing to stand up and go change. When her eyes locked on the doorway, she saw that the whole room had gone dark red. The doorway was flexing in and out. The walls were, too, caving and curving toward her before rebounding and tenting outward. She stared at it, unable to move.

She breathed in, the house breathed in around her. She breathed out, relaxing a little, and the house did, too, pooling and sloping in on every side. She put a hand up to keep it from touching her head. She felt her own hair and nothing more.

She crawled through the flexing room toward the low table they had left her. In a large bowl they had given her a chunk of honeycomb as large as her hand.

She picked it up greedily, fingers sinking into the wax. She took a huge bite, stuffing comb into both her cheeks and chewing richly, breathing hard through her nose.

I'm eating the summer, and the spring has just started.

The part of her mind that was separate, or the Eddy part, maybe, knew that it was early autumn. The baked pumpkin on the other plate was proof enough of that. But that wasn't what Etta had meant.

Etta's hand slid into the honeycomb and became gold. She was gold all over, liquid sunshine and surety and the pain was forgotten. She lay on the floor and felt it breathing beneath her. She held the honey above her mouth and let it drip down and in.

Her mother's voice was coming up from the floor. It was just the murmuring, buzzing tones, but Etta knew the sound. The words didn't belong to her, so she let them go.

The floor rolled beneath her, up under her heels and surging toward her head. It was delightful at first, but it became nauseating. She turned over on her belly, palms flat, and willed it to stop. It did not stop, but she sank into it, becoming part of the movement. She cried out a little and pushed back, wanting to stand.

Instead, she floated toward the ceiling and bumped against it, like a bee in a bottle. Her hands were sticky and the honey was gone.

Her mother's voice came again, this time through the ceiling. Etta listened hard, but the words didn't make any sense. It sounded like Ina was counting.

"What?"

Etta didn't think she made any noise when she spoke. She skittered down the wall like a spider. She stuck both hands into the pitcher of water they had left her to drink, to get the honey off. She drank the honey water immediately after.

Her mother's voice came from the water.

"What?"

Her stomach muscles clenched. Blood dripped down one leg, she felt it singing to her ankle in its life-and-death song.

"What?"

The walls flexed in mightily, touching her on all sides, threatening to squeeze her to death. Her arms were pinned to her sides and the blood surged out of her. She struggled, wriggling like a caught fish.

The voice was everywhere, pouring out of the walls and the floor.

"It's not yours. It never was and it never will be."

The walls fell away, vanishing over the horizon. She was alone in a dark, formless space. Nothing was hers.

One moment of pure bottomless terror swallowed her.

Who?

Eddy's voice spoke in her mind then, for the first time, loud and clear.

It isn't mine, either.

Eddy remembered that they had woken in the morning in their own bed, sore all over and with an aching jaw.

Ina had brought them milk and they had talked a little. Ina asked Etta what she had seen.

"Nothing, really. The room kind of came alive, and I was just caught in it."

"Like a womb." Ina smiled sagely.

"No, not like a womb."

But the smile did not fade.

Ina gave Etta a red box full of gifts. They were special, she said, because Etta had to wait to use them.

Inside, Etta found red ribbons for her braids, a necklace of precious shells, and a bottle of good red ink.

"You must wait a year to use them," Ina said. "Just as you must wait a while to use the gifts of womanhood. You understand?"

"I understand." Etta had put the box away and never opened it again. Opening it would feel like admitting something. Eddy supposed it was still under their bed somewhere. Neither of them cared if they ever saw it again.

He flexed those same low muscles against the coming storm and took a long swallow of water. Tomorrow's walk would be awful, but at least now he had a cup instead of a collection of rags.

Manhattan was visible for miles, thanks to the smoke of a thousand small fires. As he got closer, Eddy knew many of them would be lit under roasting pigs. He touched his three knives and his gun as he approached the edge of town.

No gates. No walls, either.

He looked for an open area where he could be observed and waited to be seen.

No spotters up high. No guard. The whole town was situated on a flat, grassy plain. The buildings were low and unguarded, with no obvious city gates or fortifications.

Underground, maybe?

He walked slowly, working to look unhurried. He held his pack straps and listened hard for the sound of a marketplace. His ears led him west along a gravel road.

Houses look good. Smells good. Whole place looks clean. These are good signs, right?

Fear rose anyway, closing his throat and making him sweat. He walked slowly, watching. He thought of Flora, confessing that she hadn't known the truth about Eddy at all. He stood up to his full height.

I'm just like them. They'll know that when they see me.

Eight in, eight out.

The smell of crackling pork was making his mouth water obscenely. He ran through a list of what was in his bag that he could trade. He planned to get full enough to burst on what they were flaunting.

Eddy walked, following his nose, listening to the growling of his stomach. As he grew closer, he could hear singing and the familiar sounds of a guitar tripping alongside human harmonies. Beneath that, a low, irregular drumbeat caught and lost the rhythm.

Eddy crept toward the corner of a new-looking log building, peeking around toward the sound of the voices. Near enough to make out the words, Eddy listened.

Bang away, Lulu
Bang it good and strong
What in the world will the Navy do when good old Lulu's gone?

Eddy had never heard a song like this before. He didn't think there was an official law about songs that treated sex with such careless humor, yet he couldn't imagine anyone singing this in Nowhere. For some reason, he flashed on the men dancing in the basement, dressed as women. He thought of the deadly seriousness of all the talk he'd ever heard or had on the subject of sex.

Is it funny? Is it ever funny?

He thought of a song he knew about a woman named Connie. The song was called "No Favorites," and it told the story of her Hive of thirty and how she'd never choose a favorite, but somehow all of her children were redheads.

The men stopped singing and fell to talking. Eddy emerged, cautious. One of them spotted Eddy and stood.

"A man and a brother!" he called out as he stood. The other men looked around, owlish in surprise.

Eddy raised his hands in front of him. "Good men? I'm a traveler, just looking to trade."

He tracked their movements as they stood, a few of them stepping toward him.

Eight in, eight out. Just like them. Be just like them.

Not attacking. They're excited.

He pulled his mask down and watched their hands.

I wonder if they have a grip for greeting here, like Jeff City.

He steadied himself as two of them came closer. They were both clean-shaven. One was young, not yet grown to his full height, Eddy judged. The other was taller and older, but they had the same wavy brown hair and soft brown eyes.

Father and son?

The older man spoke. "Welcome, traveler and brother. We'd be very interested to trade with you."

The younger man showed obvious interest but said nothing.

Eddy cleared his throat. "I'm tired from walking, and I'd trade for provisions, maybe a place to wash and sleep? I offer good drugs, lifesaving and relieving of pain."

The older man brought his hand to the center of his chest. Eddy studied its calloused look, saw the swollen joints in his fingers. "I'm James Johnson. This is my son, James Junior."

Eddy nodded to each. "I'm Eddy." He didn't trust his hands enough to gesture in the same way.

They stared expectantly.

"Eddy . . . who? What's your father-name?"

Eddy shrugged. "I never knew my father."

The older man looked shocked. "Oh, how terrible for you, brother. Come, have a seat at the fire. We'll eat first and then you can show us what you're trading."

Eddy followed warily and accepted the seat, his bag on the dirt in front of him.

They turned their backs to me without a thought. Trusting.

James introduced him around the circle and Eddy saw that each of them was short-haired and clean-shaven, neatly dressed and clean, to a man. There were no women. James Jr. was the youngest of them; Eddy guessed him at about fifteen.

More men approached from a nearby log cabin, carrying bowls. Eddy accepted one full of hot corn and beans with pulled pork on top, all of it in a sweet-salty sauce that he had never tasted before. He had finished his bowl by the time cornbread arrived. He took two pieces.

James Jr. had finished before Eddy.

Still growing, for sure.

The boy struck up another song, and the men joined in as they finished. The words were about marching to someplace Eddy had never heard of. As he sang, Junior began to collect the empty bowls and stack them, handing them off to another man, who took them away.

When they were done, Eddy spoke to no one in particular. "You sing a lot here?"

A short man in overalls grinned, showing a black tooth in his lower jaw. "It keeps us together."

Eddy nodded, looking around. "Only men and brothers here?"

James spoke up. "We don't trade women here, Eddy. If that's what you're hoping for, we'll have to part ways now." His tone was friendly but firm.

I like them already.

Eddy shook his head. "I take no trade in women or girls," he said.

He reached into his pack and brought out the wooden box. "I was just curious because some of the drugs I carry are made for women."

A black-haired man rose. "I'm a doctor, and I assist in childbirth. I can talk with you about them."

A man Midwife. Eddy pursed his lips.

"Alright, then. What do you have need of?"

The manwife spoke again. "Do you have deep sleep for childbirth? I've heard stories about how much it helps."

Eddy stared at him. "How can a sleeping woman give birth?"

Manwife shrugged. "The stories say that the woman can sleep while her body does the work. There's less pain and it's much quieter."

What is the difference between the woman and her body? How do they come apart?

"Could you plow a field in your sleep? Or bake bread?" Eddy looked around at them, bewildered. "Why would you want to?"

No one spoke.

"I don't have that," Eddy said, scowling. "I have dried red-raspberry leaf, to strengthen the womb. I have powerful painkillers and toothache remedy." He waited.

The men conferred openly and came to a decision to ask for two painkillers and cannabis.

"Oil, leaf, or tincture?"

James smiled broadly. "Leaf. Smoke with us, brother."

Several of them produced pipes made from corncob, and Eddy handed over a generous-sized wool bag.

The haze hung over them as the men settled and slumped in their seats. Eddy looked them over, deciding they had smoked before, but not often. The manwife had disappeared.

I can get the truth of it now, if I'm gentle.

"I've got a girl back home. Alice. She grows all kinds of plants and refines them. Like this." He held the pipe at arm's length, as if considering it. James reached for it, nodding.

"We grow a lot of food here," he said before taking a long pull on the pipe. "But none of us has training to make good drugs."

"Sure, sure," Eddy said. "Alice could travel and teach people. A lot of the people I meet on the road don't know a drug maker. Maybe she could teach one of you."

Junior scoffed a little. "Not one of us. One of the ladies, maybe."

Eddy was patiently silent. He knew better than to jump on it first.

"Yeah," said a ginger-haired man. "Ladies can make drugs."

There was some low laughter. Eddy tracked it as it circled him.

"Alice is pretty great," he said, with just the right edge of stubbornness. "Her mother did it before her, taught her."

"Was your father a traveler?" Junior was red eyed, already far gone.

"Oh, I didn't know him."

"That's right, you said that."

"Is your father teaching you a trade?"

James smiled at his son. "Well, we're all farmers, one way or the other. But I learned to butcher pretty well from my father, and I've been teaching James Junior."

Eddy nodded. "That's a fine trade. Do you hunt, as well?"

Junior scoffed. "Hunting is women's work."

The low ripple of laughs passed through the men again.

"What, do *you* hunt?" Junior looked as incredulous as a thoroughly stoned teenager can.

Eddy shrugged. "I hunt for myself when I'm out on the road. I have no woman to hunt for me."

"Yeah, but at home? Do men hunt for themselves where you're from?"

"Sure, anyone can hunt. Why should it be women's work?"

Junior shrugged. "Women are naturally more patient. They can sit and wait for hours, or stalk a wounded animal. I'd just lose interest and give up, like any man."

"I see."

A little silence passed.

"So who does the farming?"

James answered this time. "Farming is men's work. Planting seeds, just like making children." He spoke simply and directly, as if Eddy might be too slow to understand.

"Of course." Eddy nodded. "Do you keep any animals? Chickens for eggs, or goats for milk? Cows?"

"Sure we do, brother. Of course we do."

"Who cares for them?"

"The women, naturally. They have that nurturing instinct."

Maybe that's where all the women are, he thought. *Out doing most of the work.*

The ginger-haired man produced cups and dice and struck up a game. Eddy watched in silence.

The men began to drift off as soon as full dark fell. James Jr. offered to show Eddy to a bed. Eddy accepted gratefully, lifting his pack.

"So, do you live with your father?" Eddy glanced around while he asked, looking nonchalant.

Junior shook his head, a black shape against the dying light. "I lived with him when I first became a man, but I moved into a bigger dorm later. I wanted to read at night, and he's in an all-dark."

Eddy didn't quite understand until they entered the long log house where Junior slept. Rows of beds lined both sides of the room, neatly lined up. Young men were in about half of the low beds, each with its own deep fluff of down-filled pad and intricately sewn quilts. Eddy had to fight his knees from buckling at the sight of such luxurious goods. Quilts and down mattresses were costly projects; someone had to devote weeks or moons of work to even one.

Warm yellow light glowed from tallow candles all around the room. Many of the young men were sewing, but a few were reading from battered old books. Eddy looked closely, seeing that the men's hands were occupied with everything from basic mending to very fine embroidery.

Junior put his hands on the foot of an empty bed. "You can have this one. I made it for my brother, Josh, but he'll be a boy for two more years."

"You made this?" Eddy stepped forward and sank both hands into the depth of the bedding. He wanted to sink into that bed and sleep for a year.

"Yeah, I collect feathers from butchered birds and clean them up. The real work was in the quilt. I'm not much for building or designing, the way that some brothers can just add things up in their heads. But the geometry of quilts makes good sense to me. So the quilt took me one whole winter, but it turned out well."

Eddy looked at the pattern of interlocked triangles in green and blue and brown.

"It's fine work." His eyes strayed back to the hands around the room, stitching in rhythm. His eyes burned with fatigue and drug. "I thank you. I'd like to sleep now, if it's alright."

"Sure, sure. You can light your own candle, if you want to read."

I should write, he thought as he slid off his pack. Instead, he got out of his boots and into bed, fully clothed. He tied a long, loose piece of string to his wrist and attached the other end to his bag, which he slid beneath the bed.

He was sorely sorry that he could not sleep in this deliciously clean, pillowy bed freshly bathed and naked. The regret lasted less than a minute, however, and he fell into a deep, untroubled sleep.

What woke Eddy was the near-soundless stirring of the men around him at first light. Some had risen and were getting their boots on. Others were sitting up in bed, taking a little time to get more sewing in. At least two, Eddy realized, were masturbating in a businesslike manner, stroking beneath their bedclothes, staring at nothing in particular. He averted his eyes from this, focusing on the reddish light of dawn spilling through the door.

After a few minutes, most of the men had their boots on and were walking out the door. Eddy shouldered his pack and caught up with them. He expected to follow them to breakfast and be on his way.

Instead, he followed the almost entirely wordless herd of men to the edge of the forest on the east side of their town. All of them came near the woods and stopped, staring and waiting.

Eddy didn't speak but glanced around, watching their faces. The men were rapt, anticipating something without fear. They stood in preternatural stillness. The morning was windless and the birds had not yet woken.

Out of the darkness between the trees, a figure in a long, hooded cloak emerged. The men around Eddy tensed up visibly. The air surrounding them seemed to thicken.

The figure strode forth, approaching the edge of the trees. It didn't leave the forest. Between it and the men there was left a moat of brown pine needles—a boundary. Eddy stared.

White hands appeared from under the dark cloak, rising to push back the hood. The face of a young woman appeared, and Eddy was pierced with longing. He realized he had made a small sound when she appeared, only because the men around her had moaned aloud.

The woman was startlingly beautiful, black eyes like inky brushstrokes, slashing upward in her luminous skin. Her mouth had been stained, Eddy could tell, with berries or blood. She was black, white, and red; she glowed and grinned like a wolf in the dim light.

She held her slender hand before her, three fingers extended.

Her low, musical voice rippled out to them. "Gregory Ivansson. John Johnson. Ben Travisson."

The three men whose names were called fairly bolted toward her. She stayed them with the raising of her other hand. When they stood still, she reached into her cloak and produced three thick, shining, blue-black braids of her own hair. She handed one to each of the men and began to walk, leading them behind.

When they were gone back into the shadows, the other men began to mutter and groan. Slowly, they turned back toward town. Eddy craned his neck and filtered through the crowd, watching for Junior.

He spotted the younger man and hung back to walk with him.

"What was that?"

"The summoning."

They walked a little slower, letting the others pass them.

"What's the summoning?"

Junior shrugged, dejected. "The women send a summoner to choose men to mate with. They go and mate for three days, then they send them back with fresh kills. Those lucky fucks."

"How do they choose the men? What makes a man get chosen?"

"They choose a brother who's proven to produce children. When you first get called, you get three tries. If by the third try you've failed, or if the woman dies in childbirth, you never get called again."

"Have you been called before?"

"No," Junior said bitterly. "I've been a man for four years. Not once."

About seventy men here.

"How many women?"

Junior shrugged. "I don't know. I only lived with Marla and her house, and there were six there. I know there are others, but the boys are kept apart."

When they reached town, cornmeal mush was being served for breakfast. Eddy salted his and traded toothache remedy for a little more food for the road. The men were chastened since last night. There were no songs or dice games this morning, and precious little conversation. More than once, Eddy heard the three men's names uttered like curses. Their manner made him nervous.

He stood to leave, pack on his back. "Thank you, men and brothers, for your hospitality. I hope I may pass this way again."

Gruffly, with strained politeness, they paid their respects in waves and pats on the back. Eddy was glad to be on his way. He headed back out to the road from whence he had come before circling around to cut through the woods where the woman with the three braids had disappeared.

CHAPTER 11

The Book of Eddy
Summer

Manhattan isn't one town, it's two. Like me. So I'm going to change.

He didn't think about it. He didn't feel about it. He did it as a series of mechanical processes, there in the deep woods.

Binding off, shirt open at the neck. Washed face and throat, washed hands. The face in the still puddle beside the stream did not seem to change. *Look deeply for a moment too long. Rummage deep in the bag. No skirt, but there never was one in there, why would there be? Touch short hair, nothing to be done. Try to arrange the eyes to hold them open wider, try to soften the mouth.*

Will it be known?

The Book of Etta

Approaching the city of women. If they're hunters, they'll be on better guard than their men.

She couldn't make herself wait. She walked, listening carefully, straight along the path that had clearly been trod recently. Etta wasn't an expert tracker, but three men dragged along behind symbolic braids weren't stealthy, either. She followed footprints in the soft earth and the mashed-down thorny brambles that proliferated everywhere in this wet wood.

Through the trees, she spotted the wide, smooth side of a building made of wattle and daub.

Mud houses. No log cabins on this side.

Women's work.

If I see those three boys, I'm sunk. Maybe they're kept real busy.

She crossed her hands and crossed the line into Womanhattan.

Three girls were weeding in a bean patch when she came upon them. They looked up, shielding their eyes. Most of them worked topless, their hair falling in long braids. The palest of them wore white cotton shirts that covered them up, but even the freckled ones braved the sun.

"Good women?" She spoke as girlishly as she could, turning up her sentence at the end, trying to be very clear. She straightened her spine a little.

Don't hide them. Not here.

The women blinked at her.

"Good women, I am a traveler. Just looking to trade. Do you have a marketplace?"

One of them took her hand away from her eyes and pointed west. Etta nodded and smiled.

"Thank you! Good day to you."

None of them answered her.

She passed other women as she walked. Many would not look at her, and not one spoke to her. Many wore cloaks, like the woman in the woods had done. She wondered why they would bother with that, in this heat. The stickiest part of the year was on them now. Etta knew that back home, the best fruits would have just started to come in and Alice would be bothered every few hours for something that could keep bugs away.

When she thought of Alice, a set of dull claws raked inside her ribs. An echo followed when she thought of Flora, and she shut it down before Ina's face could appear to her.

Etta came to a place where two paths crossed in front of a house that had the unmistakable stink of a brewery. She stood a moment, considering.

A tall woman approached her, and Etta shielded her eyes. This woman's skin was ruddy brown, nearly as red as the deerskin vest she wore over her bare chest. Deer leggings covered her from the waist down, laced together at the sides. Her brown hair was braided double on her head, emphasizing her heart-shaped face.

"Hey, you!"

Etta smiled automatically. "Good woman! Good Mother? I am a traveler."

The deer skinner stopped in her tracks and regarded Etta. She didn't speak.

"I . . . I am looking for your marketplace, if your people would trade with me?"

"As I bleed. You are one of us!"

"One of you?"

The deer skinner stepped forward and gripped Etta's upper arm.

Eight in, eight out. Where are you right now? What are you?

"I am Etta," she said, trying to politely pull her arm away.

The tall woman let go, stepping back and looking Etta up and down.

"I am Kelda. Are there other women who travel the roads? Are you a tribe of women? Do you follow the herds?"

Etta laughed a little. "No, just me. I come from a place far south of here."

Kelda was grinning, getting happier by the minute. "A city? A fair place?"

Etta shrugged. "Fair enough. A small city, with farms and a fort."

"And there are other women there? More than you? Well, of course more than you, because they let you go! How many women?"

"I—I don't know, a lot? Lots of women."

Kelda looked joyous beyond reason. "Will you tell the sisters? You have to. Oh, we have to."

"The sisters?"

"Follow me." She was holding Etta's arm again in a grip that hurt. Etta felt the terrible strength in the woman's hand with alarm followed by envy. She looked at the woman's biceps and the feeling intensified. This tall person could be anything she wanted.

She would never be small. She would never find herself trapped—

Where are you right now?

"Where is your city?" Kelda interrupted her train of thought, and Etta was grateful.

"Many days' walk from here. Days and days to the south."

Kelda shook her head. "Yes, but I could ride there, on a horse. It's a few days from here?"

Etta blinked, thinking of a lie.

Do I need to lie here? What is this city of women going to do?

They pushed through the door of another earthen house, and Etta stumbled down a few stairs. The sunken room was cool and circular inside the square of the walls. Older women sat ringed around the room, working at small tasks. One pounded corn in a stone bowl, several knitted and sewed.

They looked up when the two women entered. Kelda's voice was loud in the small space.

"Sisters! I have found a traveler who—"

As one, every woman in the circle raised a finger to her lips and trained her eyes on Kelda. Etta found it deeply unsettling.

Kelda sighed and trudged to the woman nearest her, dragging Etta along behind her.

Etta watched as Kelda's hands flew through a series of gestures, landing on her own body several times. The old woman watched Kelda's face with rheumy eyes. When her gaze darted to Etta, Etta smiled and ducked her head a little, as though speaking to one of the Mothers of Nowhere.

Kelda tapped her throat again and again.

She's begging to talk.

The old woman sighed and made a gesture that signaled permission, even to someone who knew nothing of this language of gestures.

Kelda fetched a deep breath and fell heavily into a cross-legged position on the packed earth floor. After a moment and a few looks, Etta joined her.

They waited. The old woman finished a line of stitches in the garment she was mending patiently, without hurry. She set it aside before turning to face them.

"Silence is the way of women." Her teeth were perfect.

"Silence is our gift," Kelda said in a rush. "This is—"

"I can see that you've brought me a stranger, Kelda. I am not too old to know a new face when I see one." The old woman studied Etta's brow. Her own eyes had the same upward tilt as the woman in the woods. Etta wondered if they were mother and daughter.

"I am Sharon. And I assume you know Kelda, since she cannot hold her tongue. What's your name, and where are you from?"

"Good Mother, I am—"

The old woman raised her hand to her lips again. "We are not Mothers here, stranger."

Kelda huffed her obvious displeasure. Etta stared back and forth at both of them.

"Good woman, I am Etta. I come from a place south of here, south of the Black Mountains, the Odarks. I am looking for places that will trade."

The old woman's mouth scrunched to the side like a drawstring bag pulled tight. "If you wanted trade, you'd be in Estiel. Why are you really here?"

At the sound of the place's name, Etta's calves began to cramp.

Eight in, eight out.

"I've been to Estiel, Moth—good woman. I was seeking new places. New people."

"For what?"

Sharon's eyes held Etta's, wouldn't let her slide away from the question.

"I don't know."

"Mmm. Kelda, why did you bring her here?"

Kelda seemed ready to burst. She pushed herself up on both knees. "Sharon! This means there are other women, in other cities. We aren't the last!"

Sharon sighed and Etta watched the woman's ribcage settle like an old dog when it's done too much walking. "Of course we aren't the last."

"But everyone says—Doctor Eames says—" Kelda was spluttering now, indignant and red-faced.

"You might be too young to understand this," Sharon said, "but Doc Eames is a fool, even if he and all his folks are docs. He doesn't know the world."

Kelda's eyes turned wildly to Etta. "Did you have the plague there?"

"The Dying." Etta wondered what else people might call the event that separated the old world from the new. What other word was there for death?

"Kelda!" Sharon's voice was sharp and they both turned to face her. "The plague was everywhere. I know you know that."

"Yes, but if there are women there . . ." Kelda began. Her childlike hope was plain on her face, as unshadowed as noon.

"There are women all over the world. Every man thinks he has seen the last. You've been taught better than to believe those old men's tales."

Etta stared, stupefied.

Kelda began to drop back, her excitement snuffed.

"You're like a little girl," Sharon said disdainfully. She turned to Etta. "Are your people slavers?"

"No," she said without much force. She gathered herself again. "No, we shoot slavers."

"Mmm. Are you cutters?"

"No. No, I find girls sometimes who were cut, mostly from the south. And now I know they cut boys sometimes, too."

Sharon nodded, thoughtful. "Oh, yes, they did that in my day, as well. Fancy boys, you know. But my grandmother came here from Estiel, in the old world. She said that living among the women would be easier for me, because I was born to it. She never really adjusted to living apart, but at least she stood against that cutting nonsense."

Sharon's eyes were dreamy, faraway. "She would never let them cut my mother. Said it might kill any girl they did it to, and she was right. So they never cut my mother, and they stopped long before me."

Etta was nodding.

Sharon shook her head as if to clear it. "Are you a hunter?"

"No, I'm a raider. I find things from the old world that can be of use, like good steel. And I trade drugs made in my city."

"Mmm. Are you a breeder?"

Etta found herself tongue-tied for a moment.

the chair

"No, I have never been a Mother—"

Around the room, the old women shushed her.

"A breeder. I have never bred. I don't . . ."

Kelda gripped her shoulder, startling her. "I don't breed, either. Too dangerous."

Sharon pursed her mouth at the two of them again. "What do you seek here?"

Etta sighed, looking at the floor. When she looked up, she imagined she was speaking to Ina.

"I just want to trade for some food and a place to sleep. I'll be on my way tomorrow or the next day."

And just like that Sharon *was* Ina, her eyes narrowing at the lie, knowing Etta down to her core.

"Very well. Kelda, I charge you with taking care of our traveler."

Kelda dipped her head. "Sharon, this traveler does not know the way—"

"You don't have to keep silence with her," Sharon said.

Kelda sprang up in place. "Great!"

Great.

Kelda led Etta to her own home, an enormous stone cottage with deerskins tacked up on every side, drying in the sun.

"You must be a good hunter," Etta said, her eyes on the skins.

"The best!" Kelda swung her wooden door open and made Etta a plate of venison jerky before setting up a pot to make herb tea.

"I can trade you for food," Etta began. "I have itchweed—"

Kelda put two rough-made mugs down on the table hard. "All I want is stories. I want to know everything about your people, and the other people that you've met."

"Haven't you ever left here?"

Kelda shook her head. "Not allowed. No woman can leave Manhattan."

"But you go hunting!"

Kelda was nodding, throwing dried leaves into the dented old teapot. "Only in the forest, and if I see any man I must run from him. Doctor Eames says all men are slavers."

They're not all slavers, but I see why he'd say that.

"Is Doctor Eames the Midwife? The . . . The one who helps with childbirth?"

Kelda nodded, her chin down.

"Is he in charge here?"

"Not . . . Not exactly. He's in charge of our breeding and health. He's the only man who comes among us for anything other than summoning."

"But he tells you about the outside world?"

"Well, he tells me because I ask. He really did say that we are the only women on earth."

Etta laughed a little. "I hear that a lot. Men say it everywhere. But I've seen women in Estiel and Jeff City and other places. I've found them on the road. And I've heard from other raiders who have gone far, far away and seen more women there."

Kelda was nodding. "Really, if we were the last women on earth, we wouldn't be safe."

"We're not safe anyway. There aren't enough anywhere."

They sat with that while the water boiled. Kelda poured steaming tea into both mugs.

"You drink hot tea in the summer?"

Kelda shrugged as she sat astride one of the stumps at her table. "It doesn't taste as good cold."

Etta waited, watching the steam coil above the cup.

"How many women are here?"

"Seventeen."

Not enough.

"I see. And babies every year?"

"One, usually. Sometimes two."

"And how many not breeding, like you?"

"Well, the four old women. The two little girls who are too young. I'm the only one of age not breeding."

"Why?"

Kelda stood up and walked to the wall, touching a rabbit skin there. "It's how my own mother died."

"Oh, I'm sorry."

"It's not easy. I still have to take part in the three days of the moon. I just don't breed."

"What?"

Maybe they have it here. The thing that the Unnamed gave. Birth control.

"I provide release." Kelda said it as carefully as anyone who had ever been coached in a euphemism.

"I don't understand."

"Like a fancy boy." She was furiously blushed, the effect like a burnishing of her coppery skin. "There are other . . . you can . . ."

"Oh, oh yes. I see. Why do you . . . Why would you do that if it doesn't lead to pregnancy?"

"It's women's work. Keeping them healthy, you know. If they don't come for the moon sometimes, it makes them crazy. They can't help it. Doc Eames says it's the worst for the young men. He sets the schedule, since he knows how we bleed."

The manwife stays busy.

Etta nodded.

"But I want *your* stories! Do you have a doc? Do you have a schedule, in your city?"

Etta laughed a little. "No, we have Hives."

Kelda sat back down, her deer leather creaking. "What are Hives?"

"One woman, like the queen of a beehive. As many men as she wants, all at her disposal for breeding or labor. It's very sensible."

Kelda stared. "Do *you* have a . . . ?"

"No. My mother has a large Hive, and my friend Alice has two men. But I've never thought it was for me."

"Wow." Kelda's eyes were wide and glorious amber brown.

She'd tell me anything I asked. There's no lying in her.

"Why do you live separately from the men?"

"It causes fights. Killing, sometimes. Men are like that. They can't make peace if there aren't enough women. So we give them some distance, some order to it."

Etta shrugged. "There's no killing in No—in my town." She recovered quickly, taking a sip of the still-scalding tea. "Men get into Hives, or they . . . they, uh, fancy-boy with each other."

"Is that allowed?" Kelda's eyes were as big as chicken eggs.

"It's . . . It's frowned upon, but people understand why it happens."

Even if they never understand me.

The room was hot and fragrant with steam. Kelda stood and blithely peeled off her leather vest. Etta could not help but watch.

"You can, too, you know. I don't know if your people are very modest, but . . ."

Etta put her hands against her damp shirt. She glanced over her shoulder at the door.

Why the hell not? Eddy's not here.

As Etta rose, pulling her woven shirt over her head, Kelda grinned and set about untying the laces of her pants, as well.

When she was fully nude, Kelda stood and turned so that Etta could see all of her. Kelda's body was muscular and all-over brown. She looked as though she ran among the deer as naked as they, as wild.

She wants me to look.

Kelda dusted her calves. "My hair gets stuck to me. Feels good to let it breathe."

They were both dewy with sweat. Etta stood and slid her pants off. She hadn't had a shave since she was in Nowhere, but it hadn't been that long. She had barely regained a little fuzz.

"How are you so hairless?" Kelda closed in, openly marveling. "I've bathed with very dark women before, and they have more than you!" She pointed playfully to Etta's nearly bald vulva.

"I have the bathers shave me, at home. There are bugs on the road, and shaving helps keep them off me. I also just like the way it feels."

Giggling like a giant little girl, Kelda leaned down and gently touched Etta's leg in the hot room.

She knows exactly what she's about. How long will she play this game with me? How long has she already?

Etta looked over her shoulder again, at the door.

Kelda walked over to it and barred it with a huge split timber.

"Look," she said, her eyes overbright. "I know what you are. I knew it the moment I saw you. I only ever knew one other, and she's gone now. Can I just? Can we?"

I know what you are.

Etta reached up to cup the taller woman's cheek in her palm.

Kelda melted immediately, obediently, like butter in a hot skillet.

Etta poured herself into the taller woman's body, tasting all the strangeness of being away from home and back to the first kind of sex she knew. She brought Kelda to a quick crest, making her shake and cry out, muffling the cries with a free hand. Together, they sweated an ocean into Kelda's deerskin bed.

With her hands on Kelda's muscled thighs, she thought of Flora.

I know what you are.

She thought of herself as Eddy and invited his ghost, pretending for just a moment that he was born a man, that he was here, that his spectral sex was grafted onto her and pushed the thought of it into Kelda as she moaned.

the chair the chair the chair

Her legs cramped immediately and she found a way to stop gracefully, to stand up and lift her toes against the wooden frame of the bed.

Kelda lacked the capacity to notice. She threw a massive forearm over her eyes and panted, splayed across her hides.

When Etta could calm her calves, when she could breathe eight in and eight out, she lay down beside Kelda again.

When Kelda spoke, Etta was steeled for some declaration of love or sameness. She had had that before, she knew what to say.

"Can I go back with you? To a place where there are more of us? I want to be somewhere where we can be this way always."

Etta breathed in sharply and sat up.

"There's nowhere to go with this," she said, her voice like lead. "We have Hives. A Hive has one queen. That's it."

"But if boys can be fancy—"

"Boys can be anything. Girls can only be one thing. Like everyone says here, women's work."

"But you can be a raider, and I can be a hunter, and neither of us breeders." Kelda was sitting up now, her whole simple soul back on her trusting face. "Can't we be this, where you're from?"

Those two women who tried it, they couldn't do it. Alice. When her mother caught us, Carla looked like she wanted to eat me alive. What was it she said? That we were wasting something, like kids who ate all their honey at once.

"We can't. There's nowhere I've seen or heard of where we can be this. I don't even know what it's called."

Kelda kissed her shoulder softly. "Lie down with me."

Etta did, making a note of where her gear lay. She watched the bar on the door until she fell asleep.

There's nowhere. Nowhere.

The attack came in the hour before dawn. Etta woke without knowing what had roused her, blinking in the darkness of Kelda's house. She rolled out of bed and pulled her pants on. By the time the screaming really got started he was bound and had his boots on. He was pushing his gun back into his pants when Kelda awoke.

"Here. Here. Here." She was pushing him through a small door at the back of the cabin. The small space on the other side stank. Eddy breathed shallowly, trying to place the smell.

Kelda found her bow, not bothering to dress. "Stay here," she said. She closed the small door.

Eddy groped at his pack in total darkness. His gun was loaded. His knives were on him.

Outside, he heard the sounds of struggling. Someone ran past the exterior wall. He tried to breathe through his mouth around the stink.

She's tanning hides. That's the smell. What the fuck is going on out there?

Kelda's door thundered as someone tried to push it open against the bar they had set the night before.

Eddy held very still.

The door boomed again as someone large threw a shoulder against it.

"Open up in the name of the Lion!" The voice was muffled, but Eddy made it out.

Shit it's here I've got it.

His hands plunged into the bag again and felt around. He found the claw by the cold, smooth, foreign feel of it. He yanked it out and tied it around his neck in the total absence of light. He pushed the tanning-room door open.

Kelda stood in absolute tension, bow pulled back to the depth of her long arm. She was ready to kill whatever came through the door.

"Wait, okay? Wait. I can help." He couldn't tell if she heard him at all.

Eddy got close to the door, clearing his throat. "Get back and I'll open it. Get back!"

He waited a moment, then lifted the bar from the door. He opened it all at once and stood there, blinded by torchlight.

The man holding it was not one he had met in Estiel.

"This town is taken in the name of the Lion. All females are tribute."

Eddy laid his hand on the claw, praying for steady fingers. "I understand that. But this female is mine."

Behind the man with the torch, Eddy could see the summoner being led out in her black cloak, her head bowed. He looked back over his shoulder and saw that Kelda was still ready to strike.

He continued, "The Lion and I have a deal—"

"If you've dealt with Himself, then you know he doesn't make deals that deprive him of his claim to females. You can come and make a case for this one, if you want. But we're taking her."

There's gotta be something I can say. Some password.

Too late, he realized the man with the torch was shoving past him, into the cabin. Kelda's arrow sprouted from the man's chest an instant later.

"Kelda!"

"Run!" Kelda herself ran over the man as he fell, glancing off Eddy's shoulder.

"Kelda, wait!"

Kelda did not wait. She charged forward, nocking the other arrow she had carried from her cottage as she ran.

Eddy realized too late that the roofs of the mud houses were on fire. He ran along a disordered path, not knowing the town well enough to find his way.

A chunk of something heavy hit him on the back of the neck, just below his skull. He swayed a moment, woozy, trying to look behind him.

A group of the older women were throwing rocks. They caught him with another as he turned, just above his left eye. Blood ran into it, hot and salty, blinding him. He put up both hands.

Not me. Not me. I'm not one of them.

The claw at his throat.

"Kill the men! Kill all the men!" The screech came from all of them as they fanned out, throwing more heavy stones.

Eddy turned and ran. He made for the woods, barely keeping his feet as the ground sloped down and away from him. He didn't know he was headed to the river until his feet were in it.

Staggering, losing consciousness, he spotted a boat tied not too far from where he stood. He walked, then crawled, to get to it. His eye screwed shut, he banged into everything, thorns scraped him all over.

Into the water. Just like Estiel except this time no firelight. Can't see. Won't come up again. Go down and never come up again.

He fought to stay awake, grunting through ragged breaths. When he reached the boat, he lay for a moment in the cold river mud, face turned to the side, a terrible stitch in his ribs. After the swirling, falling feeling passed, he heaved himself over the side. The small craft rocked alarmingly, nearly dumping him into the deeper water on the other side. When it settled, he grayed out.

Hours later, the sun had risen and Eddy woke in a panic. He sat up and the gray crept into his peripheral vision again: a threat. He took a deep breath and came up slowly, peering over the edge of the deep yet narrow boat.

He saw nothing. Blinking a second, he realized fog was rolling down over the hillside.

He pulled at the boat's line and the unambitious knot loosened until it slipped off the tree that held it. He found a paddle beneath his legs and used it to push off the bank, losing the paddle in the process. Groaning with frustration and cracked with thirst, he lay back again as the current began to move the wooden craft.

Eddy lost consciousness again.

The current drifted, then grew swift. The river carried him away.

CHAPTER 12

The boat was the room. The red room, the breathing room. The boat was the room, the mushroom. Etta was having her first blood again. Eddy was paddling wildly, laughing.

The boat was the chair. Eddy couldn't get up because he was strapped into the chair. It wasn't him laughing, it was the Lion's men.

the claw the claw the claw they wore the claw

Eddy was born in the chair.

The Unnamed would have never ended up in the chair. She would have died first. Etta was only sixteen and the Unnamed would have known her for a child. She would have saved her.

But Etta had gone back to the place where she had found the moon-blood cups, with an animal's cunning that the same place would provide again. She was in a closet when they found her.

They all wore the claw but she didn't remember that. She only remembered the chair when her calves cramped in the night and woke her up. The chair with its rusty stirrups, its shrieking metal on metal. It had held her down while they came, one after the other.

the chair the chair the chair
the chair must have been made for this

Eddy was born in the chair; Etta pinned on her back with her feet splayed in rusty stirrups, blood everywhere out of her while the Lion's men pawed her nearly to death. When the stirrup broke, it was luck that shoved the jagged corroded edge into the side of the man's neck. It was both of their blood that helped her slip the other leg out. It was his gun that she had used to kill the rest of them in that blind hour. Her gun she took back from a corpse and never let go of again.

Eddy was what she carried out of there, naked and bloody as an infant, wordless as a staring-eyed newborn.

She hadn't known they had a lookout. He missed her and shot a plastic gallon of something that stood close by the river. Oil or fuel, it exploded and ran everywhere, liquid fire. Etta was deaf from the sound and almost blinded by the light. She had dropped the gun. She dove into the river with fire floating on its surface. She swam like an otter, popping up to gasp for air and then slipping farther and farther with the current.

She didn't remember that summer turning into autumn or the winter that followed. She didn't remember finding clothes and boots, huddling by the fire in a gutted house, jumping at every small sound.

When it came she didn't know what it was. It was as though she had swallowed a thunderstorm, a bag of broken glass, a live bird. It slipped out of her and hit the floor, the size of a fist and resembling nothing at all. Four days she walked in the snow, leaving a bloody trail behind her. Any predator might have tracked her, but nothing did. She remembered none of this.

Etta did not remember the day she had returned to Nowhere. She came to herself some time after that, knowing that she had shaved her head and nearly died of hunger. Her hands found her hollow belly, her fingers found the scars from the chair.

She awoke every night that year, both legs locked in cramps, screaming. When her blood returned, she waited for it to happen again. She waited for another thunderstorm with broken-glass rain, for another fist. It didn't come.

At seventeen, she knew what had happened but she couldn't remember why she knew or how. She learned to count her breath. She always knew where she was. She learned to carry Eddy strapped to her chest the way Mothers carried, the way Ina wore her wooden belly.

The boat was the chair. Eddy woke up with both legs locked in agony, his head throbbing. The motion of the small craft in the water was swift and keeling; he was going to capsize. He sat up, pulling at the toes on both feet, dizziness stealing his eyes.

Eight in, eight out.

Where are you right now?

The rapids poured over huge rocks, churning silver-white in the morning sunlight. When the cramp finally let go, Eddy held both sides of the boat and tried to look ahead. His vision was still slightly doubled and he shook his aching head, trying to see clearly. The river bumped him over a series of rises, and the last one pushed him roughly out into the water.

Choking, he went under. Sunlight on the churn became fire in the night in Estiel, but Eddy didn't remember that and neither did Etta and the most important thing right now was that neither of them could breathe.

Eddy burst to the surface, but waves overtook him. He hit slick rock hard on his right side, feeling his ribs break. The water heaved him over a short fall and he hit his head again at the bottom. He inhaled water and everything began to go black.

it isn't yours it isn't yours it isn't yours

the chair

it isn't yours

the cup
isn't yours
the book
isn't yours
the Unnamed

What was Etta and what was Eddy winked out at the same moment and then they were none.

CHAPTER 13

The fish was inches from his eyes. It bulged, mouth gasping, eyes slick and searching for the way back to the water.

Eddy couldn't breathe either. He and the fish were going to drown together. He closed his eyes and knew that the fish could not close its own.

Two broad hands came down on his ribs, on the broken side. Pain cracked out across his body and unconsciousness rolled back over him. Before he could slip sweetly out of the world again, weight came down on those hands and he vomited up river water in a hard, cold gush. It ran out of his nose and sprayed from his mouth as he coughed and struggled to breathe in. The crushing pressure came again and he got one deep, stinging breath before he passed out again.

Must be afternoon.

The light was orange and horizontal when his eyes opened again. Every breath stabbed him, so he took little sips of air. The ground was moving slowly beneath him, speeding smoothly by in a blur of grass. The motion made him retch and a thin stream of water and mucus played like a string from his mouth to the ground. Retching made his broken ribs stab him again and he brayed, curling into himself.

"She's awake."

Voices somewhere behind him. A hand on the back of his neck, warm and gentle. Eddy realized at the moment of contact that he was cold all over, drenched and shivering.

"Cover her up, we're almost there."

they know I'm they know

And darkness took him back.

Eddy awoke again in a dry, warm place. He was wearing a long gown, but everything else had been stripped off. He was deep in a warm bed, with quilts piled over him. He stirred and his side throbbed beneath a tight bandage. It held on to him the way his binding did, but his breasts were free.

He pulled his legs in and crossed his arms.

Not bound.

A candle burned in a brass holder at his bedside. The furniture in the room was wood, and all of it looked to be old world.

In great shape, though.

The room was clean and smelled like lavender. He sniffed deeply, looking for the way out.

One door, no windows.

He put his feet on the floor and found he could stand. His head was better, the double vision gone. But he felt vague and disoriented.

Where are you right now?

Across the room, a wooden chest of drawers shone. He padded to it, rolling the top drawer open. In it lay his gear, spread out on cotton toweling. His gun, his book, his knives. The book showed clear damage from the water, but it had been carefully dried. His clothes in the drawer below, washed and mended. His wooden box in the deep bottom drawer. He checked the contents and found them absolutely intact.

Where are you right now?

The door opened and a short, fat man walked in. He carried a washbasin and a handful of rags. He jumped at the sight of Eddy, who had his gun raised in no time.

"Oh! You're awake. I didn't think you'd ever wake." He put the basin down and raised his hands. "You're not in any danger from me, sister."

Eddy pointed with the gun. "Sit down."

The man moved obediently and sat on the bed, hands folded in his lap.

"My name is Neum, and I've been taking care of you for the last two days. Sister, this is a safe place. I don't mind you feeling like you need your gun, but would you please not point it at me just now?" Neum had a quavering voice and a mouth like a fat baby, pursed and pink. He was pop-eyed, but calm.

Eddy's head swam. He didn't feel like he could keep the gun raised if he wanted to. Heavily, he sat at the foot of the bed.

"Where am I right now?"

"Adam on the Ommun. Ommun, for short. It's a safe place, sister. You are welcome here."

"Ommun? How did I get here?"

Neum grinned, turning to better face Eddy. "Well, I heard that two fishermen—Lehi and Samuel, that is—found you drowning in the Misery. They fished you out and pumped your lungs, then put you in the fish cart and brought you home. They didn't know how you were drowning, though. They saw no boat. They thought you might be an angel."

Angel?

"And Ommun . . . Where are we? Are we north of the Black Mountains?"

Neum looked perplexed. "We're east of the Misery. I don't know the Black Mountains."

"The Odarks?" Eddy felt the first drips of panic.

"Oh, sure, the Odarks!" Neum brightened. "We're far to the north of them."

"How far?"

The round man shrugged. Eddy saw his wobbly chins move when he did it. "You'd have to ask the missionaries."

They're well fed here, at least. If he was tending me, he can't be that important. But still well fed.

Neum stood up slowly, palms raised to Eddy again. "I have to tell Alma you're awake. She wanted to know if there was any change."

Eddy's vision went gray at the edges. "Who's Alma?" His voice sounded far away.

"Alma is our Mother. I'll be back, don't you worry. That water's good and hot if you want a washing."

He slipped out the door.

Eddy sagged to the bed, holding himself up on his weak arms.

How long was I down?

He felt empty all over, hungry and husked out and devoid of real thoughts.

Manhattan. I was in Manhattan. I saw them summoning. Lucky fucks.

The rock that hit him in the head. He touched the spot above his eye and felt the soft, fleshy ridge of a clean-healing wound on its way to becoming a scar, the divot in his skull.

The boat. The chair. The BOAT.

With sickening clarity he remembered his body bashing into the rocks. He put a hand against the ribs he knew were broken. The gentle pressure made him wince.

The swell of his breast above his hand felt obscene, but he doubted he could bind them well in his current condition.

The door opened again and a woman's pregnant belly was the first thing to push through.

Eddy looked up and locked eyes with the most beautiful woman he had ever seen.

She was roundly gravid, with huge, full breasts lying against her belly, free beneath her green dress. Eddy could see each nipple in high relief, as long and fat as those of a nursing bitch. Her face was oval and white; her cheeks like peaches grown in the shade. Her wide doe-brown eyes were starred with golden lashes, at once arresting and innocent. Her pink mouth was generous and merry, smiling already as Eddy looked her over.

Her hair was pure glory, there was no other word for it. It spilled over both shoulders and down her back, the ends trailing the floor. It fell in dips and waves, the colors of honey and wheat and sunshine, white in some places and glinting dull red in the candlelight.

Her arms were spread wide as if she had been waiting for Eddy her whole life. "Sister, we are so glad you are with us!"

She hugged Eddy where he sat, pressing his face into the soft, mountainous pillow of her chest.

Milk. She's ready to pop, and full of milk.

When she pulled away, Eddy could see that her green shirt was damp where she had pressed him.

"We were so worried that you would never waken, and we would never even know your name."

Neum sidled in behind her, grinning.

Eddy stared, saying nothing.

"What is your name, sister?"

"Etta."

It had just slipped out. She had meant to say Eddy, but here she was. They knew her. Sister.

"Sister Etta." The tall blonde woman strode forward and Etta was struck again by how stunning she was. "I'm Alma. This is Adam on the Ommun, and you are so welcome here." She took Etta's hands in hers and looked deeply into her eyes. "How are you feeling?"

Etta winced. "Not great. My ribs are broken, I think."

"Three broken," Neum piped up. "Very bruised. But the real trouble was the head injury. Yea, that was the thing that nearly killed you. But your spirit is strong."

Alma nodded, face alight. "Yea, the spirit is strong. I dreamed of your coming."

"What?" Etta frowned, dropping their handhold.

Alma was unperturbed. "Yea, I dreamed that an angel would come among us from the numberless concourses of God the Mother and spake unto us."

"Spake?"

Honey waterfalls as Alma nodded. "Yea. Not as you speak now, but spake with authority. It will come."

What.

"But not yet. Now you must rest and get your strength." She stepped forward and laid a light hand on Etta's shoulder. "You will be well."

Etta felt a strange warmth flowing into her from Alma's hand. It seemed to move to her most painful spots and settle there, soothing the ache.

The living hell?

She looked up at Alma's serene face, her brown eyes giving away not a thing.

"The Aarons will bring you something to eat," Neum said. "Unless you'd like to join the stake?"

Etta blinked, trying to get clear.

"Can I leave here?"

Neum looked at Alma. "Of course you can. We'll not hold you. But you're not in good health. Maybe you should rest awhile and leave when you feel better."

"You were born free and you must live free," Alma said, turning back around.

Etta squinted. Alma's eyes seemed somehow brighter, as if a fire burned behind them.

"And every sister is made in the image of Heavenly Mother, thus you are God Herself. As I am. And so you are holy." She nodded as if that meant something.

"So I'm free . . . So if I want to leave, I can leave?"

I can barely stand. But I want it said.

"Neum here can get you a new pack. Yours was shredded. And you can go with my blessing."

Alma turned to leave again, but turned back, hands laid across her full-moon belly. "But if you stay, there are more blessings in store. This, I prophesy."

She swept grandly out of the room, leaving her milky smell behind her.

Neum smiled, watching her. Turning back to Etta, he asked, "Shall I bring you that pack?"

Etta sighed, sagging to the bed. "No. Thank you."

"Shall I have the Aarons bring you some food?"

"How can I trade for food? What can I offer?"

Neum's bushy brows shot up. "No, you are our sister. No trade will be had. We want to share with you."

"I . . . Thank you."

His brows settled down. "Good. It'll be here directly."

When Neum was gone, Etta dressed slowly. Lifting her arms over her head hurt, and standing too long made her feel faint. When she was back in her own pants, she hung the cotton nightdress on a hook and fished out her journal. She sat in the chair beside the bed and put the pen to the paper.

The Book of Etta
Summer

Someplace called Ommun. Some woman called Alma. Manhattan was attacked by the Lion. Paws came and burned the town. I took some injury there, ended up on a river. Misery? Saved by fishermen from Ommun.

Going to stay here until I'm well enough to move on. So far seems safe.

She thought of Alice's admonition that healing was hindered by the stoic suffering of those who would not take their medicine. Etta put a finger to the top of a som bottle and took a drop beneath her tongue. The milky smell of Alma and her hand on her gun took her into sleep.

When she woke there was a bowl of corn chowder beside her bed. It had gone cold, but she ate it ravenously. When she had finished, she picked up the wooden bowl and opened the door.

Outside her room, two young men were waiting.

"Good morning! My name is Jarod and this is Timothy. What can we do for you?"

She sized them both up.

Fourteen, maybe. No beards yet.

"I need to know where to take this. And where I can go to . . . go? Do you have an outhouse?"

Timothy took her bowl, green eyes gleaming. Jarod pointed down to the right. "Bathrooms are just down there, first hallway on your right."

Etta walked slowly, glancing to both sides.

Closed doors. No windows. A fort? Secure, anyway.

She turned the corner and found a room of indoor toilets. She poked around a little and found that each was its own composting unit.

Emptied often. No windows and almost no smell.

Looking up, she realized that air was blowing through a vent above her at a constant rate.

Wonder how that runs.

Instead of walking back the way she had come, she kept going down the hall. The walls were decorated with fabric art, Etta saw.

Embroidery, with big stitches in color. They have enough cloth and thread and dye to make things just for the look of them.

Words were spelled out in the stitches, like *FAMILY IS FOREVER* and *RETURN WITH HONOR*. Some of them looked old and yellowing, but many were fresh and new.

She was distracted from the artwork by a sound. She shook her head, still feeling not quite herself.

Can't be. Must be goats or something that sounds like it.

Etta passed by a mural painted in muted tones: a man in a strange, draped costume holding a stack of flat, yellow objects like books.

The sound persisted. Etta cocked her head, listening.

Can't be. Can't be. It'll be a trap, watch.

She followed the sound to the door it was coming from, drawn toward the impossible cacophony. She laid a hand on her gun as she came close.

Etta stood in the doorway, openmouthed.

Babies. She looked around at the toddlers and cradles, the tiny ones held in the arms of young women.

Twelve. Thirteen. Not one of them over three years old. So many.

The girls who held the babies looked stricken and tired.

"When is the next leaf coming in?"

The girl was tall, with bushy black hair that framed her face like a mane.

"I think we have another hour," answered a very pretty albino woman, her pink-edged eyes looking exhausted.

Most of the smallest babies were crying; the squalling sound had woken or disturbed the others until they all joined in. The toddlers took advantage of the chaos, running wild and causing upheaval of their own.

Etta saw that two of the small children were albino, as well.

The women noticed her finally, calling out over the noise.

"You must be the one they fished out of the Misery!" The albino girl smiled, her teeth whiter than her skin. "Would you like to hold one of them? We're trying to quiet them down."

Etta came forward without thinking, arms outstretched. The black-haired girl put a blue-eyed baby in her arms, turning to a gaggle of toddlers at her feet.

CHAPTER 14

Etta held the baby tight as she slid into a chair. The kid squirmed a little, making a noise like a goat.

She tried again to get a count, but they wouldn't hold still.

Like the locusts in Meramec. So many, shedding their shells and moving on.

She shook her head a little, as if to clear it.

Buzz buzz.

"Blblblblb," said the baby in her arms, drool running sideways and down the child's cheek. "Brrrb."

The black-haired girl stepped in closer. "That's Sarai, she's teething. I think there's an amber bracelet here . . ." She looked away, distracted.

"This is a girl child?" Etta resisted the urge to check the baby's diaper.

"Sure, sure." White hands ran through black hair. "Seven girls, ten boys, all told. Only four girls and five boys today, a bunch are with their mothers. I'm Eliza and that's Lucy." She gestured noncommittally to the alabaster woman, who turned around with her marble-white breasts bared.

"Pleased to meet you," she said, scooping up one of the squalling children and helping it latch. The second child had a harder time, but Lucy tried patiently and tirelessly until the latch was strong.

"Are these . . .? Who are the . . . Are you two the Mothers?"

Lucy nodded toward one of the towheaded toddlers. "Judith there, she's mine. And I have a three-year-old and another on the way around Christmas."

Eliza reached for the baby in Etta's arms and Etta let go. "Sarai is my child. And Brigham, over by the toy box. He looks just like his daddy, no guesswork there." She had found a piece of amber for Sarai to chew on. The child locked it in her jaws, spilling ever more spit onto her mother's arm.

"How were they born?" Etta stared around the room, trying to remember when she had seen so many children in one place.

Jeff City was close . . . but that was a whole city.

"In the usual way." Lucy smirked above the two suckling children.

"No, I mean . . . How many people are here? How many women?"

"Two hundred and twenty-nine, counting the preexistence," Eliza said, rubbing her low belly. "Seventy-eight women and girls."

"That's not possible," Etta breathed.

Eliza and Lucy tittered. "Of course it is."

Lucy pulled a child off her pale nipple with an audible pop. The baby began to fuss.

"You're full of bubbles, silly." Expertly, she laid the child over her forearm while balancing the other, and gently joggled the baby until two small burps came up.

"How many die in childbirth?"

Eliza looked at her sharply. "None, in our time. Some of our mothers did, but that was before the Prophet."

Lucy swapped the children and burped the other.

"The Prophet?"

"Alma. Did she not visit your sickbed?"

The woman with the long hair. The smell of milk.

"She did, yes. How did she fix it?"

"Oh, not her," Lucy said with an air of indulgence. "Heavenly Mother. Alma is just Her Prophet."

Etta leaned back in the soft chair, suddenly heavily tired.

"Sister, you're very pale." Eliza put a soft hand on Etta's arm.

"Well . . ." Lucy smiled, crinkling her pink eyes.

"Oh, hush!" Turning back to Etta, Eliza smiled. "Do you need help getting back to bed?"

Etta started to answer but she was asleep before the words left her mouth. The two nursemaids covered her with a crocheted blanket and went about their work.

When she awoke, men and women were filing in the doors to pick up the children. Lucy was smiling down on her.

"Are you ready for dinner, sister?"

Groggy and sore, Etta rose. "I'm not sure I can . . ."

Lucy reached out and took the arm of a tall, bearded man. "Of course. Oliver here can help you, all you have to do is take his arm."

"But Miss Lucy, I came to get my boy."

"One of your brohuz can get him." Lucy dazzled him with a smile. "Like Naham there."

A young man looked up at the sound of his name, blushing. "Yes, Miss Lucy?"

"Can you take Korah with you as well?"

"Yes, Miss Lucy."

Oliver offered his arm to Etta.

Might as well.

She took it and rose stiffly. "Lead the way."

Out in the hallway, clear of the noise of children, Oliver spoke first.

"So you were the one drowned in the Misery?"

"Yes, I nearly did."

"What's your name, miss?"

"Etta."

"Miss Etta. I've never heard that name before."

"It's the name of an old poem that my mother liked."

Oliver grinned, good white teeth above his beard. "That's right lovely. And where are you from?"

"South of the Odarks." The lie was smooth by now. "I was traveling and I ran into trouble in a strange place called Manhattan."

Oliver chuckled. "Oh, I know Manhattan, sure. My mish took me through there. Almost got summoned, but the local menfolk were too upset to let it happen. Think they liked me on account of I'm so tall."

"You know Manhattan?"

"Sure, sure. My second or third mish, I think. And then I stopped by that way again on my fourth mish on the way home, to get something to eat. They were good brothers there, but unlucky."

"That's about right," Etta said.

Oliver had led them to a huge, open room. Long tables stretched across the space, laid with overlapping tablecloths in blue and green. Candles were lit at regular intervals, making the large room seem warm despite the steel floor and high, vented ceiling.

"My seat is over there, near my wife," Oliver said. "But there will be space there, with the mish boys. I'll introduce you."

He led Etta slowly and gently toward a table of young men. "Gabriel, Rei. Can you two steward this young woman, please? I'd like to go join my wife."

Gabriel rose from the table. He was a strikingly beautiful boy with fine bones and long blond hair that fell straight over his shoulders and down his back.

"We'd be honored, Miss Etta. Please join us."

Rei was olive skinned and shy looking. He grinned a little, half rising from his seat. "Miss."

Etta sank into a chair and took a long drink from a glass of water at her place. It tasted sweet and clean.

"Is your water from the Misery?"

Gabriel reached for his own drink. "It's from the cisterns, down on the lowest level. Plenty of rain this year."

Etta drank again.

"The Leaf Society needs to hurry it up," Rei grumbled. "I'm starving."

As if called, young men began streaming out of the kitchen carrying bowls.

"Oh, thank Heavenly Mother," Rei said.

Food arrived in bowls and tubs, covered with napkins and towels. Smells hit Etta in the face: eggs, butter, spinach. She reached for the one nearest her before she realized that no one else had moved yet.

Rei looked at her with sympathy. "I know, miss. Only a minute now."

Etta's mouth watered. She waited.

Alma glided into the center of the room, golden and serene.

"Bow your heads, children. I'm going to offer a blessing."

All around, people crossed their arms and bowed their heads. Etta was too fascinated to do the same.

"Dear most generous Heavenly Mother, we thank thee for this food and for our life together. We ask you to bless the hands that prepared it and bless the food so that it may strengthen and nourish our bodies. We thank thee also for sending us the stranger, Etta, so that she may speak unto us, as was promised to us. We pray these things in the names of thy children. Amen."

"Amen" chorused around the room.

Rei whipped the towel off the platter nearest him. "Scramble, miss?"

He held out a huge spoonful of eggs mixed with vegetables. He could barely take his eyes off the food.

"Thank you," she said, proffering her plate. With grim patience, Rei served her cornbread and fruits, some of everything on the table, before serving himself. Gabriel waited for his own turn.

No one spoke for a while. Etta found that she was very hungry, but watching Rei wolf his portion down made her think he had been a long time on the road.

"Seconds, miss?"

Etta swallowed, washing the fluffy eggs down with a swig of water. "I'm not even sure I'll finish what I've got here. But thank you."

Rei piled more on his own plate, nodding. "I put in a long day in the fields, miss. I'll finish anything you leave behind." He smiled as he began shoveling again.

Well then.

In the end, she left only a few bites uneaten. True to his word, Rei scooped them up. Gabriel stacked their plates and put them at the end of the table. "Make it easier on the leaf," he said, smiling.

Young men rose up all over the room, collecting the plates and serving dishes that they had distributed. Etta watched it.

So organized.

Something about the scene teased her memory. She thought she had seen something like this before. Or not seen, but . . .

"Come out, you cooks, come out!"

People around the room were taking up the song, clapping their hands in time.

"We won't shut up 'til you come out. Come out, you cooks, come out!"

A small group of middle-aged women emerged from the kitchen at the far end of the room. They all made the same gesture: right hand palm to the chin and then away from the face. There was a burst of polite applause and the women disappeared again.

"Would you like to come with us to Deseret tonight?"

Rei was standing and offering his arm. Gabriel rose hastily, looking slightly ashamed. "Yea. You could come along, since you don't have a group of your own."

Etta glanced around, seeing everyone group and pair. "I'm actually pretty tired . . ."

Not sure I can find my way back to where I was without help, though.

"Oh, it isn't long!" Gabriel was solicitous. "Just prayers, really, before bedtime. We can walk you back after. You don't look so strong just now."

Etta managed a weak smile. She thought about the Mothers of Nowhere, who wove and knit after supper, sometimes telling stories to anyone who joined them.

Not homesick, exactly. She insisted this to herself.

Just unfamiliar.

She accepted Rei's arm. Gabriel passed his through her other one and she started a little, feeling very penned in.

"Lean on me," Gabriel said. Up close, his eyes were two colors, like Alice's. Blue with an inner rim of gold.

Eight in, eight out.

They're too nice. That was Eddy's voice. *You know they want something.*

Where are you right now?

I don't know, actually.

She let herself be practically frog-marched to a smaller room with old-world upholstered chairs. The two men helped her into one and sat on either side of her, looking pleased with themselves.

A pregnant woman welcomed everyone by name as they came in. Her voice was low and musical, but Etta saw that her top lip was seamed off center, and her speech was not quite clear.

Born cloven. They must have doctors here. Cutters, even. Maybe that's why—

"Our traveler, Sister Etta."

Etta's head snapped up at the sound of her name.

The cloven woman was beaming at her. "You are welcome here among us. The Prophet said you were foretold to her. She told every priest and bishop that you would be a blessing to our people."

Bishop.

The word made her think of suicide and for a moment her mind groped blindly at the thing, feeling its contours and unable to find its name.

Mormons. Just like the ones the Unnamed lived with, the couple. Honus. Jodi.

Her mouth hung open for a moment before she thought to close it. She tried to run through the details of the story, but only the most personal parts really stood out.

The Unnamed loved Jodi but settled for sleeping with Honus. Honus thought he could have two wives. Loved Jodi and the Unnamed both, but neither of them would have it. A man with two wives. What an idea.

She tried to focus on the cloven woman's blunted, cottony speech but found that she could not. When Alma swept into the room, the hush got Etta's attention first.

Every head turned to face Alma. She had changed into a long white nightgown. Etta could make out the darker spots of her areolae beneath the translucent material.

"Forgive the intrusion, Sister Moses. I wanted to give our visitor a blessing before I went to bed."

"Not at all, Prophet Alma. You bless us with your presence."

Everyone turned to stare at Etta as Alma drew near. Etta looked up, unsure.

"If you two young men will assist me?" Alma said.

Gabriel and Rei were out of their seats at once, standing at Alma's sides. Alma placed warm and gentle hands on Etta's head.

"Sweet Heavenly Mother, we ask thy blessing on this woman as she heals from mortal wounds, that she may speak unto us the truth that only she knows. Let her be strengthened and fortified in our fellowship. Let her . . ."

Alma's voice died away for a moment and Etta opened her eyes, wary. Beneath the gown, she could see Alma's belly contracting hard. Alma let out a long, gentle breath.

"Let her guide us as Moroni did the Nephites. In the name of thy children, we pray. Amen."

The names meant nothing to Etta, but they elicited sighs from around the room. Etta glanced about her, feeling embarrassed. She looked back at Alma to see that Gabriel and Rei had each unbuttoned a corner of Alma's bodice. Alma squeezed both her own breasts with a sigh, and a tiny jet of warm milk hit Etta in the face.

What in the living fuck?

She was too stunned to wipe her face for a moment. Then Alma, rebuttoned, crushed her in another fragrant embrace.

At least I can wipe it off on her.

Alma whispered to her softly, "I know our ways are strange to you. Don't you worry." She moved her hands from Etta's head to her biceps and once again Etta felt the flow of that curious warmth, flooding toward her injuries. She felt comfortably sleepy again.

No som tonight.

No som here at all, Eddy's voice corrected. *It isn't safe. I can't believe you did it in the first place.*

She thought she wouldn't sleep, but exhaustion stole over her the moment she fell back into bed.

Etta did not dream.

She woke with her heart pounding, her body panicking without her. The room was too dark to see anything.

Early? Late?

She hadn't seen the sun in days. For a moment, she had a steep feeling of vertigo, not knowing which way was up.

Maybe we're miles beneath the ground.

She thought of the deep but wide-open sensation of being underground at Meramec.

She kicked the covers off and thrashed herself to the floor. Her ribs sang out in agony at the sudden exertion, and dizziness rolled after. On all fours, she shook her head.

Eight in, eight out. Eddy's voice, calm and secure.

She concentrated on breathing in and both legs locked into rigid cramps. She sucked whistling breaths through clenched teeth and flipped over, trying to pull her toes up.

Eddy's voice couldn't reach her. She wanted her mother and couldn't even allow that thought to form. She pounded one fist into the floor, fighting someone who wasn't there.

She must have made enough noise to be heard outside in the hall. Neum came around the door, lips pursed and brow furrowed.

He reached for her arm and she yanked it away, causing another bright flare of pain at her ribs.

Neum looked her over and realized the source of the problem. Expertly, he wrapped his hand around her right heel and pushed the sole of her foot up toward her knee with the lever of his forearm.

She felt the muscle shudder for a moment and let go. He felt it, too, and moved to do the same with her left foot. Both legs relaxed and she lay slack, trying to regain her breath. She wiped the sweat from her forehead with the back of her hand, waving him off when he tried to help her up again.

"Are you alright, sister?"

"What do you people want from me?"

Her voice was mean with pain and worry, but she was too far gone to care.

"Why did you bring me here? Why are you taking care of me like I'm one of your own?"

She was standing, but weaving on her feet. He held out both hands as if to catch her.

"Because it's what we do. We help."

"Bullshit." She slumped, both elbows on the bed, fighting to drag herself into it. "Nobody helps."

"Sure they do! That's all the mish does! Go out and help. They've helped people all over, and sometimes the people come back here."

Gingerly, afraid of her lashing out, he offered her water from the pitcher beside her bed.

She accepted it with a huff.

Get hold of yourself.

Why is he here? Was he outside the room all night? Eddy's voice, steady and wary.

"And anyhow, Alma told us you were coming."

At the sound of Alma's name, Etta's face soured. She remembered being hit in the face with warm milk, the absurd intimacy of it.

"What is . . . Why is she . . . ?" She didn't even know how to ask the question.

Why do you all treat her like some kind of thing that's not even human? She's like the biggest Hive queen, Mother, head Midwife, council leader. She's everything to you people. She's just a woman.

But the warm feeling of Alma's hands came back to her as she thought it.

"I want to leave here."

Neum stood up. "I'll get you a pack ready."

You'll end up crawling. Eddy's voice steadied her. *Just go talk to Alma. Ask for that.*

"No." She took a few deep breaths. "Can I . . . Can you just take me to Alma?"

"Sure I can!" The little man brightened considerably. "All the women are there, anyway. That's why I was awake, otherwise I'd be long asleep right now."

"What?"

"Alma is in childbed, sister. Come." He offered his arm and she took it.

Where are you right now?

The walk seemed to take forever. Etta came to understand she had been asleep only an hour or two before waking up. She was still deeply tired and in a lot of pain.

Remember her belly. She was contracting hard, clearly headed for labor. Do they have Midwives here?

Death is always in the room. Eddy's voice, Ina's words. Etta shook her head. *Fatigue is making me crazy.*

Us.

She could tell they were getting close. She heard the long groans and knew the sound. She had attended births in Nowhere as many did, hanging nearby. They sang and drummed and whispered and hoped, as if their collective wanting could seep beneath the door and reach the woman and child as they struggled toward life.

Most of the births Etta had been to ended badly for one or both.

She expected Neum to drop her in a chair near the door, but he pushed it open and guided her inside. Wordlessly, he closed it behind her.

In the room there were only women. Alma was walking, supported by the albino girl from the nursery, Lucy, and another whom Etta did not recognize. They led her across the room and back, contractions doubling her over. Against the walls, women sat in chairs and on stools. Many prayed, eyes closed and lips moving as they murmured. Others were riveted to the sight of Alma as she writhed and fought to walk.

Etta stared for a few minutes before Eliza caught her attention and offered her a chair. Eliza stood, letting Etta have her seat. Eliza settled herself on the floor and leaned back. After a few minutes, she reached up and rested her elbows on Etta's knees.

Etta was shocked at first, but she remembered the easy intimacy of women at births back in Nowhere. They held each other and rubbed each other's shoulders, sharing food and drink and forgetting all old gossips and rivalries at these events. She'd always felt on edge at those times, even when she was just a girl. She knew early on that the touch of a woman meant more to her than the comfort the others came for. She was worried that her need was clear on her face; that someone would see her feelings as sharply as she felt them.

The thing in her that was Eddy chuckled a little. *You've never been as obvious as I would be. Lucky.*

She ignored that. This was not a place for him.

Alma's typical radiance seemed dimmed. She was pale and sweated like a cheese in the warm air. Her glorious hair was wound into a thick braid that swung below her knees, counterbalancing as her back bent. She grunted and groaned like any woman giving birth.

Etta looked over at the table beside the bed. She saw a clean, sharp knife, white cotton towels, string, and a ready supply of clean water.

Seems like they know what they're doing.

They must, with so many babies around here.

Etta's eyes darted around the room, looking for what was different.

They must know something we don't.

Alma's groaning slipped lower and she began shaking her head as if to say no, over and over. Etta had heard enough stories to know that was a sign that the moment was near. Lucy and the other girl helped Alma to the bed, where she climbed laboriously to her hands and knees. The two attendants pulled her gown up over her head and Alma was there in her full nude splendor, warm and round and ripe in every direction. Her body rippled like a snake. Etta could see the baby crowning.

Lucy put her hands on either side of the child's head and waited. Alma pushed when the contraction came, without a word passing between them. The baby's head was out but the shoulders took longer. Two more pushes and the child slid free into Lucy's hands.

"A girl!" Lucy's cry was pure joy. She held the child over her arm, sweeping the mouth free and waiting for the child to breathe. The baby gave a small cry in the shock of the cold.

All around the room, eyes were wet.

A moment later, Alma grunted again and the other young woman, a brown-haired and plain complement to Lucy's luminous whiteness, came around to deliver the placenta. She blocked Etta's view for a moment, and she and Eliza craned their necks, trying to watch.

This is it, Etta thought. *If their Prophet is going to bleed to death in front of them, this is when it will happen.*

The brown-braided woman came away holding another baby. This one was smaller and paler, nearly blue. Hastily, she flipped the infant over, tapping smartly on its back until it blew sticky fluid from its mouth and began to cry.

"Another girl!"

Alma sobbed, her face hidden from view. Women rose all over the room, blocking Etta out again.

The third baby came as an afterthought, long after they all believed it was over. Women all over the room gently rubbed vernix into the first two children's skin and wiped them clean, wrapping them up to be held. It was Eliza who caught this last child, another small one. This one was born wiggling, silent but clearly very much alive. People turned to look only as Eliza's voice rang out, breaking.

"Our Prophet has had another girl!"

Eliza put the tiny, perfect baby into the arms of another and helped Alma with the afterbirth that finally began to make its appearance.

Alma turned over, red-faced and slick with sweat. She looked exhausted but vigorous.

She hardly bled at all. Etta searched the bedclothes, watching folded sheets being taken away to make the woman more comfortable. *She looks fine.*

Alma held her arms out and two of the babies were placed there. The third she instructed Eliza to lay between her knees, which she brought up to make a cradle. She looked them over, nodding approvingly.

"I haven't had three since my twentieth year!"

Lucy mopped Alma's brow for her and offered her water. Alma drank without taking her eyes off the babies.

"Three girls! We are so blessed! Let it be known that it was young Shemnon who fathered these. Any woman seeking a strong seeder should get herself sealed to him quick!"

A giggle rippled through the room.

So she does have a Hive. Or at least, it's not one man she's tied to. Otherwise she wouldn't have to call him out. And others can have him, too.

"It's not Shemnon, Prophet. It's you!"

Alma sighed, bringing the two nearest girls to her breasts and yelping as milk let down and she contracted again.

"Still, they help a little. Three seeds at once! Not bad."

Eliza spoke over her shoulder to Etta. "The prophet normally has two at a time. Yea, she's very pleased with Shemnon."

Etta had a startled moment before she could answer. "How many living children does she have?"

Eliza laughed a little. "Living children? They're all living. What a question! This makes thirteen. Most of them girls."

Thirteen living children. Etta thought of the women of Nowhere, how they preened over two or three children in the house. How the Hives of women with even one child swelled and exploded, men living in the house next door, waiting.

Lucy leaned over Alma. "May I have the honor of nursing your third, sister? She seems mighty hungry."

The tiny third-comer was indeed crying weakly, demanding to be fed.

"I'd be much obliged, Sister Lucy."

Lucy swept the child off Alma's knees and brought her to the breast. The infant fought for a few minutes to latch, but quickly fell to mashing her tiny fist into the woman's flesh, breathing furiously through her miniscule nose.

The older women in the room dried their tears and picked up the dirty linens and tools.

"We'll take these to the leaf," one silver-haired woman in a long dress said to no one in particular. The room emptied somewhat. Etta stayed.

She sidled closer to the bed, entranced by Alma's glowing appearance.

"I've never seen a birth go so well." Etta watched the two pink mouths working tirelessly at Alma's nipples.

Alma's eyes met hers and Etta realized with a sense of unreality that the woman's eyes were green.

Weren't they brown before? Brown like a fawn in the spring?

Alma's hand shot out fast and closed around Etta's wrist. Etta felt as trapped as a mouse under the eyes of a hawk.

"Yes, they were brown before. They change."

"How did you—"

"Not now." Alma's gaze was intense, holding her in place as though she were bound there. "Now is the time for other things."

Alma's hand on her arm felt white-hot. Etta stared back into the woman's murky green eyes, uncomprehending.

Alma's voice was low and steady. She cradled both children with her drawn-up thighs, holding on to Etta. "I know what we have to do, and this is the only time I'm going to have enough power to make you ready to do it. Yea, you have been taught by your Mothers. And so you are ready for the terrible battle to commence."

"What?"

One child fell away from the nipple, milk-drunk and asleep in the ease of newborns. The other followed seconds later. They pillowed against Alma's body. Her hands held Etta in place.

"It is the teaching of the Mothers. You must lead them. Hush now. Just hushhh."

The final sound she made filled the room, as the sound of beating wings on a thousand bees.

Etta struggled to free herself. *What the living hell is this?*

Alma's hand was so hot it was burning her. The heat shot through her fast, along the lines that carried panic and pain. Etta's heart pounded. Her arm thrummed and her feet jittered.

Run, damn you! Run!

Her eyelids twitched out of sync. Alma's grip grew stronger.

Without her volition, Etta's leg sprang up and stomped onto the bed beside Alma. Alma moved her inexorable grip to Etta's calf and clamped tight. Etta yelped.

The other women in the room kept their distance, watching transfixed.

"Is it not written in your law, ye are goddess?" Alma's teeth clamped on the final sibilant, holding it like a cat hissing in the dark.

"What?" Etta was locked into her body, thrumming with something she could not control.

Alma squeezed the belly of her calf muscle tight and Etta felt something burst out of it, like the noisome fluid in an abscess lanced with a hot knife. She bellowed and broke free, slipping to the floor.

Three women carried her back to bed. Alma fell asleep, arms curled around two of her three newborns. All over the tunnels of Ommun, people made ready to celebrate.

CHAPTER 15

In Nowhere, births were celebrated. Healthy births were not as rare now as they had been two generations ago, but they were far from certain. Half of the male children lived, and most of the mothers of boys could come through the fever just fine. Women who gave birth to girls, however, were prone to the sudden bleeding and loss of consciousness that was described in the Unnamed's earliest notebooks. Girl children died three times out of every four. The community contributed every way they could, and they took in women and girls whenever possible. But Nowhere remained a town of men run by a handful of women.

Etta had seen more than a few towns in her time on the road. Before Estiel and before Eddy, she had made contact with people in towns along the rivers and prosperous places like Jeff City a few times a year. Places like Manhattan, mostly: faring no better than Nowhere, but dealing with it in their own way. Building their own bridge between men and what few women they could keep.

Jeff City had made her suspicious. At first, she had been convinced she had finally stumbled into a place where they could cure the fever for good, or where people had become immune. Discovering Flora, learning what a horsewoman was, had dashed those hopes. Even cities that seemed to have enough women turned out to be some kind of trick, like Flora. Or the result of kidnapping and hoarding girls. Nowhere Etta had ever seen was like Ommun: full of women and girls who were born there and stayed freely, because they wanted to.

Lying awake in bed, Etta considered Ommun.

I was hoping for this.

Were you? Eddy joined immediately, to Etta's complete lack of surprise.

She sat on the edge of her bed and it was as if he sat with her.

Yes, she thought stubbornly. *This . . . and other things.*

Remember what Kelda wanted? What Alice always wants? If there were enough women, would anyone care if we kept our own company?

Etta turned her head to the side as if Eddy were something she could avoid. To change the subject, she touched the place where her ribs had been broken.

She felt nothing.

If we had all this, no one would care who slept with who.

She gathered her courage and hit herself in that same spot with her fist. It hurt a little, but only as much as her own punch would in an unwounded spot.

That's right, Eddy's voice said.

She touched her forehead to find the divot where the rock had cut her, tried shaking her head vigorously to scare up the dizziness that had followed her for days.

The divot was there, but no pain and no dizziness followed.

Right. Eddy sounded satisfied.

Etta sat back down and pulled her toes in, arching her feet hard and shortening her calves as much as she could. She waited for the cramp to begin, wondering if the triumph of being right would be worth the pain.

She couldn't have fixed it with her bare hands. It's just not possible. Ina tried medicines and massages. Alma couldn't have done it just with her will.

She held the curl in both legs as long as she could. Nothing happened.

It's real, Eddy's voice said, as flat as a trader examining his goods. *It's real and it's what they have here. That's why.*

Etta took long, deep breaths.

Eight in, eight out.

We don't need that anymore.

Etta snorted.

They're still wanting whatever it is they think you have.

Etta considered this.

Women are the thing that's always wanted. What is there besides that? They already have enough of us. Enough babies.

Eddy shrugged with Etta's shoulders.

So?

So.

Etta thought of Nowhere. She thought of the few men who had been taken in to the small town—the ones who had skills that were needed, and who had convinced the women of the council that they were not slavers or rapists. One had been a knife sharpener with good tools. A couple had been builders.

What do you have to offer these people? You mention good drugs, they don't want drugs. You ask them what they're after and they tell you a lot of nonsense about angels and dreams.

What was it the Unnamed said about these people? About their god?

She could remember nothing. Only the sex. Only Roxanne, the Unnamed's first companion. And Jodi. Only the winter that Jodi's baby had died.

Nowhere had no gods. Etta knew them from books, and people kept some festival holidays, retold old stories sometimes. Older folks liked to argue about the deals people had made with the gods of the old world, and how, if they had been true once, they were surely broken now.

Etta had heard stories on the road about gods who had died, who were coming back someday. She heard about good gods and bad gods. Women with Hives would spin up tales about goddesses.

I've never seen anything with my own two eyes that would make me believe any of that.

Until today. Eddy sounded almost smug.

Bullshit. I didn't see anything.

Didn't see three living babies come at once. Didn't see her lay her hands and make wounds heal up.

"Fuck."

She had stood up and walked to the dresser. She opened the drawer and put her clothes back on, wanting to be out of the gown now that she could move freely, without pain.

Fine. Fine. Fine.

She held her bindings in her hands and thought about it.

Come on.

Not yet.

They put their hands on their gun and slept fitfully the rest of the night.

They knew it was morning because Neum came to get them. They were already up.

"Someone's doing better," Neum exclaimed maternally. "Are you ready?"

They knew they would be taken to Alma once again. They weren't ready to settle for anything else.

They walked with Neum, arguing.

Let me do the talking, Eddy's voice said. *I know what this is about.*

Ha. Sure you do. You know what I know.

I listen better than you do.

It was Eddy who spoke to Alma, as she lay in bed with her hair spread out around her. Gabriel and Rei were there, combing her golden hair on either side of her bed. The three babies were in the enormous bed with the prophet, who gazed serenely up at Eddy.

"How are you feeling today, sister?" Alma's voice was soothing, baby-soft.

"Much better." Eddy stood still, trying to size her up.

"I knew as much. I knew that Her will would be done."

"I don't know what was done, or how, but I feel better. And I thank you for that, and for treating me as a guest here. But I have to know, today, right now, what you want from me. It's hanging over me, and I can't stand it anymore. What is it?"

"She rose again on the third day," Alma said, nodding to Eddy.

"What?"

Rei and Gabriel exchanged looks.

"It's only important if you know the story. Etta, come here, sit with me and my babies."

Eddy did not want to go but found himself walking forward anyhow. She was too lovely, too motherly, to refuse. He tried to harden his face.

She laid her soft hand over his. He shivered, despite its immediate warmth.

"You must lead the young men on their mish. You must go tonight, while the power is still in you. You must be Moroni, and lead them into battle."

"What? Battle with what? With who? I've never—"

"Shhhhhh." Alma's full pink lips pushed forward as she put her hand on one of the babies, who had begun to stir. "That's not for me, that's for the mish. It's only for me to lay your calling on you."

I wonder if these Mormons are even the same people that the Unnamed knew. But he knew they were. There was something about their assuredness, their earnestness, that rang the same bell.

I want to leave this place, anyhow. If this is how it happens, then fine.

Alma nodded to Gabriel and Rei, who dropped their work and rose. "These two will be your companions. You may take all the Aarons and Deks you like. No other women must go among you, however. You are the only one like you."

That's the truth.

He didn't know what to say to her. He didn't want to accept what she clearly thought was his duty, but he didn't want to reject it, either. He wanted to follow these boys out, but after that, who knew. He raised a hand to her, almost a wave.

"To the square," she said, smiling, and waved back in the same way.

Mystified, he followed the two younger men out into the steel hallway.

Eddy saw people carrying enormous quantities of food, roast ears of corn and smoking sweet potatoes. He saw a cow and a goat carved in white butter on slabs of wood. He heard people singing and followed the boys toward the songs.

The children seemed to be leading, singing a silly-sounding song about popcorn growing on a tree, using their hands to tell the story. Everyone looked clean and freshened, bright faces smiled everywhere around the large spaces. The main hall overflowed with people, and Eddy stared at so many women, so many children.

Alma walked onto the dais, serenely and without any sign that she had given birth to three only the night before.

She doesn't even look pale.

People grew quiet. Alma wore the smallest strapped to her chest and had the other two in her arms. On the stage, two young women took them from her gently and held them. Alma put her hands up and silence reigned.

"We gather here today for the naming and blessing of my three, and to send out a mish!"

Applause came from everywhere and a group of men shoved one of their own forward. A tall, gangly man-boy stumbled up toward Alma, grinning and trying to regain his balance. Women laughed a little, but Eddy could see more than a few of them sizing him up.

"This Dek, Shemnon, fathered the three. And so he will help us bless them, won't you, dear?"

Shemnon grinned and Eddy saw that his two front teeth had been knocked out.

The two women holding the babies brought them in front of Shemnon, who laid one pale hand across their two foreheads. Alma came around and he reached over shyly, putting his palm against the baby lump slung low across her chest.

Tension gathered as they waited.

Alma's voice was soft but low, and carried miraculously well in the open space.

"Dear most loving, most fertile Heavenly Mother. We thank thee for thy endless bounty of children, particularly on this day when thou hast seen fit to send us three blessed girl children. We ask you, in the presence of their father the Dek, to bless them each in turn."

She laid one hand on the child she wore. "Bless Alma the younger, who will carry on my work and be a Mother to many."

She lightly touched the next child to her right. "Bless Emma, who will be a prophet in her own time and lead the people with wisdom and gifts of healing."

A sigh rippled through the crowd at that.

Alma ignored it and touched the last child. "And bless Etta, who takes the name of a stranger who will carry our story to places and people far distant, who will be a story keeper as well one day.

"We pray these things in the names of thy children. Amen."

The tension broke and a celebratory mood returned as people began to fall to the feast that had been laid. Eddy watched as the children were given bracelets that tied around their tiny wrists.

Now that their names have been given and their fates laid, they have to be marked.

He thought of Ina, telling Etta as a child that she could be a Mother or a Midwife, but the choice would not really be up to her.

Does anyone get to choose what they are?

He thought of the bindings waiting in his bag. He thought of Flora.

Doesn't seem like they choose here, either. Men are "Deks" and boys are "Aarons." Everybody is "leaf." This is all arranged for the many, and the few have to fall in line.

No different from Nowhere. Or Estiel. Or Manhattan.

When Gabriel found him, Eddy was sitting with a piece of buttered bread, not eating.

"I've got two Aarons who want to go," Gabriel told him breathlessly. "And six Deks, including me and Rei. I told the Aarons to pack our supplies. Alma says we leave tonight. Are you prepared?"

Eddy looked around, feeling supremely out of place.

"Yes, I'm prepared."

Gabriel's excitement was clear in his wide blue eyes and easy grin. But Eddy thought it was more than that. He looked eager, like someone who looked forward to relief rather than adventure.

Eddy didn't want to endure any sort of good-bye. He didn't want another moment's nonsense, another ritual that made no sense to him. He was tired of references to stories he'd never heard and feeling like an outsider who was a little too welcome to stay.

The hell did she name the baby after Etta? What was she trying to achieve there?

The boys and men joined the three of them as they gathered a pack and a bedroll for each.

Rei led them to a doorway and looked over the group.

"Alright, Aarons and Deks, I know nobody wants to leave when they're putting together such a mighty party. But the spirit says we've got to go today. So we go. Etta is our leader. Gabriel and I are her companions. The rest of you must stain us, and follow. Agree?"

Heads nodded. Eddy looked them over, nonplussed.

Stain? I think he means support, somehow.

He turned to Rei. "Where are we supposed to go?"

He looked blankly back, his dark eyes trusting. "You'll know the way. You've been appointed to take us there."

Eddy felt something flop over in his belly. "Take us out of here, Rei."

Rei turned to the door and wrenched it open, using the big handle as a lever. The room was very small, and they crowded into it so that Gabriel could slide the door closed behind them. Rei put his mouth to a horn in the corner and hollered into it.

"Take us all the way up, men!"

When the room jerked upward, Eddy was the only one to yell out his fear. The others laughed a little.

"It's only a lift," Gabriel said, pulling his long blond hair out of the straps at his shoulders. "Don't worry, we're fine."

The motion of the small room smoothed out and Eddy fought the feeling of unease as they gained altitude.

Eight in, eight out.

They ascended a long time. When he could trust his mouth, Eddy asked, "How does this work? How far down are we?"

"It's pretty far," one of the younger boys said. "I made the climb lots of times. Takes about an hour. This here lift has to be pulled up by three men who know how to work the pulley. They're just about the strongest in Ommun. You just tell them how many are going and when, and they hoist you."

By a subtle shifting of pressure, they knew they were reaching the top. The lift juddered to a stop, lowering back down a small measure to line up with another door.

Eddy prepared his eyes for the blinding sunlight, but it didn't come. They were still below ground.

A long grotto extended ahead of them, with spaced support columns erected throughout. In it, Eddy saw carefully tended patches of vegetables and grains.

"How . . . ?"

Gabriel came up behind him. "There's vents to let in light, and a very careful schedule. This way, no one can tell we're here."

They followed the others toward a short staircase that ended in a flat door overhead.

Eddy squinted up in the dark and saw that Rei was turning small metal wheels in a lock to make a pattern that would spring it open.

The sunlight did cut in then, pure white and dazzling.

Out on the ground, Eddy staggered. He looked around, taking in the wild-seeming fruit trees, the smell of the nearby creek. He turned in circles, trying to find any sign at all that hundreds of people were living below their feet.

He remembered what it had been like, waking in a strange place. He had known they had to be hidden, probably underground. But he had never imagined that secrets like this could exist. How many other cities had he walked over? How many of them were full of women?

When the entire party had come through, Rei set the door down. The door itself was metal, caked over with a heavy couple of inches of soil. Grass and weeds grew all over it, and as it flattened it became almost indistinguishable from the earth that surrounded it.

"Who locks it behind us?" Eddy almost whispered.

Rei shrugged. "One of the farmers. They saw us go."

"How do you get back in?"

"You have to know the signal." Rei stared straight ahead, but when Eddy looked at Gabriel, he winked.

"Which way?"

Eddy's head spun. He tried to remember what he had been told, where he was. He wanted to head for home.

Destiny my ass.

"South," he said.

They walked south all day.

The Book of Eddy

Maybe you just show up one day and everyone thinks you're part of a story that's already happening and what you really think doesn't matter. Maybe that's what happened to the Unnamed. I wonder if she ever thought we'd be reading about her, years later, trying to be like her. Did she even want that?

She says she wanted to give people birth control. But when that was gone, she wanted to bring babies or maybe keep them from dying. She didn't want to be any kind of story. Did someone make her into it, like Alma is trying to make me?

Make me. I was made. I made me.

What was in him that was Etta looked sideways at that, but he ignored it.

They walked a long time. As the men began to talk in small groups, Eddy came to realize they had all traveled this way before. Even the youngest of the boys had remembrances of where they went, what they found to eat.

She turned to Gabriel and Rei, whose spoke so softly and so closely that their hair almost touched as they walked.

"What do you search for? Are you raiders?"

Gabriel nodded, then tossed his long hair over both shoulders. "We raid old-world goods. And we rescue people who need rescuing. But Ommun is rich, and we don't need for much from the old world anymore. Lately . . ."

He bit his full lower lip and looked to Rei.

Rei filled in. "Lately, we've lost most of the mish to the Lion."

Eddy's body was cold all over.

"The Lion of Estiel?"

"You know another one?" This from a wry, grinning preteen. Eddy fixed his gaze on the kid and the kid looked away, abashed.

"He's all over these towns," Rei explained, "taking all the women from the ones that will surrender. Burning out the ones that won't. And most of these places hardly have a handful of women or girls, they get left with nothing at all. Manhattan—"

"I was in Manhattan. I was there when it was taken."

Dark looks circulated through the men.

"They didn't have much to begin with. They had worked out a hard system. I couldn't have lived there, myself. But it worked for them," Gabriel said, looking chastened.

Rei's voice was uncertain. "Was it burned out, or did they—"

"It was burning when I left there. They gave me this." Eddy poked the scar in his forehead where the rock had left its mark. He felt no pain, no echo from the back of his head at the sudden impact.

"We ought to go that way, to see if anyone is left." Rei pulled a long, rolled piece of hide out of his pack and laid it on the ground, kneeling.

Eddy looked it over, not understanding at first. It was a map, but it was so different from the old-world paper maps he had tended carefully over the years that he didn't recognize it at first. Leaning down, he saw that it encompassed a large amount of land, spanning from Estiel to south of the Odarks, and east to a body of water that he knew from maps was called the Atlantic, but he had never seen it.

The boys and men crowded around, discussing the best route to Manhattan. When they had settled it, referring to incomprehensible symbols used to mark food, shelter, and danger, Rei rolled it back up and they got moving again.

In some deep woods, they reached a stone cottage that was known to all of them. The younger boys split up to gather wood and build a fire, fetch water, and catch something for dinner.

Eddy squatted in the dark little house beside Rei and Gabriel. "Can I see your map again?"

Rei unrolled it and Eddy stared again. "What is this?"

Gabriel laughed a little, following Eddy's point to a black blot on the map. "Niyok. It used to be a huge city, but it's mostly burned. Not much raiding there, but every mish eventually goes to see it. Nobody believes how big the buildings are. And there's this woman in the water. Green. Huge, taller than a tree."

Eddy shook his head. *Nothing these guys say sounds real.*

"Where else have you gone? Have you been to Utah?" Eddy was thinking of the Unnamed, trying to make her map overlap theirs.

"Sure, we've been to Uta, that's where the Prophet used to live."

"Alma?"

Rei shook his head. "No, the old Prophet. The two of us have been to Ido and seen the farms there. Lots of people living there. Good land, and they do alright."

"Have you been to an old-world city called San Francisco? Where the western sea is? The . . ." He struggled to remember the name. "The Pacific."

Gabriel shook his head again. "I've never been to the Spific, but other mish have told me they went there. But the cities on the sea are all crumbled, and at the edge the water is rising. There's nothing there. The water rises in Niyok every year, too."

Eddy's heart sank just a little. He hadn't known he hoped to see the Unnamed's city some day until he knew he never would.

They looked over the map in silence for a moment, until Gabriel's finger landed on a point near the Misery.

"We're here." He dragged his finger up the map and tapped a star-shaped splotch a little north of where they were. "This is Jamestown. Jacob and Esau said it's been taken, but the Paws haven't set out to return to Estiel yet, so there's still time."

"Time for what?"

Everyone turned to look at Eddy. Gabriel's eyebrow came up. "To save them. What did you think we were going to do?"

Eddy swept his gaze around the knot of men and boys. No one had a trace of mirth. "How . . . How are we going to . . . Have you done this before? Do you know how many men the Lion has?"

Rei came forward smiling and put his hand on Eddy's shoulder. Eddy shrugged it away and crossed his arms.

"Of course we have. This is our mish now. It has to be, or the Lion will take every town along the Misery and eventually come to us. We're hidden and protected, but like you said, he has a lot of men. We've had trouble with the Paws since my first mish, seven years ago."

"Yeah, me too. So what do we do?"

Gabriel grinned a little, his gold cap of hair catching the sunlight. "The same thing we always do, but with you, this time. Like the Prophet said."

The arms bunker was too far away from the underground city, the boys grumbled. They all talked about the first time they had seen it with a kind of reverence, passing it from mouth to mouth—a fable told by every Mother at bedtime.

"Enough guns for a thousand mish. Rows and rows, all different kinds. Whole rooms of just ammo. Just like home, all set aside for us by the old world. They said that when they found it, it breathed in like a living child. It was waiting for us, because they knew that we would have to fight, isn't that right?"

The hatch was concealed just as the other one had been in Ommun, but the approach was more complicated. One of the younger boys pestered Rei until he relented, letting the little redhead do the job of opening it.

Located at four points around the hatch were steel posts, each housing a metal toggle switch under a cloudy plastic cover. Eddy watched as the boy paced carefully between them, flipping them all up and then down in a careful sequence. When he was finished, he nodded his coppery head at them and stepped back. After a few minutes, the hatch came up soundlessly and two older men appeared beneath it, smiling through their beards.

Eddy descended the steel rungs of the ladder, feeling like he was in a dream. Rei stayed up top with the boys, and Gabriel followed downward.

Unlike Ommun's steel gray, everything in this bunker was white. The walls were lined with bright-white, unblemished plastic that baffled the light that seemed to come up from the ground. Eddy stared down at it, uncomprehending.

"Where does the light come from?"

One of the bearded guardians shrugged beneath his flannel shirt. "From the sun. The machine is old, but it never stops working."

Eddy thought of Alice's glow paint, and the thin glass bulbs he found in houses, that gave off a golden glow in pictures he'd seen. The brightness in the armory was terrible; he knew he'd have a headache if he stayed too long.

"We need to be outfitted for a mish not far from here. A rifle for every man, with .22s for the little ones. Pistols all around, as well. Armor we'll have to tie and drag up."

The beards were nodding, opening large drawers in the walls.

Inside were untold numbers of black guns, every shape and size that Eddy had ever seen and quite a few that he hadn't. His knees wobbled.

"You have . . . You have . . ."

Gabriel looked at him with alarm. "Are you alright? Can you breathe okay?"

Eddy slumped against a wall, thinking of the deals he had seen made for even broken and rusted guns. The way the Lion's eyes had raked over Eddy's revolver, the eyes of his Paws darting toward it, unable to look away. Knives were better, less dangerous and more useful in every way. But guns were like the Lion's cats: a symbol of danger at your disposal.

Guns make us men.

Eddy's hand brushed the flat front of his jeans before circling to the back.

"Do you have ammo for this?" Eddy's mouth was dry.

Graybeard took the revolver and expertly knocked out the cylinder with a flick of his wrist. "Sure, plenty. Plus lots more like this one, not many can handle 'em. You want a set?"

"I want a dozen."

I want one for every woman in Nowhere and every woman I meet on the road. I want to come back here every summer and get more.

The armor turned out to be black vests and helmets that they tied into a brutal garland. Gabriel carried the end of the rope up the ladder, and the boys hauled the train through the hatch. Rifles were handed up next, up a line of men through to the boys, one at a time. Handguns were loaded into two bags that Gabriel packed out.

Eddy took his two guns: one new and one old. The bearded men had given him a new kit to clean them with and shined up his old ones. They scoffed at the handmade bullets he still had in the chamber and gingerly tipped them out, filling the cylinder with machine-made old bullets from the old world, uniformly cruel and stamped, each one exactly the same.

They loaded his bag with boxes of more of them, and exactly twelve revolvers, as he had asked. They weighed him down terribly, and he couldn't think of what to say. His thanks would never be enough. He strained and grunted to get up the ladder. He hoped his straps would hold out until he made it back to Nowhere.

It's like carrying a little girl on my back.

A couple little girls.

He adjusted the straps over and over, trying to settle the weight. Gabriel unrolled the map again and showed them the way they would follow to Jamestown. They walked through the night, by the light of the moon. They knew Jamestown by its fires, dark-blue smoke against a light-blue dawn.

Eddy slept fitfully, his back humped over on his pack. He woke twice thinking his legs were cramping, but it was only memory that seized. He found his legs curled and painless, and he thought of Alma's face. He kicked at the dirt and tried to go back to sleep. All around him, boys slept utterly at peace, as if they had been bred to lie beneath the trees and never think of danger.

When they were all awake it was nearly dark again. Gabriel and Rei divided tasks and Eddy watched, fascinated. They had obviously done this before, maybe a hundred times. They sent two of the youngest boys as scouts to determine how many men and where they were concentrated. Two others were sent to figure out where the women were being held. All four came back in short order, with the same story.

"They're in that big building on the far west of the main drag. A school, I think. There are bodies all over town, and there's a lot of screaming in there."

Gabriel shot air out between his front teeth and stared at the ground. "They're breaking them here? So they're not for the harem. Must be trade."

Eddy watched him and Rei plan rapidly between the two of them.

"So we come in through the windows?"

"Yeah, like that time in Olathe?"

"Yeah, but this time no flash. We can get the doors open and cut them down quick."

Rei turned to the younger boys. "Remember, the women will be tied or chained. They can't run, and they'll duck down when it starts. You're watching for movement. Assume all of the men will have guns, but we'll have more."

Eddy felt out of place, not sure whether to lead or follow. "So what do I do?"

They turned to him as if they had forgotten he was there.

"Have you ever shot a man before?"

"Yes."

"As long as you're prepared to do it again, that's what you're here for."

Show them? Why not show them. It might open the door.

"Wait, I have this."

He dug in the pocket of his jeans and pulled out the claw, its string balled up and tangled to the bail. He let the pendant fall and it swung there like a hanged man. Gabriel's blue eyes followed it.

"How did you get that?"

"What difference does it make? I got it. I could pound on the door, get them to open up, take them by surprise."

Rei sized him up, his dark eyes narrowing. "You traded for that."

Eddy shrugged. "I might have taken it off a dead Paw."

"But you didn't." Gabriel stood with his shoulder lined up with Rei's. "Because they don't leave behind their dead. And he only gives those out to men who trade for women. That's the mark. That's what it means."

Shit.

"I was doing it for a good reason. I was getting someone's little girl back. A baby, not even really talking yet."

They seemed to shrug as one body.

I don't have to explain myself to them. Doing what I'm supposed to do.

But he saw their estimation of him drop in that moment. It rippled through the boys and something was gone, whatever charm Alma had placed on his presence on this mish was dimmed to the point that it might as well have never been.

Gabriel eyed him, appraising. "Sure. Sure, you get them to open the door. Get them talking, feeling like you're a brother. They'll be open. Guns down."

Eddy nodded, thinking with giddy sickness of the rounds and rounds of ammunition at the ready.

Hardly have to stop. Reload and keep going until they're all gone.

When it was all quiet, they sent Eddy to the door of the large building. There was a single sentry posted, and he was too young to have a beard.

Eddy raised his hand and put the other to his claw. "Hey. Didn't I meet you in Estiel?"

He started, yanking a gun that had seen better days out of his waistband. "What?"

Eddy stepped a little closer, pulling the claw up off his chest. "When he gave me this. The Lion. I thought I saw you there."

"I'm from KC. I've never been to Estiel. Might go there soon. Who are you?"

"Oh." Eddy forced a laugh. "I'm from near Estiel. I'm not a Paw, but I heard you guys were here. I wanted to join up and go to Estiel by truck rather than on foot."

The kid smiled and lowered his ruined gun a little.

Eddy popped his chin, smiling a little. "Who's your commander?"

He cocked his head.

That isn't the word. Damn it.

"I'm with Zander and Harrin. And Carl is leader."

Always four.

"Can I go in and see them? I want to make sure they don't mind taking me along."

Don't move. Don't cross your arms. Look sure.

Eddy relaxed and avoided the urge to look around. He managed a small laugh before popping his chin at the guard.

"What's your name?" Eddy's voice was easy, untroubled.

"Jeff."

"Jeff. I know they're probably asleep. My name's Eddy." Another step forward. "I won't even wake them. I'll get some sleep, too, and we can go in the morning."

The kid looked over his shoulder at the door. He shrugged a little and turned back, stuffing his gun back into his pants. "Sure, what the hell."

Eddy managed a smile, dropping his claw back down and half expecting his heart to bounce it away again.

Jeff disappeared into the doorway, shoulder first. He put his head back out and waved for Eddy to follow.

Eddy walked in, seeing humps of people in the half-light of a single hanging lantern. The room stank of every fluid discharged by the body. He put the back of his hand to his mouth.

Jeff pointed. "That's Carl over there. Wake him if you want to. I'm going back out to guard." He nodded to Eddy before turning around again.

Eddy heard the muffled sound of Jeff being knocked out and dragged away, but no one stirred. He stepped in the direction of where Jeff had pointed, still barely seeing anything.

His foot crushed something soft and he stepped back quickly, squinting down. It was the hand of a young girl who lay splayed out on the floor, blinking at the ceiling. She was naked. She made no sound at all.

Eddy stared down at her, the yellow lantern a slick of shine in her wide eyes. She was terribly thin, a plate of bones between her withered breasts and a deep V where her belly should be. Her hair was shaved.

As his eyes adjusted, he took in the room around him. There were more women than he had thought at first, he saw. Once he knew that their heads were shaved he could make them out, a company of skeletons sleeping with their arms crossed like bats. They all looked near death. Two men slept fairly near to one another, each with a woman or girl beneath their heads, meager pillows.

I could cut their throats now, in the quiet. Warm the girls in the spill.

But something in him wanted to see their terror when they awoke to the sound of shooting, to see the world taken from them in an instant.

He made his way to the back door and tapped three times. The signal.

They came in, bursting through with the starlight, at front and back.

Eddy saw one of the men scramble to his feet, the weight of his gun pulling his untied trousers down as he struggled to stand. Eddy opened his mouth to say something, some sardonic dismissal to be the last words in his enemy's ears. But he never got it out.

Gabriel and Rei and their complement of boys opened fire, their guns spraying bright flash and thunder like Eddy had never seen before. He threw himself to the ground, hands over his ears. The girl nearest him was screaming, her mouth wide open, but he could hear nothing at all.

Wetness splashed on the back of his neck and he glanced, up, catching the blood in his mouth. The gunfire had cut the first man in half and most of what was in him spilled across the floor. The second man had barely made it onto his knees before gunfire caught him in the neck and face and he fell forward across the girl beneath him.

Most of the women had been tied or chained, as Gabriel had guessed. Only two had even half risen. One of them was bleeding fast from her neck; she wouldn't make it. The other looked unhurt, but her eyes were shiny like peeled eggs.

They got the boys to quit firing, with some difficulty. The guns sprayed bullets as easily as dry dandelion fluff when blown firmly. They obviously enjoyed the feeling. Holes dotted the walls all around them, from knee level to above Eddy's head.

Eddy's hands shook and his veins were full of ice. He had a hard time gaining his feet. His mouth was dry as cotton and he couldn't hear at all.

He stared around him at the utter carnage. The boys had been directed to free the women, but most of them sat unmoved, not seeing the change.

Rei lit more lanterns and his black hair shone as he lifted one high, counting.

"Eight." He looked over to Gabriel. "Eight who will make it. None look to be pregnant."

Gabriel nodded, kneeling down to speak to one of the women. "Sister, are you okay?"

She flinched away from him. Eddy couldn't guess her age but saw the way the loose skin in her face bunched when she grimaced. Older than him.

No one spoke. The smell of blood held sway over all.

Eddy went back and found the woman he had stepped on when he came in. She lay exactly as she had, her blue-white skin spattered with black blood. He sat down beside her head, trying to think of what to say.

You're safe now.

But she isn't.

She can come with us. With them. That will be better.

It will.

The boys found blankets and offered up their coats. One by one, most of the women were coaxed into sitting up and covering themselves. Gabriel offered food and they jumped at it. When he saw this, he ordered a cooking fire built and sent two boys out to hunt.

Eddy laid a wool blanket across the woman spread out on the floor. He stared into the hollow of her collarbone. She didn't take food or water. She wouldn't look at anyone or answer questions.

When they had all eaten what they could and the boys had dragged the dead men out, Gabriel took Rei and the boys outside, leaving only Eddy with the women. Some of them had gone to sleep. Three sat grouped together, talking low and quiet.

Eddy lay with his face beside the woman on the floor, his body away from hers as if they had placed beds head-to-head. He crossed his arms across his chest. He was still shaking.

He spoke to her in a low voice, not sure why he was doing it.

"I've never. I mean, I've shot men before. But not like that. I've never seen guns like that. I can't. I mean, how can you walk around with something like that? I can't even hear. I can still see the flash."

The girl flexed her jaw. Eddy could hear the creak of muscle over the sound of grinding teeth.

"I thought we would come here and save you from the Paws of the Lion. But I just didn't expect. Every time I think I've seen the worst thing, I see something else."

The floor. The floor that breathed. Lying on the floor bleeding my first and going with it, trying to go with it.

He tried to slow his breathing, to place his thoughts in order.

The chair.

This girl was just in the chair.

Eddy sat up and unbuttoned his shirt. He came around to face her, lining himself up to meet her eyes as they stared straight up.

"I'm not one of them," Etta said. "See that?" Etta was still bound, but the truth was clear.

The terror was something that Eddy had felt. Etta felt light and free of it.

The girl on the floor cried without sound, tears sliding into her ears.

"I'm not one of them."

She sat down beside her and waited until the girl's sobs finally made sound.

Later, nearly dawn.

"What's your name?" The girl spoke without being spoken to, spooking Etta a little.

"Etta. I'm from a place far away from here. What's yours?"

The girl shrugged. "Girl. None of us have names."

"What?"

"Girl. Birthmark girl. Green-eyed girl. Black girl. Things. Not names."

"What did they call you?"

Another shrug like a pile of sticks being dropped in a bag. "Nothing. Girl."

"Are you from here? From Jamestown?"

Her chin like a blade, chopping up and down as she nodded. "Born here. Property of Archer, like everyone else. And then property of the Lion. And now. Who knows?"

These were not questions.

"You're not property. Not at all. If you go back to Ommun with these boys, you'll be . . ."

The word is free, but I don't know.

"You'll be alright. Not property."

The girl did not look at her, but she did not look as though she believed.

"Do you want a name?"

Another shrug. "You can call me anything."

"No, I mean . . ."

There's nothing I can give her that's for her. It would be for me, just to feel better.

They sat in silence a long time.

"You won't be hungry. They have plenty to eat there. And a safe place to sleep. Beds with quilts." Everything she offered sounded ridiculous.

The girl didn't nod. She looked at nothing.

"You don't have to go with them. You could go out on your own."

Sit right here and die, more like.

Etta pictured her, sitting in this spot, leaves blowing through the open door and into her unflinching face. The moment she died would go unmarked.

"You'd have to watch out for Paws."

And every other man on earth.

No shrug. The girl made no sign that she had heard.

When Gabriel realized that many of the girls were too weak to walk back, he set about starting the truck that the Paws had come in with. It had high wooden sides on its bed, big enough for everyone to ride in. Once he got it running, the boys hopped up into it and helped the scarecrow girls climb in. Etta helped the girl from the floor, standing in the dirt and lifting her whole weight. Her body felt as hollow as a bird's.

Etta climbed into the cab with Gabriel. She felt a pang for Flora, remembering their rides.

The roar was terrific, and she knew they wouldn't be heard.

"Why bother?" Etta stared out over the tall weeds in the culverts that lined the roads. She didn't want to speak, but she had to.

"What?" Gabriel kept his eyes on the road.

"Why bother with this mish? The Lion. Those girls. The trouble was just as bad before."

"How do you know?"

She jerked her head back toward the whistling rear window, the boards that enclosed the bed. "Get a look. That's not new to them. One girl told me they don't even have names, they never have. Why didn't you come for them before this?"

Gabriel shrugged, wrestling the wheel over the rough fields. "We didn't know. We watch for the Lion."

She didn't like the answer but she didn't know what to do with it. She settled back and rode.

I need to go home.

Getting the girls down the hatch and into Ommun was quite a production. A couple had to be lowered in slings made of bedsheets. The women of Ommun came out, their braids shining like the scales of shiny fish, their smiles concealing their horror with long-practiced kindness. The girls from Jamestown were fed again and clothed in long woven dresses. They looked like the figures Etta sometimes found in old-world stores; tall, faceless woman-shaped objects that clothes hung off of in long, rat-gnawed shreds. The activity around them gave the impression of life, but Etta could not tear her gaze away from the eye-holes of the woman she'd stepped on, the girl from the floor.

No name.

Etta slipped away from the tumult, the preparations for whatever feast was about to come.

One more night in these featherbeds, then I'm going home.

But the night was going to pass too slowly, and she needed to steady herself.

She followed the rattling sound to an open vent, felt the air blowing on her face. Standing beneath the grate, she rolled and lit a joint. She hit it over and over until the fog settled into the dips and valleys between her thoughts. She slid her back down the wall and sat on the floor.

The sound of singing came low and sweet, echoing through the metal hallways and stretching out between the minutes like warm caramel pooling in her ears. When she could feel the bones of her legs bounding against one another in their abundant flesh, when she knew she wasn't one of the scarecrows, she rose.

The main hall was thronged with people. Men came to sit or kneel beside the women of Jamestown. Etta listened and gathered that they had all been given names. Coral. Sarah. Leah. The girl from the floor was being called Sheba. The men who spoke to her were quiet and deferential.

She looked right through them.

Etta felt that she was dragging chains behind her. The chains were stories. They were the burdens of Chloe and Flora and Alice, of every nameless woman she had ever failed to help. She was dragging the chair and her mother and the Unnamed and every woman she had ever known. She looked at Sheba and she was so tired she couldn't move at all. If air were water, if today were the day she jumped into the Misery, she would sink, she would drown.

Alma was there, glowing and nursing one of her infants as she spoke. Etta couldn't follow it. She heard buzzing like a thousand bees until her own name broke through.

"And Sister Etta. Like Nephi, took upon herself the guise and the voice of the enemy in order to bring us another mish victory. Just as it was revealed to me."

There was another ripple of incredulity through the crowd. Gabriel turned to look at her, and Etta tried hard not to laugh. She saw Rei's face suddenly take on surprise and remorse, looking at her and trying to convey some kind of forgiveness.

More stories that don't mean anything. More names. More calling a past that anyone could see a vision of the future. Didn't she say I was Moroni before?

But inside her, something tickled near her heart like a bare branch scraping the side of a house in the wind. She stood on tiptoe and felt no ghost of a cramp.

Is this how it happened with the Unnamed? Did they make her out of a person and into a story?

In full view of the room, she lit up again and inhaled deeply. She made her way to Sheba, reaching out to take the gaunt woman's limp hand. Into it, she pressed a vial of som.

"All I can give you is a choice in whether you want to go on or not. That's the only real gift anyway."

Vaguely, by a circuitous route, Sheba's eyes found Etta's. They saw each other for just a moment. Etta thought of a deer sliding between the trees, its round black eyes.

Shouldn't have done that.

Had to.

She stumbled over her own feet, following the Prophet as she dismounted the stage. She elbowed her way into the room.

"Alma." Her voice sounded rough and too heavy in her own ears.

Alma lifted her rosy, golden head and smiled. "Sister Etta. I knew you would come."

She had to blink again and again; her eyeballs felt furred.

"Did you know? Did you."

Alma gestured and the room cleared itself. Etta came to the bed like a moth toward a campfire. She felt like she was rocking, waving with her whole body toward Alma and back.

"Will you stay with us?" Alma was smiling.

Smirking. Like a cat that's just eaten.

"No. I have to leave here. Do it again."

"What?" Alma's wheat lashes beat against her cheeks. "Do what again?"

"What you did before. Fix me. I'm tired of dragging this ghost around. All these ghosts. Take them away, if you can."

Alma's laugh bubbled up out of her throat. She grabbed Etta's arm, and the heat beat up toward her face like a blush. Alma's face pinked, too. Etta surged in place, throbbing like her whole body was a sore tooth.

"I don't know which one you are. It's all ghosts in there." The heat faded from Alma's cheeks. She turned to work on someone else.

Etta shook herself loose. She decided to become Sheba, the nowhere ghost, the no eyes and no mouth, nobody and no body.

Did I really think she'd lay her hands on me and I'd walk away Eddy, perfect Etta, someone else in some other world?

She smoked until she fell asleep, not caring who smelled it. In the morning, there was a burnt circle in the bed and the room smelled like a chicken on fire.

The walk back to Nowhere took too long. Eddy was weeks on the road, weighed down by the guns he couldn't wait to trade and use. Some days he didn't walk at all. He raided ghost towns and read books, examined the tools of the old world and tried to see what kind of life they had.

The Book of Eddy

Sheba is still looking up at me. I wonder what she did with that vial. I wonder if Alma will explain away how Sheba died and what it means. How it fits some story that was already known and told. I could go home peddling bullshit about my travels, my visions and what they mean. I could turn the Unnamed into Nephi and all that, make it a story that we know but nobody else. Is that what keeps them together?

Why couldn't she fix me? She fixed the chair.

I was born in the book. Not in the chair. Etta was wrong about that. I don't know if she's the ghost or if I am, but we're both going home. She's going back to Nowhere. And someday soon, I am going back to Estiel with what I've got on my back.

Not like those rattling bastard guns that cut them all up. But enough in my revolver to change the way things run. Even a Lion will die if I shoot it enough times.

And then, his whole Hive will walk down the stairs and add themselves to my chains.

I'm going to go home and tell my mother my name.

I'm going to walk into that basement and meet the men who are women. I am going to dance their ghost dance to their dead music.

I am going to walk through those gates and tell them I am Eddy, son of Ina. I am going to ask Alice to live with me. And Flora. Maybe I will have a Hive after all. Who's going to stop me?

He was ready. He was bound and masked and had his guns loaded behind him. He hefted up the pack and winced at the weight settling back into the sore grooves in his shoulders. He couldn't wait to put it down. He was so tired of carrying everything.

He knew something was wrong before he could see it or smell it. He waited for the feeling to settle into anticipation or just the anxiety of meeting Ina and explaining himself. He walked slowly, expecting the faded white sign that read "Nowhere" to rise into view over that next hill.

He crested the hill and stopped.

There was no spotter in the tower. The gates were wide open. Ashes from the cornfields blew into his open mouth.

CHAPTER 16

It was hard to find an entrance to the tunnels with so many landmarks razed. Eddy searched frantically for long minutes, the stink of burned houses choking him.

A trapdoor finally appeared beneath a drift of ashes and he wrenched it upward, flinging himself headlong down the stairs so heedlessly that he tripped. He pulled himself up from the dirt and blinked into the darkness. By feel he managed to get a torch out of the sconce on the wall, but dropped it a second later. In the light of the sparks from his flint, he saw it lying there and struggled to light it. Once he had the hope of a flame, he crouched and began to crawl.

"Hello? Anyone?"

He couldn't hear anything over the pounding of his heart. His breathing was hard and ragged, so he held it. He could see his pulse in his eyeballs.

"Hello! Hello!"

A dim echo returned his own voice to him.

Fuck fuck living fuck.

He crawled as fast as the small space would allow him. He worked his way to the juncture beneath the schoolhouse and shouted in each direction in turn.

"Hello! Damn it. Hello! Anyone?"

From far down the western tube, he heard someone answer.

"Your name?"

He breathed in sharp and held it.

This is not the moment.

"Etta! Daughter of Ina!"

For a moment she heard nothing and fought terror that the Lion's men were in the tunnels with her. But then the grunting of the men in the tunnel came close enough and she heard a voice she knew.

"Rob?"

Rob, son of Marcia, emerged, filthy and with one arm bandaged. Behind him, Aaron and David dragged themselves into the slightly roomier space of the juncture.

Etta hugged Rob, and over her shoulder saw Tommy the bather crawl slowly into view. Something was wrong with his face.

"What happened?"

Tommy shrugged. Rob spoke first. "We were attacked. It was those men you were talking about, the Lion? They knew everything, where everything was kept. They took the women and girls first, then they emptied out Alice's place. Her garden, everything."

"Alice? What about the Mothers?"

Aaron was nodding, his cheeks hollow under his beard. "Them, too. Ina and Lisa and Bronwen. All gone."

I told them this would happen.

But would it have happened if I hadn't brought Flora back here?

"Where are the rest of the men?" Etta looked around, unbelieving.

"Some of them got away," Tommy said. His speech was mush. Etta guessed someone had kicked him hard in the teeth. "Just ran. Most of them are dead."

Etta waited for rage or sorrow to take her, but nothing came. Her stomach contracted into a tiny ball.

"We have to get them back. The women. We have to attack the Lion. I know the way."

The men looked at each other. Doubt and fear passed between them in the deep shadows of the torchlight.

"I don't think you understand," David said slowly. "They were all armed. They killed dozens of people, just in the first few minutes. They burned down our whole city."

"I understand perfectly," Etta snapped back. "Because I've seen it before."

For a few minutes, she told them about her experience with the Lion. She sketched Manhattan and Ommun lightly, leaving out things she couldn't explain. They settled in, sitting down. It made her furious.

"Don't sit down! We can't lose any time! We have to go now, back to Ommun. We can get supplies there, and guns. We can make a plan."

No one spoke, no one stirred.

"What are you doing?" She was screaming at them now. "Are you going to stay in this grave like you're already dead? Come on!"

Tommy scooted forward, putting his light bather's hand on Etta's knee. "Etta. Etta, come down here."

Etta fumed for a moment, then knelt.

"They're scared. I'm scared. We've seen things . . ." His voice cracked and he stared at the floor for a moment. "We've seen things happen to people we love that we'll never get over. Things that don't even bear thinking of."

Tommy's eyes were glassy and he wasn't looking at her.

Sheba on the floor.

Eight in, eight out.

Where are you right now? Where are they?

She started again, softer. "Look, men. It's early morning up there. They're all gone. What's done is done. There's nothing for you here, probably not even anything to eat. Ommun has enough food to feed every traveler. They're strange people, but they're good. And their town . . . it's full of women. More women than I've ever seen in my life. Go there with me. Whatever happens, whatever you all choose, they're our best hope now."

They softened to her. She coaxed them out into the light. Before noon, the smell of Nowhere burning was gone from their noses and only clung as a memory in their clothes and hair. They walked the road in a short V with Etta at its point.

They walked for a few days, talking little. Etta hunted and fed them, the men gathered nuts and fruits as they went. On the fifth or sixth night, Rob was ready to talk a little.

"They really did come out of nothingness. No spotter saw them. One moment we were all asleep and the next minute there's screaming and gunshots from everywhere at once."

Etta nodded over a cup of wild mint tea. They had eaten a couple of squirrels and were still awake, staring at the fire.

"I heard Janet screaming first," Aaron said softly. "I was in the Hive house next door, but by the time I got there, she was dragged out and they were all dead. I took to the tunnels right away. But her baby . . ."

Janet had been five moons gone, Etta remembered.

"They didn't . . ."

Aaron shrugged. "As far as I know, they took the women without hurting them. But still."

There were grim nods around the circle.

"Even the Mothers, they all fought." David was staring at the fire. "I saw Carla bite a man until he bled. He slapped her, but with his open hand."

"They must have had orders to bring them to the Lion," Etta mused, still feeling nothing. "Had to be."

"Maybe that's where Alice went," Tommy said. His broken mouth made her name "Alish."

Etta looked at him sharply. "What?"

He took a gulp of tea. "It makes sense. She and that Flora disappear weeks ago, and then these men show up and they know everything—"

"Alice and Flora left?"

Tommy looked guilty.

"There were rumors," Rob said reluctantly.

"All kinds of rumors," Aaron added.

"People said they went after you," David offered, miserably.

"People also said they were in love." Aaron's eyes were bright in the firelight, accusing her.

"Right," Rob said. "But Emory said you had had a plan to trade som with the Lion. And I think they decided to do it without you."

Now it came. The rage like a firestorm from one side, and the sorrow like a sunless sea on the other. Etta was hot and cold and lost within it. For a moment she thought she might pass out.

"Etta? Etta, you okay?"

Rob put his hand out to her and she smacked it away with a force that scared him.

"Look," Eddy said. "I'm going to tell you this one time, so all of you pay attention. My name. Is Eddy. And when we're out here, I'm a man. You understand?"

They didn't, that was plain on their faces. But no one argued.

"We'll make Ommun tomorrow," he said. "Get some sleep."

In the morning, they got started in the blue light before true dawn.

Eddy walked out ahead by himself, but after it got light, Tommy jogged up to join him.

"You know I've bathed you for years."

"What's your point?" Eddy did not deign to look at him.

"I know what you are. What's all this about?"

They walked in silence. Eddy clenched his jaw over and over, chewing on his empty mouth.

"Why would you want that, when all anyone in this world wants is a woman?"

Eddy did look now, to see if Tommy really was this stupid.

"I saw you dancing." Eddy looked ahead again.

"What?" Tommy sounded confused, but defensive underneath.

"In the spring. I left the main hall and I heard music. Old-world music. I looked in a cellar window and I saw you dancing. As a woman. You and another. Fancy boys."

Tommy didn't speak for a few moments. "Yeah. Yeah, that was me. That was me trying to be the thing everyone wants. Like Breezy."

"Like the women stolen by the Lion."

"Not wanted like that," Tommy began truculently.

"Being a woman means always being wanted like that. There is no such thing as safe wanting. Safe wanting always turns into ownership. Desire turns to chains faster than you can breathe in to say no. Be careful what you decide you're going to be. Outside the walls of a city like Nowhere, women become things. You don't have to be born a woman. The Lion's men keep boys, too."

Tommy looked at her with his mouth open. "But they can't . . . They can't bear children."

"No, but they can be the thing you want in every other way, can't they? You can't, but the same is true of a lot of us. In the meantime, you can dance and sing and wear your hair long." She thought of Kelda. "You can be used. You can provide release."

"Stop it." His voice was cold, shaken.

"I didn't start this."

"I didn't understand." He was trying to get in front of Eddy, to look him in the eye.

"You still don't."

The people of Ommun were not as joyous to greet a company of men as they had been to welcome the women of Jamestown, but the last refugees of Nowhere were warmly received.

Eddy watched, bemused, as each of the men in his party struggled to take it all in. The food. The enormity of the underground city. The children. The women. Alma.

Once he knew they were cared for, Eddy left to find Gabriel and Rei. They were at Deseret by the time he caught up with them. He waited outside the door.

"I'm ready to lead another mish," he said as they appeared.

Gabriel looked pointedly at the claw Eddy was wearing. "To where?"

"To Estiel. It's time to kill the Lion."

The two men exchanged a glance.

"They took my home. My mother. Every woman from Nowhere. Nobody near Estiel is safe while this is allowed to go on. His time has long since come."

Gabriel stepped forward, pushing his long blond hair back off his shoulders. "Sister Etta, I don't think we can do that."

Impatient, Eddy stepped closer as well. "You have more firepower in a hole in the ground than he has in his entire operation! Remember how you cut down those men in Jamestown? This will be like that. A slaughter. Him and his cats."

Rei spoke up shyly. "It isn't up to us. The mish has to be called. Blessed. The Prophet has to tell us it's Mother God's will."

"Fine." Eddy exhaled hard through both nostrils. "Fine, I'll go talk to Alma."

"Do that," Gabriel said. The two men walked away together, leaving Eddy alone.

Eddy waited outside Alma's room for a long time before he was granted an audience.

Better not show her how annoyed I am.

"How are your three babies?"

Her brown eyes smiled at him as she gestured to the two in bed beside her. "As well as I could want." Her voice was like music. "What do you need, Eddy?"

The room spun for him a little as he wondered whether he had ever told her his name.

"I need . . . I need another mish. A big one. I need to fight the Lion and free my people."

Alma softly clucked her tongue. "You don't need that at all," she said evenly. "You need to stay here."

"What?"

"I spake your destiny unto Etta, and she fulfilled it like a good sister. Now, I must tell you to fulfill hers."

"What?"

She laid a hand on one child, watching the other. When she looked back up, her eyes had gone green again.

He stood transfixed, like a mouse watching a hawk dive down.

"Etta will be the mother of warriors."

"No."

Alma actually laughed. "When we say no, Mother God sends the whale to swallow us up."

Eddy felt beads of sweat roll down the backs of his thighs.

The whales in that textbook. Long as a house, warm-blooded in the dark sea. Birth live young.

It won't swallow me.

Alma settled her golden head back on her enormous stack of down pillows. "Eddy will fight the Lion, oh yes. You'll never bend your will to Hers. Eddy will go in blazing and righteous and fight Samson's fight. But the Philistines won't cut your hair, they'll let it grow. And then the warriors will come. Part your own red sea and they will come."

the chair the chair the chair

"It is the destiny of every woman, child. It is your crowning glory."

"Not me," he croaked. "I don't have to be that."

"Every time you say no, the whale swims a little closer." Alma giggled like she was watching a naughty child try to get away with not eating their vegetables.

Eddy tore from the room without another word. In private, he opened his pack and pulled from his wooden medicine chest a set of tiny red envelopes made of fabric. Each of these smelled strongly of licorice bitterness. In memory, Alice spoke.

"Sometimes it's for the best. We all want a healthy child and a happy ending. But sometimes you're not going to get it. Everyone knows the Unnamed did it, and Midwives can do it with knives, of course. They don't do it much, but I've heard."

Alice. Alice gone from her greenhouse, gone to the Lion.

"But for the women you meet out there, if they're already bleeding or if they can't get free, this will do it. Brew in hot water and drink. The taste is awful, and sickness comes quick. They'll vomit and they'll shit. But they won't be pregnant anymore. Warn them, make sure you warn them."

I've been warned. I know what to do.

In the morning, Alma made it crystal clear. No one could follow him. No one could help him. Avoiding Etta's fate was an affront to their god.

They had one more private moment together. Alma cut through the crowd and put her hot hand on Eddy's bicep.

"It will happen," she hissed. "Don't you understand? I can't change it once it's been spake. It will happen."

Eddy stared back at her and said nothing.

"It would be better for you if it happens here. Not there."

He yanked his arm away from her and walked to the lift.

He waited a long time before he realized that no help meant no help. He made the exhausting climb up ladder after ladder alone. The stores of guns and ammo would not open for him, but he still had what they had given him last time. The climb was torturous under the added weight, and he had to rest many times. When he got out, he was glad he had started early.

◆ ◆ ◆

The Book of Eddy
Summer

Nothing she said matters. It's all made up, her stories of whales and soldiers and funny names. Her eyes must just be something else in the stew of their blood, the gene squares in the Physicians' Desk Reference. *Just like the albinos. They've crossbred too many times and made her crazy. Fertile, but crazy.*

I'm going to get my mother. And Alice. And Flora. I'm going to walk out of there with the Lion's entire harem and they won't dare refuse me entrance to Ommun then. I'll be the richest man on earth.

It's ten days walking, maybe more. Plenty of time to plan it out.

He thought of nothing else. He scraped his memory raw, trying to recall every detail of the huge building the Lion occupied. The place he had seen the catamites at play. The old metalworker's shop.

Won't kill anyone I don't have to. But I'll probably have to kill everyone who has a gun.

He thought hard about the Paws he had met. Some had guns, but many only had knives and other short-range weapons.

Need to get up high. Pick off a few at a distance. That first.

He thought of the best places near the Lion's stronghold, where he could get the advantage and keep it awhile. He tried to see the whole thing, the glass and boarded-up windows. The stink of the cats. The Arch.

The Arch. The black rainbow. The metal skeleton.

It was guarded, but by how many? Metal plates shed like scales off it all the time, so there were plenty of places to hang on. How many could he kill there?

He couldn't swim the river with the guns, so he stole a boat from the dock and floated soundlessly down toward the Arch in the middle of the night.

When he reached the Arch, he saw one guard. As he crept closer, he could hear the man snoring. His knife slid between the man's ribs and he didn't even scream. He wiped the blood off on his pants and retrieved his pack. He climbed.

The thing was not exactly solid. Parts seemed to sag under him and grind against one another as he came up. He tried to triple his own height and get his body behind some of the sections that still looked secure. He waited for daybreak.

The first men out were farmers. They emerged to feed chickens and milk cows, and Eddy let them pass. He waited.

When Paws began to appear, he waited.

When he saw three Paws moving a group of catamites across the green, he opened fire.

They ran in all directions, looking wildly to discover the source of incoming bullets. One pulled a gun but dropped quickly after. Wounded, but Eddy couldn't see where. He waited.

I can do this. I am this. This is now.

As he'd planned, the chaos brought more of them pouring out of the main building. Gripping his perch with his legs, he shot with both hands, emptying the cylinder of the revolver first and the clip of the newer gun long after. Shakily, he stowed one and reloaded the other, then switched.

Another two rounds of this. He wasn't killing as efficiently as he had hoped, but he had done some real damage. He was breathing so fast and shallow that he began to see spots.

Eight in, eight out.

He climbed down, worried that he would fall. Two loaded guns in his hands, he walked toward the Lion's home.

One lone man came out from behind the hulk of a car, raising a deer rifle at Eddy. Eddy shot him in the face.

He came to the open door of the Lion's den. He smelled the oily garlic-sweet stink of the cats. Darkness within, but no sound.

He stood at the doorway a long time, waiting. Nothing came.

He swept the room while his eyes adjusted, panting again and frantic. The smell was everywhere at once, and his frenzied imagination told him the cats were everywhere.

The cats were nowhere.

He backed toward the staircase, guns raised, wind whistling in and out of his nose.

Eight in, eight out.

Where are you?

I'm now. I'm here.

The stairs were closed off from even the little light that came through to the main foyer, and he held his eyes wide open. When he saw a muzzle flash and felt the air slamming around him, he shot back blind and heard the groan as someone slid to the carpeted floor.

At the landing, a boarded window admitted slivers of white light. They striped the wall like the coat of a tiger. Eddy turned and took the next flight up.

He climbed and climbed, like the way out of Ommun. The final landing was lit with oil lamps of some kind.

This is it. Fuck my destiny.

The double doors burst open and Eddy pissed down both legs as the lion and the tiger sprang at him at once, their chains flying out behind them. He had never known pure terror like this. The moment stretched out for an eternity as the massive animals bounded and leapt at him, their teeth and claws filling the world and all his senses as he fired fired fired fired.

Three bullets caught the lion in the air and the big cat went down, blood black in its deep chest. The tiger was hit only once and landed heavily on top of Eddy, the rich doom of its reeking breath puffing into his face.

Claws sank into his right shoulder and he screamed in a voice he didn't recognize. His left arm went up and he fired into the tiger's chin a dry and useless click from a dead revolver.

The tiger's snarling head came down, wide as the world, targeted with a million years of predatory instinct on Eddy's slender neck.

Right arm searing with a vast and unbelievable pain, Eddy raised the newer gun as far as he could and shot the beast in its groin and thigh until the clip was empty.

He felt the animal's blood pouring out, hot on his belly. Its terrible weight pinned him down and crushed the breath out of him as the monster collapsed. Eddy bridged and bucked, trying to slide out from under, but his crazed breath dragged the animal's fur into his mouth and he choked on it. As he chased what was left of his mind down a small black hole, he could swear he heard his mother's voice.

CHAPTER 17

In the red haze of fever, Etta knew a few things only.

Flora was there. She tended Etta most of the time, she was pretty sure. She could feel Flora's fingers checking her pulse, wrapping delicately around her wrist below her leather bonds.

Ina was there. Etta could hear her, but never close by. For days, she wondered why she did not come to her living daughter. Later, she thought it might have been because Ina would have killed Etta to spare her what was to come.

No sign of Alice. She knew Alice was here somewhere, because she never felt the pain of Flora cleaning the wound in her shoulder at all. Only Alice could do that.

In the pounding madness of the fever, she saw the tiger again and again. When the fever subsided, she knew the tiger was real.

"What?" asked the silky voice of the Lion. "You thought I only had one?"

He walked the chained cat into her room often. The smell of it kept her nightmares florid and active.

In her terrible weakness, Etta struggled to look around the room and get a sense of where she was. Out the window, she could see only sky, ceaseless blue, every day. She was restrained all over and wore diapers like a baby. Flora tended to her gently and carefully, but everything itched and ached down there anyway.

When the fever was gone, Flora gave her a drink that knocked her out cold and she woke up in a different room. This one was bigger, nicer, and stocked with old-world treasures that made Etta's mouth go dry. She was restrained, but Flora came and let her use a bedpan. In the mirror, she was painfully thin and she flinched from the length of her hair.

How long have I been here?

Flora would not answer any question she was asked. She would smile sadly and shake her head, that was all.

On the third day in the new room, she was given a long silk nightgown to wear after a warm sponge bath from Flora, who would not meet her eyes. Flora carefully locked Etta's wrist cuffs, one at a time, to the foot of the bed while she cleaned her back.

Flora laid her down and locked her wrist restraints over her head again.

"Flora, I'm much stronger now. I could walk out of here, if you'd help me."

That same sad shake of her head. Etta fell into a fitful sleep.

The next days followed the same. Flora came and cared for Etta, keeping her clean and comfortable. When Etta's wrists were wet, she tested her restraints to see if she could slip free with a little help.

She looked up at Flora, her eyes pleading. "You could get me a little grease. Soap. Anything. I could slip my wrist out and they'd never know it was you."

A look of consternation flitted over Flora's face, and she bent down to dry Etta's wrists carefully.

"You have to do this job, I know that." Etta spoke through her teeth. "But you don't have to be good at it. That is a choice."

Flora looked at the floor, shrugging.

"Are you not allowed to talk to me?"

No answer, not even with her eyes.

"You know why he's keeping me. Look at me. Look, Flora."

Flora's eyes flashed back to Etta's. Etta saw that her roots were grown out and there was stubble on her chin. Her eyes were like cored fruit.

"Kill me," Etta said. "Say I got free and tried to kill you. Just kill me so I don't have to do this. You know what's going to happen."

Flora nodded, tiny up and down with her chin.

"Don't leave me to it." Etta was pleading now. "Help me. In any little way, Flora. I'm begging you to help me."

Etta thought she saw something coming back into Flora's eyes. Some hint of the woman she had been.

But there was a sound of footsteps outside the door, and Flora turned to leave at once.

Etta awoke the next day, knowing it was late night. A candle burned across the room. She could see the Lion's outline, his broad back turned to her as he flipped the pages in a book.

"Your breathing changes when you're awake."

His voice startled her. She tried to sit up but found that she was bound tight.

She said nothing.

"I've been reading this diary, this Book of the Unnamed Midwife," he said. "Is this your hero? Was this what you were planning to become?"

Etta didn't answer. She looked out the window and saw that just a little bit of the waning moon was visible outside.

The Lion closed the book and turned around to face her. He was still just a dark shape, backlit by the candle.

"Well?"

"Well what?" Her voice sounded screechy, like she hadn't used it in days.

He didn't answer.

Her whole body tensed. She shivered and she hoped he couldn't see it in the poor light.

"There are two things you can be," the Lion began. He turned and picked up the candlestick and walked slowly across the room toward her. "You know that, right?"

Mother or Midwife

Eddy or Etta

alive or dead

"You can be useful to me by telling me what I want to know. Or you can be useful to me the way every other woman is useful. You get to choose, right now. Do you understand?"

Etta looked at the face behind the candlelight. He looked perfectly rational. Calm and controlled. She shook like a leaf.

"Yes. What do you want to know?"

He reached behind his back and pulled out one of her revolvers. He laid it on the cover beside her. She ached to put her hands on it.

"You had a bag full of these when you got here. They're clean, and they're filled with old-world bullets. Perfect condition, and you've got hundreds."

He took the gun and put it in the drawer at her bedside.

She watched the gun, and when he tilted it against the light, she saw that it was loaded.

"Where did it come from?"

"I have a secret," she said, her face boiling hot and her whole body cold.

"Yes?" He leaned in over her, prowling like one of his cats.

"I give birth to guns. I bleed bullets. I was born to destroy men. Like you."

He looked away, disappointed for a split second before turning back to her with a predator's grin.

The Lion of Estiel blew out the candle and climbed into bed with Etta.

CHAPTER 18

Etta was born in the bed.

She was not born right away. She was conceived over and over, and the Lion always asked the same questions. Her answer changed, but she never told him the truth.

He worked on her the way a man chops down a tree, cutting wedges out of every side, trying to make it fall in the direction that he wanted. She knew she would fall, eventually. All she could do was hope to take his house with her when she went.

A few of the times she thought she would get loose, he noticed. He saw the strain in her muscles and laughed at her, buckling her restraints down until they bit into her skin. Then he took his own bites.

She vacated herself. Eddy sat beside the bed, in a chair, taking it all in.

They would not die, he told her. The Lion would not kill them. They were useful.

Etta did not want to die. Eddy wanted to leave. Together, they decided what they would do.

Flora came one day to clean Etta up. Flora disinfected the places where Etta was wounded and put a steaming hot cloth between Etta's bound legs, pressing the heat to her torn and aching flesh.

Etta watched Flora's face as the woman looked dispassionately down on her body. She tried to lie still, not to flinch or tense up. She was worried Flora would see how much weight she had lost.

Flora caught Etta staring up at her intently and flinched herself. She looked back into Etta's eyes for a searching moment.

She can see us planning, Eddy mused from his chair. *She knows us.*

Etta hoped Flora could see every moment of what she was planning to do. She hoped Flora would be ready when the time came.

Two endless nights later, Etta could rotate her bony wrist inside the restraint cuff, even buckled to its smallest diameter. She had everything she needed. Her body was slick with sweat and blood and the mess that a man makes. Etta's own sweat slipped one bruised arm out of the leather that held her and slowly, meticulously, she freed her other limbs without a sound.

The drawer rolled out slickly and the Lion's breath did not even hitch in his deep sleep. Etta had the gun in her hands and under the covers in one fluid motion. She rested the barrel against one of the low dimples near the base of his spine and pulled the trigger.

The gun dry-fired, loud in the dim room.

Too light you should have known it was too light oh fuck oh fuck.

"Your breathing changes when you're awake." The Lion's voice was calm and unsleepy.

Etta kicked at the sheets and furs on the bed, trying to get to her feet. She was stiff and clumsy and succeeded only in landing on the floor, shoulders down, ankles still caught.

She kicked again as he rose on the other side of the bed, smooth and calm.

She pulled the drawer of the nightstand out and it clattered to the floor. Smooth, old-world bullets hit the carpet with small thumps and rolled away unseen.

The Lion circled around the wide, low bed and stood over her.

"You are wasting my time. You're not even an amusing waste of time. Why don't you tell me what I want to know?"

He leaned down over her and she clutched her gun in both hands. He did not attempt to take it from her.

He wrapped his hands around her bony ones and pushed them to her chest, the gun an unyielding weight between them. He leaned on it with all his weight, moving one leg over to straddle her trapped feet.

"Where did you get them?"

Etta said nothing, fighting to breathe around the crushing weight on her chest.

"Where. Did. You. Get. Them." With each word, the Lion let up a little and then pushed back down, forcing air out of her lungs in agonizing rhythm. The weight sunk in lower and lower as her ribs collapsed. She could not breathe in.

"I'm going to let you breathe in just one more time. If you tell me what I want to know, you can go sleep in the harem. Your mother is there. I'm sure a few friends of yours, too. If you don't, that'll be your last breath. Ready?"

Etta smelled him, his hot heavy breath and the scent of his skin. She smelled it on herself and she thought of hunting in the early morning.

The smell of men. The smell of predator. Flora, asking whether I want to be hunter or hunted. I want neither. I want to be something else.

When he let up, breath rushed into her as unwillingly as the filling of a bellows. Her mouth and nose filled with him, with his cats, with her own terror.

"I'll tell you!" Her voice was pinched, afraid. "I'll tell you where."

He pushed down hard, the gun grinding into her sternum. She felt something pop inside her chest and knew he had broken a rib. He knew it, too, and he smiled.

"Where?"

"Get my map and I'll show it to you. It isn't a town. I have to show you."

He stood up, pushing off her chest, and she wheezed her high-pitched agony. She pulled the gun off her chest and felt the imprint of it in her skin. She laid it down on the nightstand and struggled to breathe, swaying on her way to her feet.

From the collection of her belongings on the desk across the room, the Lion found her stack of folded paper maps. He unwrapped them.

"Show me."

Etta walked unsteadily toward him, her eyes held wide.

If I got into the harem I could come up with a plan. More of us there. Maybe Alice. She could poison him, I know it.

"Show me." His hand covered the back of her neck and pulled her down toward the papers. "Right now."

"Alright!" She squeaked the word and felt shame cover her in fire. She touched the maps, spreading them out, looking for the right one.

"And if you think you can just put your finger on the map at some unknown spot," the Lion said, his mouth beside her ear, "and expect me to run out the door and go looking for some made-up place, think again. You are going to mark the route. You are going to get buckled back in for the night. Then you are going to ride on the hood of my truck until we get there. And if we don't find it, we are never going to find out whether you're a breeder or not. You understand me?"

She opened the map that showed Ommun and its armory, marked in the symbols of Nowhere's raiders. She saw her notations for food and safety, and the symbol she had made up for their wealth of weapons: the peaked shape of a bullet. She leaned forward, her hand hovering over the map.

"It's right here." Her finger extended to point to the spot. She put her other hand down for balance so she could lean forward.

Maybe Ommun can protect itself. Maybe Alma really is . . .

Etta shook all over, unable to control herself.

Don't do this. Eddy's voice was hard beside her. *We said we'd die before we did this. All those girls in Ommun. Sheba. The baby with our name.*

She drew in a shaky breath, deciding.

As she leaned forward, she felt a lump under her left hand. Something was folded into the map. What was it? Her mind raced, trying to place the feel of it.

"It's this road," she began, her voice husky and barely audible. "South of . . ."

The Lion leaned closer, his grip on her neck weighing her down. "South of what?"

Her right hand was pointing out the road that led from the Misery to Ommun.

Her left hand was squeezing the lump through the folds in the old-world paper. The object poked through, then slid as its sharp edges sliced through the map.

Once her palm was on top of it, she knew what it was. An arrowhead. Made from folded scrap metal and sharpened to a fine, thin edge.

Etta's voice grew stronger as Eddy situated the arrowhead in his palm. "The city is called Ommun," she said with some strength returning to her voice. "It's underground, right here."

Right hand guiding. Left hand rising.

The Lion was staring intently at the map, looking at her hand-drawn symbols.

"Is that a bullet?" He reached with his free hand and tapped the map.

"Yes, that's what it is. That's where they are." Driving upward, Eddy thrust the arrowhead with the heel of his left hand, slamming it into the Lion's armpit.

The grip on her neck loosened as the Lion staggered back in shock. Etta pushed him in the center of his chest while he was vulnerable and ran for the gun.

He clawed with both hands at the arrowhead, trying to get a grip on it in the slick warmth of his own blood. Etta hit the floor, sprawling, trying to find the bullets that had gone wild.

The Lion made for the door, slipping in his own blood. Beside it stood a rifle. Eddy had put the arrowhead into the underside of the Lion's right arm. He could pick up the gun, but he fumbled with it, bellowing.

Etta found one bullet and Eddy fitted it sightlessly into the chamber. Eddy stood up and Etta took aim.

Across the room, the Lion's blood poured out of him. There were sounds on the other side of the door.

The rifle slipped and slipped again in the Lion's grip, but his finger was on the trigger. The shot was deafening in the small space, but the bullet sank into the bed a few feet in front of Etta.

Eddy shot and Etta saw the bullet take the Lion's nose, crumpling his face in the center. Blood poured from the hole, cascading over his white lower teeth. He sat down hard.

Etta sat, too, shock taking over. Still naked, she could feel a bullet under her thigh. She loaded that into the gun and cast about for others. She found four.

Shouts filled the hallways and lights danced crazily on the peeling wallpaper. She fired at a shadow and ran in the opposite direction.

She didn't know where she was going. She thought maybe the women were kept on the same floor, but she had no way of knowing where. Looking down, she tried to see where the tracks in the ancient carpet were heaviest. Eddy tracked the footsteps of men as he tracked deer in the woods.

The hunted, now. He saw a man standing above a chair that blocked a pair of double doors.

The man guarding the harem was ready for her. Eddy came striding down the hallway naked, past all thought, and shot him in the throat after he missed her by inches.

The harem was awake. There had to be thirty of them, sleeping grouped and doubled in the beds that seemed to fill the room. Ina saw her and whooped, somewhere between joy and anguish. Etta's mother made her put on a robe.

When Etta spotted Flora, she raised her gun and fired again, aiming for the horsewoman's eye. Ina grabbed Etta's elbow and the shot went wide, all of them cringing away from the sound.

"No," Ina told her. "We need her."

Eddy believed that.

Etta had no words. Across the room, she locked eyes with Alice. Alice looked away hurriedly.

The harem left their room, the smaller ones carried and wrapped in sheets, and made their way down the hall. Etta went first, knowing she had two more shots. Ina followed behind, whispering to Flora.

"Here," Ina said, pointing to a closed door.

Etta tried to open it, but it was locked. They heard the tumbler turning and Etta stepped back and shot the man who threw the door wide. They had to shove him out of the way to get into the armory.

Almost every woman got a gun. Etta found the one that had belonged to the Unnamed and took it back. As they pillaged, Etta dimly recognized Kelda in the crowd. She had found a bow and was easing a tight quiver onto her back.

Back in the stairwell, they shot two more. Ina, whispering to Flora, stopped them at the doorway on another landing.

"Here."

The direction was unneeded; the stink told Etta this was where the cats were kept. She knocked on the door and shot their keeper as he bellowed and tried to raise his gun. They shoved his corpse back into the room where the animals were caged in huge welded scrap-metal enclosures.

"We should free them," a dark-haired woman said.

Etta found a few words, parceled them out grudgingly. "Let them starve."

They closed the door.

The women poured out of the ground floor into the warm night air. They shot more guards and picked up a couple of confused catamites on their way to the truckyard. Word spread fast among the catamites and they came teeming, shouting, toward the street. The boys of Nowhere who had lived ran to join them.

Eddy stared around, dumbstruck. *Where is everyone? Why aren't we being shot at?*

Etta looked around, dazed, tried to remember how many men had been here. How many had she killed? Escape couldn't possibly be this easy.

Maybe there are a lot of them out raiding right now. Eddy was not interested in analyzing this too long. He jogged across the truck lot. *Maybe not that many men want to live like this.*

Etta looked ahead, watching Flora's faded red hair bouncing on her back beside Alice's matted curls.

The yard was deserted and most of the keys were hung on a pegboard. After a few minutes' discussion, they found that only Flora knew how to drive.

"See," Ina said. "I told you." She was so small without her belly, her triumph so pitiful.

They piled into a yellow bus that roared to life and blew black clouds out of its exhaust pipe. Etta told the directions to Ina, and Ina sat behind Flora to help her get there.

In one of the sagging seats, Kelda opened her arms and Etta sat down beside her, not giving in to her embrace.

"I thought I would never see you again," Kelda said, her voice thick.

"You won't." Eddy stared out the window. Etta felt herself crying and didn't bother to wipe her face.

They rode the bumpy road without talking for a while. Around them, women and girls and boys wept and talked and slept and whispered.

Alice came and sat in the seat in front of them, pushing a sleeping boy toward the wall.

"Why did you try to kill her?" she asked.

Etta did not raise her head. "She wouldn't help me. She was there, caring for me, so that I could be kept."

Alice put her hands against the seat and leaned forward. Etta could see how dirty Alice was, how thin.

"I made the drugs that kept you under," she said. "Kelda washed your sheets. Even your mother cooked the food you ate. We all helped. None of us could get you out."

Etta said nothing. Across the aisle, she could see her mother's head bent forward as she slept. The back of her mother's neck was too thin, too fragile.

"Flora was the only one who would do it. Everyone else was too afraid. The Paws who took her were awful, and they'd bring her back hours later. She . . . She took the worst of it. Because they knew what she was. They knew she wouldn't get pregnant. Etta, she . . . she doesn't deserve this. Not now."

Etta didn't answer her. She shrugged Kelda's arms away. As she stood, she saw Alice take her place beside Kelda.

She walked up to crouch beside Flora in the driver's seat. They didn't speak for a long time. The bus crawled over the rough trail in the darkness.

"They burned Nowhere," Etta said.

Flora snorted a little. "I hardly got to see it at all."

Looking up at her, Etta saw finger bruises low on Flora's neck.

"I'm not going to apologize," Etta said. "You could have helped me. But I'm not going to try to shoot you again. I . . . I understand. Doing what you have to, to survive. I understand better."

Flora nodded after a moment. "I could have. You're right. I was so scared, Eddy. I just wanted to live."

Eddy stood up beside her. Gently, moving slow and with the beats of his heart, he put his hand on Flora's shoulder.

She sighed deep as a sob.

Eddy spoke after a while, when he realized he didn't know where Flora would try to take them. "Do you know the way?" Out in the night, the moonlight green flashed in the eyes of some animal as it crossed their path.

"Back to Nowhere?"

"No."

They talked for a few minutes, Eddy giving every landmark he could think of to help her. Flora promised to wake him if they got lost.

Eddy came back to sit in the seat that Alice had vacated. She was asleep, but Kelda's eyes were big in the dark.

"Where are we going?" Kelda finally asked.

Etta stared out the window, trying to figure out how long it would take to get them back to Ommun.

"Toward destiny."

ABOUT THE AUTHOR

Photo © 2016 by Devin Cooper

Meg Elison is a high school dropout and a graduate of UC Berkeley. Her debut novel, *The Book of the Unnamed Midwife*, won the 2014 Philip K. Dick Award. Its sequel, *The Book of Etta*, is the second novel in the Road to Nowhere trilogy. The author lives in the San Francisco Bay Area and writes like she's running out of time.